ANY PATRON, RESIDENT, OR MEMBER OF the visiting day public wishing to view the real-life results of a masterly crime is urged to present themselves at the Market Square, close to the great Hawksmoor church of Christ Church Spitalfields at 11 a.m. tomorrow. An authentic experience is guaranteed. Attendance not recommended for the young or for those of a squeamish or nervous disposition. A modest FEE of one half of one guinea is PAYABLE TO THE OFFICER AT THE SITE.

From the Classifieds

THE LONDON MERCURY

PAST*WORLD*

A MYSTERY OF THE NEAR FUTURE

———◆——

A NOVEL

BY

IAN BECK

(AUTHOR OF MANY DIVERSE TITLES)

———◆——

PUBLISHED IN NEW YORK
BY BLOOMSBURY

MMIX

BLOOMSBURY

NEW YORK BERLIN LONDON

First published in Great Britain in 2009 by Bloomsbury Publishing Plc
Published in the United States in 2009 by Bloomsbury U.S.A. Children's Books
175 Fifth Avenue, New York, New York 10010

Library of Congress Cataloging-in-Publication Data
Beck, Ian.
Pastworld / by Ian Beck. — 1st U.S. ed.
p.   cm.
Summary: In 2050, while visiting Pastworld, a Victorian London theme park,
teenaged Caleb meets seventeen-year-old Eve, a Pastworld inhabitant who has no
knowledge of the modern world, and both become pawns in a murderer's diabolical
plan that reveals disturbing truths about the teenagers' origins.
ISBN-13: 978-1-59990-040-7 • ISBN-10: 1-59990-040-8
[1. Science fiction. 2. Amusement parks—Fiction. 3. Genetic engineering—Fiction.
4. Murder—Fiction. 5. London (England)—Fiction. 6. England—Fiction.] I. Title.
PZ7.B380768Pas 2009   [Fic]—dc22   2009008706

First U.S. Edition 2009
Typeset by Dorchester Typesetting Group Ltd
Printed in the U.S.A. by Quebecor World Fairfield
2 4 6 8 10 9 7 5 3 1

All papers used by Bloomsbury U.S.A. are natural, recyclable products
made from wood grown in well-managed forests. The manufacturing processes
conform to the environmental regulations of the country of origin.

IN MEMORIAM
ELLEN ALICE BECK
JANUARY 1913–OCTOBER 2008

A TRUE ACCOUNT OF THE FANTOM AND HIS CRIMES
AND ORIGIN, AS INTRODUCED AND COLLATED BY
CHIEF INSPECTOR CHARLES CATCHPOLE OF
SCOTLAND YARD (PASTWORLD DIVISION); AND
INCLUDING SOME DOCUMENTARY EVIDENCE SEEN
AND QUOTED HERE FOR THE FIRST TIME

⇝ FOREWORD ⇜

In presenting this story I would not wish to take any knowledge for granted on behalf of the reader. Most will be familiar with the crimes of the Fantom, and with the history and geography of the theme park known as Pastworld, but it was important to write this account for everybody and not to presume any knowledge of either the place, or the criminal and his crimes, on the part of any present or future readers. I would therefore ask those of you who are only too aware of these things to bear with the author.

The popular press carried garbled and sensational reports on the case of the Fantom and I was anxious to counteract such stories and present the truth as far as I could.

My involvement in this mystery began by chance during an early morning shift at the Buckland Corporation's Comms Centre when a warning signal lit up on my console. I have no wish to overplay my own role in the drama, but I cannot escape responsibility for some of what took place. It was my brief at first to find missing persons and through that quest I was able to help bring the Fantom if not to justice, then at least out into the open. I leave it for posterity to judge if I succeeded or not.

The words you will read are all mine except where I quote from various official sources and from Eve's journal.

I am grateful for the grant of monies from the William Leighton Foundation, which bought me the time to study and collate those various documents. Certain scenes and events are, of course, conjecture on my part, but a conjecture that is always based on the facts as they have been related to me by eye witnesses.

I hope that this account can stand both as an entertainment in its own right and also as an official record, but even more importantly, perhaps, as a warning: a warning of the vanity of progress and science, and of the fate that may await those who meddle with the building blocks of human nature.

CI Charles Catchpole, Scotland Yard (Pastworld Division)
July 2050

⟶❈ CHAPTER 1 ❈⟵

It was the cold hour before dawn. The streets of Pastworld City were laid out below the Buckland Corporation passenger airship like a map. At first little, if any, detail was visible through the early morning gloom and fog. There were just the regimented lines of grey slate roofs, with their yellow London brick stacks, and smoke curling up from artfully distressed terracotta chimney-pots. Flocks of mech pigeons were tucked in neat, dormant rows under the eaves of buildings. Few sounds were to be heard at that early hour, only the drone of the airship's engines and the mournful moans of the foghorns, which seemed almost to be searching for one another, somewhere along the silvered and twisted ribbon of river. Further away in the distance, from the deep, slumbering darkness at the centre of the city, could be heard the faint tolling of a single church bell.

There was little human movement.

Much nearer to the centre of the city, at the very hub of things, an eagle-eyed passenger would have spied a lone and sinister figure moving fast through the twisted streets and alleyways. He was the virus of the place, infecting the veins and arteries of the city. The shape and detail of his figure were hidden by the flapping of his long black cloak and his tall black evening hat. Every so often he turned and looked behind him, and the street lights caught in dazzle on his eyeglasses, which contained nothing but plain glass, for his vision was more than perfect. The lower part of his face was hidden behind a layer of dark silk, a scarf perhaps or a foulard, intended as a mask. He carried something bulky across his shoulders, well hidden beneath the folds of his cloak.

Ahead of him another figure, a piece of city shadow, suddenly detached itself from the shelter of one of the stone doorways and darted out on to the cobbles before him, blocking his way. The masked man quickly registered the outline of a youth: a pair of long skinny legs in shabby trousers, and a pair of worn boots; in fact the typical legs of a street urchin, a dip or a pickpocket. The boy's skin, in the almost-dawn light, was as grey as the surrounding stone, his face as sharply sculpted. He was a simple, cheerful-looking ruffian, of about seventeen. He wore a butcher-boy cap pulled down tight on his head. Its peak, which was broken down and worn by use, cast a deep shadow over the boy's face.

'Spare us a copper then, mi—' the boy started to say in a cheerily casual sort of way, but then he sputtered into silence when he saw the figure who stood in front of him.

'Nothing with me, I'm sorry,' said the cloaked man, hesitating, and with a hint of the mechanical response in his voice. There was something about the boy, something familiar. He riffled through his mind, and a flurry of boys like this one, so many boys, flickered through his head, but there was none that matched him, just an inexplicable image of an old black book. He dismissed it, shook his head and moved on swiftly.

The boy stood stock-still, frozen to the spot. He waited a moment and then he let out a sudden cloud of breath in relief. He watched the cloaked figure melt away into the fog. The boy shook himself and briefly laughed out loud. *He must be slipping*, the boy thought, *he saw me close to and didn't realise who I was.*

A Buckland Corp. passenger airship, the first of the morning, passed low overhead, its gondola lights briefly rippling across the street. The boy watched the ship pass right over him on its way to the Arrival Dock. Then he set off, his boots clattering across the cobbles. The metal heel tips scraped and rang, and he ran away as fast as he could.

While he ran the contours of the fog shifted and swirled around him. To Japhet McCreddie, known to all as 'Bible J', the fog was a living thing. The fog was his friend; he thought of it as his 'familiar'. It was a faithful beast, which prowled back and forth with him all day, followed him on his various quests around the city, shielding him, and all the other thieves (and worse) who thrived together in the shadows of Pastworld. It loomed all over the centre of the city, only too happy to swallow everything up, to make and keep secrets, and to smother the truth.

Not a hundred yards ahead of him was the exact place where the denser fog started, pumped up unbeknown to him through grilles from a system of pipes and ducts somewhere below the pavement. It hovered in a single, mechanical and severely straight line, right after the bridge. It nudged against the railings and the iron lamp posts with its beast back. In the fog there seemed to be no backwards, no place where he had come from, and no forwards, no visible place where he was going to, and that always suited Bible J's purpose. For the moment, time and place were suspended; he was just a very lucky boy hidden in the fog.

———◆———

The cloaked figure hurried on. The streets widened and the bright pools of light from the gas lamps became more frequent. By his movements, by the sudden lurches and flits of his figure, he appeared both young and vigorous. The bulky thing that he carried across his shoulders did not seem to slow him down at all. He made his way up a rising street towards some temporary hoardings that surrounded a towering building.

He had just left a butchered and dismembered body, minus the head, in plain view. Its various parts were spread out wide in the shape of Vitruvian man down in the area of the city known as Shoreditch. It was a reminder to all of his followers, and to anyone else, of his ruthlessness at dealing with attempted betrayals. It was also part of another message, an elaborate signal of his return from the dark, from the wilderness, a sharp return to business as usual that he would soon confirm to the Inspector, and to all the other fools who were after him.

The cloaked figure stopped in front of a plain wooden door set into the hoardings.

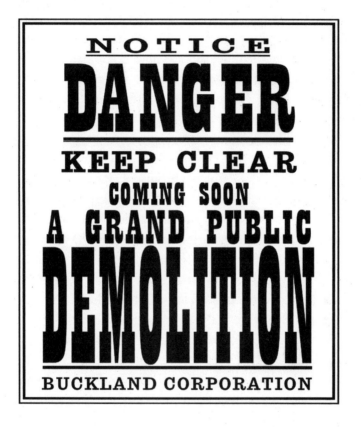

NOTICE

DANGER

KEEP CLEAR

COMING SOON

A GRAND PUBLIC

DEMOLITION

BUCKLAND CORPORATION

was printed in thick black lettering inches high on hundreds of identical posters pasted in rows all over the temporary walls. The entrance was lit from above by a single lantern. He looked around, waited for a beat, then furtively prised open the door. Once inside he shut the door, and set off in the darkness across the wasteland and then into the building itself.

He ran up a wide stone staircase. The stairs, once brightly lit, were in almost complete darkness, but did not slow him down. His cloak billowed and rustled as he climbed. The whispers of sound were reflected back from the surfaces around him, from the marble-clad walls and the metal banisters. He crossed a landing and climbed higher. Here there were service stairs, wooden and bare. He did not need to stop to catch his breath. He climbed another staircase and then another, and on, higher and higher.

Finally he reached a narrow hallway. There he stopped and pulled an iron carbide official police issue lamp out from under his cloak. He shone the light around the walls and across the ceiling above him. Its beam bounced back on to his white shirt front, which was splashed over with red.

There was all the evidence around him of preparations for the coming demolition. The hallway floor was covered in fragments of fallen ceiling and lengths of aluminium ducting for the coils of now mostly dead and useless cable. This was the last of the old twentieth-century 'new builds' and now the tallest building in the city, its once proud modernity was reduced to scattered lumps of decaying plaster.

This was where he thrived best: in a lost or secret place. Either somewhere very high or somewhere deep underground. In the murk and dark, in the chaos of half completion, of hasty closures, of sudden blocked-off passageways, dank tunnels and dangerously high roofs.

Dust motes floated in the lamp beam. He disturbed some nesting pigeons; they were real pigeons too, not Buckland mech birds. They flew up and hit the ceiling in their panic. The confusion of their wings caused fresh falls of plaster dust. A large, sleek brown rat scuttled across the floor. It stopped in front of him, as if barring the way. It lifted its head, its eyes seeming to glow red, and opened its mouth to reveal two rows of even, sharp teeth set in a fixed grimace. Then the rat said menacingly, 'No entry. Restricted area. Restricted area.'

❧ CHAPTER 2 ❧

FROM EVE'S JOURNAL[*]

I am Eve. I have no mother that I remember and no real father either, unless you count Jack. My memories of being little, or of being a child at all are few if any. At present I am five feet and seven inches tall and as far as I know I am seventeen years old.

I will try to write down all of the things of interest that happen, as slowly and as carefully as I can. I feel I must record my story. Others perhaps will read it. I cannot know of course who they will be.

It is early morning and the sky is filled with tumbling, ragged white clouds. I watch the clouds chase and rush after one another, and as I watch them I am almost bursting with love for all of Nature's creation. I cannot bear to think that the day will come when I will see all of this no more.

---

[*] *Ledger content. Unless otherwise stated the transcribed ledger/chronicle is in the original, all hand-written on antique wove paper in sepia-coloured ink.*

From the earliest days that I can remember Jack has always been there. I suppose I assumed he was my father, but of course I found out that he wasn't. He said he was my guardian, that I am an orphan. Imagine a shabby, rounded man, with thick glasses. Jack has terrible eyesight and is nearly blind, and he is so tender to me. Sometimes he is like a grumpy old toy bear that growls when you turn it over.

He is always fearful of the big city outside our windows. I have only the haziest memory of going anywhere else at all, although recently I have experienced what appears to be a returning memory or sensation. It is the smell of a particular kind of smoke and of myself jumping over some sparks and flames. Odd but it seems very real to me. Despite everything, despite the blank slate of my past, I somehow manage to understand almost the whole world around me. Perhaps it is just that Jack told me so many things, taught me so well in his way, because I often feel as if those spoken memories, those shared conversations make up my entire childhood.

I seem to have just woken up a couple of years ago as a fully grown fifteen-year-old.

I remember one particular day very clearly. I stood at our attic window and noticed everything around me as if my eyes had just opened for the first time. I remember I watched a great passenger airship as it sailed past, and Jack said to me, 'Here they come. Do you see?' and he pointed at the shape as it crossed the grey sky. I nodded and repeated, 'Here they come.' Why that is so clearly imprinted I have no idea, unless it was because that day there was another man in the room, and as a rule we never have any visitors at all.

I remember that our visitor, a well-dressed man ('our smart visitor' I called him) took me by the shoulders, turned me away from the window and looked into my face, then he said, 'My, those eyes, Jack. She'll break hearts with those,' and Jack agreed and sighed.

I pass my days and nights calm and steady and quiet in our attic rooms. I do think it strange that I am never ever allowed to go out on my own. I am only ever allowed out with poor, fearful Jack.

'This is a big and dangerous city,' Jack says.

'Dangerous even for me?' I asked once.

'Yes, dangerous for a girl like you – double dangerous,' he replied, scrunching up his face with anguish. 'You have no idea,' he added, 'there are people out there who would mean a girl like you nothing but harm.'

I accepted his explanation, but inside I feel a strange confidence that I will be safe, invincible, if ever I do go out on my own. And oh, I want to do so very badly.

Jack keeps me close to him always. As time passes, measured by the ticking of our mantel clock, he seems to become more and more scared for me. On the rare occasions when we go out it is always now in the evening.

I am sure that the two of us are barely visible to passers-by on the dark, crowded streets. We walk together in the fogs that seem to arrive exactly on cue. Jack's eyesight is getting so bad that I have always to lead him by the arm.

A strange couple we must seem to anyone who cares to notice us. The halting, rounded Jack, and myself tall – 'willowy', Jack says.

I am always eager to explore everything. I am tempted to be wild: I am fidgety, and constantly dream of running away, slipping the leash in the fog, and escaping. I want just to run, skip and jump.

On our walks Jack looks around us. Peers as best he can into the cold gloom, ever fearful, ever worried, and never relaxed. Sometimes he stops and talks to an acquaintance; there is a woman we sometimes see who must live in the maze of streets somewhere near to us. I call her the lady with the cat.

'Chilly this evening, Jack.'

'Yes indeed it is, my dear.'

'Out with your girl, then?'

'Yes, she's very kindly walking with me, poor old dog that I am.'

'You're an old dog, Jack, and I walk a cat, not very well matched, are we?'

Jack chuckles nervously at comments like that, but I can tell he just wants to tuck his head down into his collar and keep walking.

Later

Everything has changed. I will explain as best I can.

Jack went out early alone and he came back trembling and agitated and preoccupied. He sat me down, and squinted at me as best he could through his thick glasses.

'I have to tell you something, Eve,' he said, in an

unsteady voice. 'You may often have wondered why I look after you so carefully. The truth is that someone is after us. They have been for a long while now. I have deliberately kept this from you, Eve, just for your own protection. I have always been so very, very careful for you, but anyhow this bad, bad person has got a sniff of you, and as soon as it can be arranged we will have to move somewhere else. Somewhere far from here.'

He stood and paced up and down in a twitching panic. I could make no sense of it at all. Here was my mystery.

'How would such a dangerous person know anything about us?' I said.

'He knows,' Jack said nodding. 'As I said, he's got a sniff of you.'

Something alerted me in those repeated words: 'a sniff of you'. That surely means it is not 'us' at all but just me alone, myself — someone is especially after me. It was suddenly clear to me.

I am a deep secret.

I am a hidden person.

I am to be kept safe for ever. I was a fairy-tale princess, like Rapunzel, locked away from the world in her high tower.

Except of course that when I caught a glimpse of myself in the overmantel glass, I saw that I am not a fairy-tale princess at all. I have no cascades of golden hair to spill out of our window all the way down into the cold street below. No, I am just myself. It was just me I saw looking back. Me, all drab in my plain cinnamon-coloured day dress, standing in our shabby attic rooms, with poor half-blind

Jack to protect me.

'Why,' I said, 'would anybody even know about me, let alone wish me any harm?'

Jack shook his head. 'There are some things you are not ready to know yet.'

A few days have passed and the mysterious friend of Jack's, the smart visitor, has been to see Jack once again. This time they sat together talking urgently while I stayed very quiet and made, at his request, a nice pot of Assam tea. I watched them but I said nothing. They spoke in careful, low voices, and the smart visitor was clearly as agitated as Jack. It was then that I found out something strange and new about myself. If I watched their mouths very closely as they spoke, I could read their lips. I could make out and read the words as if they were unrolling inside my own head on a printed page.

JACK: 'I'm that attached now, I couldn't do it, and I can't go back, surely you can understand? You've got a child yourself.'

THE SMART VISITOR: 'I do understand, of course I do, but you can't compare the two. It's either that or one day he'll come for her and you will be in the way, and that will be the end of you.'

After an awkward taking of tea during which our visitor simply stared at me and shook his head, he finally made to leave. He shrugged himself into his overcoat and they spoke again hurriedly in the little vestibule that led to the staircase but now their backs were turned and I could make out nothing more of what they said.

I said nothing to Jack about my sudden ability to read lips.

When the visitor had gone and Jack turned his face back to me he looked collapsed, vanquished, twisted in grief at whatever the smart visitor's news had been.

I went to the window and looked down on the busy street below. I watched all the bustling people going to and fro. When I finally turned away from the window and looked at Jack, he was sitting with his back to me, slumped and cowed in our dingy room. Jack turned awkwardly in his chair, squinting at me against the bright light from the window.

'Sorry, Eve,' he said.

'Why should you be sorry?' I replied.

'Can't explain,' he said quietly.

In the evening we had a cold supper of sliced mutton, pickles and bread. We ate in silence. Our cutlery clattered on the plates. Jack breathed heavily not looking at me.

Since that day Jack has remained in a watchful and preoccupied state.

'He'll come for her,' the smart visitor said, 'and you will be in the way.' Who is going to come for me? I wish it could be my rescuer. At last my own gallant knight on a white charger will come. But it seems more likely from the fear on Jack's face that he will be our nemesis. An evil enchanter, another kind of pale rider altogether, who will destroy poor Jack and take me away with him. These thoughts leave me both excited and fearful. They have also concentrated my mind and I now know just what I must to do. I have to save myself and poor Jack from such a fate at all costs.

Jack spends his days now poring over the daily newspaper and the weekly magazines. He holds his reading glass in his trembling hand over the pages, as close to the light as he can get, very obviously looking for something. He won't explain to me what or why. He mutters as he reads, 'Phantom, all over the phantom,' and 'Damn my failing eyes.'

I am resolved. Tomorrow I will simply go. I will vanish, run away and take my chances. I will at least spare Jack the fear, the danger of discovery and destruction. I will rescue myself from my high tower and spare Jack any more responsibility.

It is something I have never ever done before; I will go out and away, alone.

I have achieved it, so much has happened. I must write it all down very carefully.

The very next morning after I determined to run away, I looked out across the rooftops and I saw that snow had fallen in the night. It was soft and thick and spread evenly like a dimpled sheet across the roof tiles. I opened the attic window a little and breathed in the frosted air, and I looked forward in excitement to running away, out into that bright white morning.

I had planned carefully what to take. I would need to wrap up warmly, so I took my winter coat from its wooden hanger and untied the camphor bag that protected it from moths. I packed a small leather bag with a change of clothes and all of my own money from the savings jar. Then I left the coat and bag tucked behind a chair in the parlour.

Jack went out early to the nearby grocer's shop, and he was soon back with a packet of tea and a few rashers of bacon. As he patted the snow from his coat, he said, 'My, it's brisk out today, Eve,' and then he unfurled his morning paper as usual and studied it near the even white light from the window.

I made a pot of strong tea, and some toast, and griddled the bacon for our breakfast.

I said, 'Shall I read to you some more this morning?'

'Yes, that would be lovely, but no more of Mr Sherlock Holmes, he's a bit too close to the bone, Mr Dickens I think.' Eventually after breakfast he settled himself in his high-backed chair, and put his feet up on a cushion. He crossed his arms over his rounded tummy and nodded for me to begin.

'Great Expectations. Chapter 1.

'My father's family name being Pirrip, and my Christian name Philip, my infant tongue could make of both names nothing longer or more explicit than Pip. So, I called myself Pip, and came to be called Pip . . .'

As I read on through the hour I saw Jack's eyelids begin to droop and flutter. Then the familiar little parps and snorts of his snoring began and in a few pages more Jack was fast asleep. I kept on reading aloud while I pulled from out of my bodice the note I had already written. I propped it up against the now cold brown teapot.

Dear Jack,

I am going away.
Don't worry about me.
Don't look for me.
Protect yourself.

Your loving Eve

Then still reading aloud I struggled my way one-handed into my warm coat and picked up the bag. Then I stopped reading, lay the book down and let myself out of the door very quietly, shutting it with just the slightest click. I was sure that no one from the downstairs lodgings or the shop below saw me leave as I slipped . . .

. . . out into the street.

I had resolved to run away to the circus. I had no plan in my head at all except to find a circus. I would vanish into the big city somewhere. I would work and travel around from place to place.

It was quite a shock to step out finally into a busy street alone and in broad daylight. It was so rushed and hectic. Ragged urchin boys sped past me on the slippery snow-covered pavement laughing, and pushing one another. Street singers were gathered in a cluster singing loudly. Hawkers were selling things: safety matches, and bootlaces, and hot chestnuts. The snow blew around in sharp little flurries and swirls. My face tingled and I felt suddenly a great rushing sensation, as if I were properly alive for the first time. My senses quivered; the cold air felt like a tonic. I found that I was very fast on my feet without Jack to hold me back. I ran, I skipped and jumped over the snow.

A man in the street was selling mince pies, they were lined up neat and warm and inviting, all steaming on a tray which hung from a strap around his neck.

'How much?' I asked.

'A penny, miss,' he said smiling back at me.

I handed him one of the bright pennies I had taken from the jar and I felt a twinge of guilt at the thought of Jack sleeping unaware in the parlour. I looked into all the shop windows while I feasted on my hot mince pie. A ragged man sat on the pavement propped up by the red posting box. He looked up at me as I passed with a sad expression on his face. I stopped then, only too aware of the warmth in my own hand from the little pie and the frosted look of his blue-white skinny fingers. I walked back a pace and handed him another coin, this time a whole silver sixpenny piece. I touched his hand and felt the sudden chill, his fingers were as cold as the icicles on our guttering. At first he smiled and nodded gratefully, and then a sudden change came over his face. A change that suggested he had recognised me, although as far as I knew we had never seen each other before.

'It's you,' he said his eyes wide. 'You're the one,' and he nodded.

'I can't think what you mean,' I said smiling back at him and hurried off.

'Come back,' he called out, but I kept walking.

Some minutes later I saw that the cold beggar had managed to follow me. He was looking in the window of a baker's shop. He could get a half loaf and a lardy cake at least with my sixpence, and even a bag of broken biscuits too. He turned and our eyes met. I looked away, a little disturbed by the way he stared at me, like a hungry wolf in a fairy tale. I set off down the street again hurrying away from him between all the bustling shoppers.

I arrived at the market place. This is where I knew the circus would be. There were rows of big shops behind the busy crowds. A muffin man with a tray balanced on his head, pushed and dodged his way through. A man in a long overcoat kept pace with me for a moment. His waist was wound about with sacking and across his shoulders he carried a pole strung with a row of dead rabbits all tied by their little hind feet. I turned away from those sad little dead creatures only to find myself face to face with with a pink pig's head hanging on a hook along with a row of others in the window of a pork butcher's. I could clearly see their pale eyelashes. A long row of pig carcasses hung from a rail below. A large crusted raised pork pie sat on a china platter below them. I hurried further into the crowd, away from the smell of blood and sawdust. In among the market stalls was the winter fair with street entertainers and a little circus of sorts.

Near to me there was the first of a group of brightly painted wagons with canvas covers. A tumbler in a bright harlequin costume stood in front of the nearest wagon, while another played a battered cornet. There was a banner stretched above them, with the words JAGO'S ACCLAIMED PANDEMONIUM SHOW lettered across it.

The performers had attracted quite a crowd of Gawkers who were watching them all in a jovial crush. Aware of the possibility that the beggar might still be following me, I went in deep among them.

'Sorry,' I said, 'I am so sorry, excuse me, please,' and I pushed my way forward as far away from blood and pig carcasses and ragged men as I could get. Most of the people I jostled and bumped past seemed jolly enough, all out to enjoy themselves on a bright, crisp morning, but there were some other, rougher-looking folk among them. Men and women with deeply hollowed eyes and sunken cheeks. They were starved-looking people with thin wrists and knobbly bones that seemed almost to poke out of their filthy clothes.

A covered wagon was stationed at each end of a small stage and a high tightrope was strung above the stage supported by two striped poles. A harlequin on the stage played a loud roll on a snare drum, and another stood holding on to one of the support ropes, shouting in a raucous voice, his face vivid white with make up, his thin mouth painted a cheerful bright red.

'Roll up, roll up,' he cried. 'See Jago walk the rope. All the way from the far Indies, to be here with us today in cold old London town, all that way, from the heat and dust of that far country, just to walk a high rope for you, fifteen feet in the air, and no safety net, roll up now, come on, roll up.'

The canvas opened at the back of one of the wagons and another harlequin stepped out on to the little stage to applause. He had a dark face in stark contrast to the other white-faced harlequins. As he stood balanced on the lower part of the rope. I noticed his soft shoes and the way he curled his toes around the rope. I supposed it was to grip. The Indian harlequin carried a parasol, covered in bright

{ 26 }

diamond patches of coloured cloth. He waved the parasol about as a counterbalance as he inched comically up the rope towards the top of the support pole. I pushed forward further, squeezing my way nearer to the front to get a better view. The drummer kept the snapping drum roll going all the while.

The Harlequin made to walk right across the rope but he seemed to lose his balance, he fell forwards almost tipping himself off over the crowd. First he leaned one way, and then the other, flailing his arms, with a frightened expression on his face. A silence fell over the section of the crowd near the stage. I gasped, along with several others. Then someone laughed and we all realised it was a trick. He was only pretending to fall. The crowd loved this and laughter rang out. There were oohs and aahs, and more nervous laughter. I had never seen anything so frightening or exciting in all of my poor, dull, closed-off life.

One of the harlequins came among us with a collecting box. I put in some coins from my coat pocket, without looking, not quite knowing exactly how generous I was really being. The harlequin smiled as I dropped them into the box, he had a kindly face under the stark white make-up, a friendly face.

The rope walker finished his act above the heads of the crowd. I couldn't see how he did it, but by some clever trick the Indian harlequin seemed to fall to the stage in a kind of slowed-down motion. I joined in the wild applause; I felt safe, suddenly warm and happy, huddled close in the crowd watching these colourful entertainers.

The drummer put aside his drum, and pulled a small

table to the front of the makeshift stage. The table was laid with a large fine cloth; the cloth was blue, the blue of the sky, the blue of infinity, the blue of serenity, and it was covered over in tiny silver stars. The Indian harlequin, the one I imagined was perhaps Jago himself, raised his hand, his long bony finger pointed upwards, to concentrate his audience's attention, and he hissed 'Sshh.'

The crowd quietened down, the cornet player switched to a violin, and started to play a sad little waltz tune. The harlequin Jago reached under the blue cloth, and then pulled out . . . nothing. He held his hands out to the audience, and showed them front and back – nothing. He pulled his ragged sleeves up a little to show that they also concealed nothing. He bent forward to the crowd and to me in particular. He put his hand behind my ear. I felt his fingers brush past me with a tickling sensation on my skin and he pulled as if from nowhere a single white egg. He held it up and showed it round, first to me and then to the audience. The egg shone out clear white against his skin.

There was scattered laughter and applause. 'Just an egg, you will allow,' he said. 'An egg and nothing but an egg?'

'Oh yes,' I said eager to join in.

He raised his hand high above his head, and slowly brought it down, he tapped the egg lightly on the edge of the table, cupped his hands, and in an instant . . . a white dove emerged.

He released the dove, and it flew up and round in the cold air and finally settled on the top of one of the striped support poles. We all applauded wildly; I had never seen anything so amazing. The other harlequin continued to shake his collecting box. Another was starting to pack away their bright equipment into the wagons; it seemed that they were getting ready to leave. I felt a surge of disappointment. Soon they would all be gone. I determined that I must be part of them. I would follow them and I would watch them again and join in again, make myself useful, make myself indispensable.

Then I caught sight of something which alarmed me. It was the ragged man again, the one I had given sixpence to. He was staring at me and at the same time moving steadily in my direction through the crowd. I was gripped by fear. It was as if something were suddenly released inside me, as if an alarm had finally gone off. This feeling energised me further, heightened my reaction to everything. I just knew that the ragged man meant me great harm. It is typical somehow of my particular turn of mind that I could watch the harlequins preparing to leave with sweet regret, while at the same time closely watching someone that I somehow knew instinctively to be murderous, bearing down on me, with such strange and cruel intent on his face, but that is what it's like to be seventeen and suddenly awakened and in love with life.

Jago pulled the blue cloth from the table; it unfurled like a flag. Meanwhile the table itself was hurled into the back of the wagon. It seemed that there would be one last trick. Jago shook the cloth out to its full size until it was a big square banner. He turned the cloth round front to back — nothing. The audience waited. In fear, I turned again and scanned the crowd. All the faces were looking, mesmerised, at the performer above them on the stage; all except one. It was the ragged man. He was looking directly at me as he pushed himself forward through the last few people in the crowd who separated us. I turned back to the platform. I looked up at the harlequin. He seemed to single me out with his dark eyes. It was then that I felt a strong bony hand grip my shoulder. I turned and looked into the dirt-streaked face of the ragged man. Close to, it was a frightening face. The beggar opened his mouth and showed his yellowed and crooked teeth.

'Well, well, what have we here?' he said. 'I've found you, I know it, the pretty blue-eyed girl herself.'

The harlequin looked down at me from the top edge of the stage, and he raised one eyebrow like a question mark. I felt the hand of the beggar tighten further on my shoulder, and I looked up at the harlequin and I quietly said the words 'Help me.'

With a sudden movement the Harlequin threw the blue cloth, and it fell over me like a waterfall. As I was enveloped by the cloth I felt a strong counter grip on my waist. My shoulder was pulled from the beggar's hand, and my feet lifted off the ground. I heard the ragged man give a surprised yell of 'Oi'. His hands tried to grab at me wildly under the folds of the cloth, but I felt a rush of strength and movement, and the world suddenly turned upside down. There was a flash of the bright cold blue sky and then there was darkness, a rush, and a sudden soft landing. I found I was lying on a pile of dusty velvet behind the tailboard of the circus wagon. My eye was close to a peep hole. I was able to see everything from my sudden new position as the cloth fluttered and tangled up around the beggar, and then fell to the ground.

The harlequin picked up the cloth, and twirled it in front of the crowd, front to back, back to front, nothing, it was empty.

'The lady vanishes,' he called out.

It must have seemed to them that I had indeed simply vanished into thin air. The large crowd roared their approval. There was applause and laughter. Clearly for them my disappearance and the confusion of the ragged man all seemed to be part of the show.

The beggar looked round him and then shouted out in a fury, 'All right, that's enough. Show's over, now you give her back to me.'

The harlequin cried, 'Sshh, the lady's not for returning,' pressed his finger to his lips and raised the blue cloth over his own head and held it there for a moment, then let it fall to cover himself completely. There was silence. The ragged man stared at the cloth, with a puzzled expression on his face. Then he reached forward and grabbed at the cloth, which spiralled to the ground, to reveal . . . again nothing, for the harlequin was gone too.

By now the wagons were on the move. I saw the other two harlequins running away back into the crowd and heard the crowd roar their approval again. I watched as the ragged man kicked at the folds of the fine blue cloth, and then he picked it up, and shook it as if perhaps expecting either myself or the harlequin to fall out on to the ground. Then he began a furious pursuit, pushing through the edge of the crowd, elbowing people aside. He shoved his way through, and suddenly the ragged man was within grabbing distance of the tailboard of the wagon where I lay hidden. It was then that the dove that had been born fully grown from the egg flew past the beggar and, as it did so, pulled the fine floating length of blue cloth from his hand, in its beak and flew with it under the canvas cover of the wagon. The beggar, with an amazed expression on his face, tripped and fell headlong across the cobbles, into a puddle of filthy snow melt, and then we rattled fast out of the busy square and turned into the traffic.

I was squashed down among deep piles of soft fabrics, folded costumes and rolls of velvet inside the wagon. I sat up as we turned the corner and sneezed in all the general dustiness, and the dark conjuring harlequin with the kind eyes popped his head through the canvas flap from the front of the wagon.

'Are you all right? Sorry about grabbing you like that, only it looked to me like you needed it. Don't worry – we'll shake him off soon enough.'

I felt dizzy, both from the motion of the wagon, and also from the sudden lurch in my circumstances. I crawled forward to the front so as to hear him better. The wagon was full of entertainer's paraphernalia; piles of costumes, striped poles and ropes, glass globes and silver stars, and a giant cut-out pasteboard moon with a smiling face.

'I should hold tight if I were you,' he said. 'Our horse may be skinny, but she's fast. Why was the ragged man after you?'

I looked at the narrow back of the harlequin blankly. I was unsure now of anything and anyone – I had been *rescued, saved, but by who?*

'Well,' I said. 'My guardian had warned me not to go out on my own. He said that someone meant me harm. I took no heed though and went out alone. The next thing I knew that man had grabbed hold of me.'

'Don't worry, you'll be safe with us,' said the harlequin. 'We know those ragged men, only too well. Why would anyone want to do you harm I wonder? From your clothes you don't look like a Gawker — you're a cast native, a dweller?'

'I've lived here all my life,' I said, puzzled. What was a cast native?

'A native then, just a bit off your usual beat,' he said with a smile.

I sat alone in the back of the wagon while it rattled away. When we finally came to a stop, it was already dark. There was an odd brackish smell, which I discovered as I climbed warily out of the wagon, was from the river Thames. The horse was let out of its shafts and stood chewing out of a feed bag. We had fetched up under some trees, in what appeared to be an enclosed park. One or two simple tents and some other wagons were pitched around us under the wide branches. There was a small fire, which gave off more smoke than flames, a pot was hung over it, and I could smell something cooking and the smell reminded me of how hungry I was.

Jago sat on the front step of the wagon. He seemed to be only a little older than myself, and he was petting the white dove which shone bright next to his copper-coloured skin. He looked over and smiled at me. One of the other harlequins

{ 33 }

was standing a little way from the fire. He had a spoon balanced on his nose. He flipped his head up and the spoon suddenly twisted up in the air end over end, and then it landed back on his nose, balanced just as before. He extended his arm, dropped the spoon down into his hand and held it out to me.

'Have something to eat,' he said, and winked at me. I took the spoon warily, as if half expecting it to jump out of my hand and back up on to the harlequin's nose.

Jago smiled, stretched forward with the dove now sitting happily on his shoulder and ladled something out of the pot on to a plate and handed it to me. It was a kind of aromatic stew, with yellow rice; it smelled wonderful. There were pale shapes of what turned out to be chicken in the middle of it. I wolfed it down fast. It stung my tongue and there was heat in it from spices. Then he held out a mug of tea, and I went to drink it, but he thought better of it and he took the cup and threw the tea on to the fire so that the ashes hissed. Then he filled the mug again this time from a dark bottle.

'Try that instead,' he said.

'Mm, it's bitter,' I said, 'sour too.'

'It's just beer, plain old English Ale.'

I sipped at the liquid again, I had never tasted beer before. I sat down near the fire, which by now had faded down to a few wisps of smoke. Then Jago took the cup of beer back from me and drank down the rest himself.

'I'm Jago,' he said, and wiped his thin hand across his mouth.

I nodded. 'I thought you were. My name is Eve,' and I took his hand in mine for a moment. I had never seen or touched skin so dark before.

A passenger airship passed over the trees, and it was low enough for the passenger gondola to almost touch the treetops. The wind from the propellers thrashed the leaves back and forth. The lights shone down across the tents that were pitched among the trees.

'A lovely name, for a lovely girl,' Jago said. He looked up at the airship. 'And still they come,' he added, watching the airship as it passed over us. His narrow face broke into a grin and I saw how neat and white his teeth were. 'I wonder why you have been sent to me, Eve?'

'I have run away to join your circus,' I said.

❖ CHAPTER 3 ❖

OBSERVATION ROOM 1,
BUCKLAND CORP. COMMS CENTRE 6.40 A.M.

Sgt Charles Catchpole was drinking a strong coffee, his first of the day, and looking at the image of Pastworld on the Comms screen. Dawn was breaking over the shadowy city. It was a view that never failed to engage him. The rows of yellow gaslights were softened, blurred by the machined fog. The muffled barges, and the haze of steam from the gasworks all made a subtle picture, an aubade worthy of J. M. Whistler. Catchpole's dreamy gaze was interrupted when the alarm signal lit up, a sudden flicker of light, and movement on the bank of screens at the workstation.

He put his styrofoam cup down on the desk top, pressed the lid carefully back into place. He brought up the image, selected it as a central feature and ran it across six of the smaller screens. A pursuit spy, one of the newer Espion cameras, was transmitting a movement-triggered image, from a restricted zone.

He reached forward for the alert signal tag. He checked the coordinates and zoomed in on the image. Immediately, Catchpole switched to a Code Orange. This would automatically trigger interest from DI Hudson in his cubicle down the corridor. He kept the live Espion feed up, minimised it and noted the earlier mech circuit pattern as well. It wasn't a minute before his partner, Hudson, appeared. The bright bank of screens reflected as intense blue squares across his wraparounds as he entered the room.

'What you got?' said Hudson as he eased his bulky frame into a chair by Catchpole's desk. He sat with his arms folded in a 'this had better be good' stance.

'Well, look at this.' Catchpole tapped the central panel of screens with his coffee stirrer.

'About fifteen minutes ago I noticed that one of the sentinel mechs had been activated on this circuit loop. I checked back on it and read the timeline, and it wasn't a malfunction, it was an intruder. A minute later an Espion camera was triggered by exceptional movement, and this feed has been coming in ever since.' Catchpole brought it up on to the main screen again. In green-tinted night vision, they watched the picture of the upper level of the old Tower 42 building. A figure in a billowing cloak stood still and high on the ruined top.

Hudson said quietly, 'Let's get a closer shot and go for a match.'

Catchpole moved his hand across the screen on the console and the image shifted, sparked for an instant with little flickers of white and then settled. A masked face with bright shining circles for eyes came into close view.

'God it looks like him all right,' Hudson said. 'He's back.'

The image of the masked figure's head froze onscreen. Catchpole shifted the still image away into a separate window.

Hudson was right; it certainly looked like him.

Catchpole shifted his hand again and focused in on the figure. On the closer image the 'o' shape of the mouth was clearly defined behind the thin mask as he calmly breathed in and out.

'He's holding something,' said Hudson. 'Check it.'

Catchpole focused on what was held in the figure's hands. While they watched, the figure placed the object very carefully on a flat iron protrusion, the top edge of a girder, just above his head.

'Oh God,' said Hudson.

Then the figure vanished; he simply stepped off the edge of the building.

'Now,' Catchpole said, 'who else would do that?'

'Looks like he's really back,' Hudson said, 'better get hard copy of this. Print it all up and we'll take it over to the Inspector on the next flight.' At the mention of the Inspector, Catchpole's spirits rose. If pursuit was back on, officially, that would mean a visit to Pastworld, and a change of outlook, a change of clothes of course, a change of era, and perhaps even a change of everything else as well . . .

⚜ CHAPTER 4 ⚜

The Fantom looked down at the rat. 'Well they know I'm here now all right,' he said. He shone the lamp up through the ruined ceiling. The lamp light picked out a ladder. The Fantom tested it for weight, then climbed swiftly up. He pulled himself on to the remaining support beams into the windy darkness above. The pigeons flew through one of the great gaping holes into the sudden freedom of the open air.

He continued up among the broken roof beams and the huge rivet-studded metal girders. He crossed a fragile timber platform that bowed and buckled under his weight.

From his position he looked down from the full height of the tower. He stood uncertainly for a moment on the very edge of a steeply curved iron support. The sad moan of the fog horns rose again from the river somewhere below. The dawn breeze ruffled his cloak, so that it billowed out in a swirl. He removed the bag from his shoulders and placed it at his feet, then he pulled out a gold watch on a chain from his waistcoat pocket and checked the time. He waited, watching the second hand – waited for the artificial sun to rise behind the clouds.

Far below him, under the cobbles and the stone, underneath the tangled map of streets, the city changed gear; the secret systems shifted and, perfectly on cue, a light grew in the sky.

At the right moment he stood up tall and pulled something out of the bag at his feet. He held it very carefully in his hands and allowed time for it to be seen, for they would surely be watching now. Then he reached up and put the severed head on to the girder above him with its blood-shocked grin facing outwards. He slipped the bag back across his shoulders. Then with his tall figure haloed by light, he climbed with care up the last few feet to the pinnacle of the ruined dome. He stood grudgingly admiring the beauty of the perfect sunrise. He looked across at the wheeling birds over the river, at the view of the whole city. He took it all in, his eyes aqua blue and sharp behind his mask. He raised his arms and held them out wide. He spoke out loud, 'Alas poor Yorick,' and laughed, and after that he counted in perfectly measured seconds, 'One, one thousand, two, one thousand, three, one thousand,' and so on under his breath, as someone had once taught him. When he reached the number ten, his figure, perfectly silhouetted against the orb of the bright, newly risen electric sun, simply stepped off the skeleton dome, straight out into freefall through the cold morning air . . .

⇥ CHAPTER 5 ⇤

A circus wagon pulled away from one of the busy market squares and turned off into the thoroughfare. A ragged man, tubercular-looking with a long neck and skinny limbs picked himself up from a cold, wet, puddle of snow melt. He had been close to his prize, close enough to touch her. He walked away like some dripping, bedraggled scarecrow back through the crowd of warm bundled up and mostly indifferent Gawkers. Some of them laughed as he passed. One or two even tried to give him coins, they had enjoyed his performance as the patsy to the conjuror so much.

The ragged man had no desire to end his life cut into pieces, with his heart removed like the others before him. He had a difficult decision to make. He had the choice of reporting his sighting of her now and letting the message travel up the chain of command or he could walk back to the place where he had first seen her. He knew that there was a good chance that there he might find the secondary prize, her guardian.

It was a cold day and he shivered as he walked, his wet rags hung heavy on his frame. He was lucky that at the moment his tattered boots were still just watertight. If he caught sight of the guardian too, it would surely mean a reward. Not the first prize but something substantial. She had been outside all on her own and that must mean that the guardian would be trying to find her, or at least have raised some sort of alarm. Better still, there was always the chance that she might come back. In which case, he would be able to take her and him together, there and then. Simple.

The pie seller's pitch was not far from the red postbox where he had first seen her. He made his way back there. He felt bitter at the way she had been taken from him after he had been so close, and by a dirty conjuring trick too. He would know that conjuror anywhere and if he ever saw him again he would finish him. When he finally reached the postbox he saw that it was half hidden under a fall of fresh snow.

Opposite was a row of dark shops, some with bowed window fronts, and all with beautifully lettered fascias in gold script, or decorated capitals. The row of shops offered everything from groceries and ironmongery to ladies' fine hats. There were modest lodgings and rooms above the shops. Their hipped roofs and red chimney pots peeped out in patches under the settling snow. The street looked like a Christmas card, which is just how it had been planned. The beggar set himself to wait. He stood as still as he could shivering. His feet were numb, and his hands looked blue-white under his half mittens. He did not have to wait for very long.

An agitated-looking man wearing spectacles and carrying a white stick soon appeared at the top of the short flight of steps from the lodgings entrance beside the grocer's shop. The man was untidily dressed. He wore no overcoat, just a woollen scarf around his throat and a tweed jacket. The ragged man watched the figure struggle down the icy steps of the lodging house, one hand firmly on the iron rail the other probing with a white stick. The man's head jerked from side to side as he looked up and down the still busy street. The ragged man watched him until he had reached the middle of the pavement then he moved away from the postbox and fell in step, shuffling through the snow at a safe distance behind the blind man. The beggar watched as the blind man stopped people in the street, asked them something and then moved on. Finally the blind man reached the public house on the corner, the Buckland Arms, and went inside.

The door of the public house was firmly closed. The ragged man could smell sour, vinegary beer fumes and the winter warmer, Buckland punch. The glass panel on the door had etched and engraved glass patterns all over it, protecting the privacy of the Gawkers. There were slivers and gaps in the pattern, little bevels and edges of clear glass. The ragged man put his reddened eye to one of the clear sections and looked in. The bar was crowded with Gawkers, men in bowler hats and checked tweed jackets, men in cloth caps and white muffler scarves, women sitting laughing together at round marble-topped tables, all red-faced and fiercely jolly in the warm amber lit interior. The ragged man shivered, and pulled his dirty scarf tighter about his neck. The blind man went from person to person from table to table, all along the side of the saloon bar, even talking through the little hinged and bevelled windows that opened into the public bar on the other side. He asked his question. With each answer came a shake of a head. Finally the blind man turned away from the bar making as if to leave. The ragged man dodged back from the heavy doors. His excitement rising, he ran lightly ahead and waited in the middle of the pavement where he was sure to be accosted. A gust of warm air and a spiral cloud of fine sawdust from the floor billowed out with him as the blind man pushed through the door and retraced his steps.

The blind man came up to the ragged man, the white stick held out in front of him prodding the skim of snow on the treacherous pavement. 'Excuse me, friend,' he said, 'I'm looking for a girl.'

'That's what they all say,' the beggar replied, baring his yellow teeth as he gave a shifty little laugh.

'No, I'm serious,' said the blind man. 'You can see well, I have no doubt, sir, so please try and help me. She's my only daughter you see and she's gone and run away, the silly girl. She's seventeen, and a very slender girl, and bright-eyed. Have you perhaps seen her?'

'I wish I had, I really do,' said the ragged man. The cheeky cockney laugh was absent now, replaced with a sense of threat. He moved closer so that for a moment the blind man and the ragged man stood facing one another in the middle of the still busy pavement.

'Tell you what, spare me a copper coin,' the beggar said, 'and I'll help you find her.'

The blind man peered at him closely and then reached his free hand forward and felt for the beggars arm. He felt ragged clothes, he felt the texture of coarse and tattered greasy fabric. Then the blind man sniffed, and even through the cold air, he picked up a stale and unwashed smell.

'Oh,' said the blind man quietly, 'you're one of them,' and he backed off fearfully, his black boots slipping a little on the icy cobbles. 'I have no coins,' he said matter of factly, 'nothing to give you today, I'm afraid.'

'Tight-fisted like the rest of your type,' the ragged man said, his voice now a knife in the air, 'I hope for your sake you find that girl.'

'I hope to God you don't,' the blind man muttered under his breath.

———◆———

The ragged man stood in the shelter of a shop doorway. He pulled a packet of cigarette papers and a little rough leather pouch of tobacco out of an inner pocket. He rolled himself a cigarette. He struck a match against the brickwork and lit up, his face rosy in its sudden flare. He breathed in the warm smoke, coughed a little and rubbed his bony hands together. He settled to wait, smoking and watching the steps that led to the blind man's lodgings.

Within an hour the blind man let himself out of the door, turning awkwardly he stumbled down the steps once again supporting himself on his cane. The ragged man stepped out of the doorway. The blind man held a white envelope in his free hand, held it free of his flapping coat, his chin tucked down to hold his scarf in place. He made his way slowly, warily, towards the postbox. The ragged man moved quickly into place a few yards from the postbox. The blind man drew nearer. The ragged man walked forward directly into his path and bumped against him just enough, nudging at the arm that held the envelope – just enough to dislodge it from the blind man's nervous grip so that it fluttered down to the ground and sat on the snow, white on white. The blind man called out in anguish. The ragged man picked up the envelope at once. It had an address written across it in large childish-looking writing.

'I am so sorry,' the ragged man said, smoothing his voice, 'you seem to have dropped this. Here allow me to post it for you, sir.' The ragged man quickly tapped the iron mouth of the postbox with the edge of the envelope to make it sound as if he had dropped it in.

'There! It's away now for you, and just in time for the last post too,' he said, slipping the envelope into his own pocket.

'Did you post that for me?' said the blind man. 'Well thank you, sir, that's very kind I'm sure.' The blind man stood still and stared after the retreating stranger. He could make out only a dark shape against the white like an upside-down exclamation mark. He sniffed the air suspiciously, but this time he smelled only the lingering smoke of the man's cigarettes. He made his way carefully back to his lodgings, tapping his way with the cane across the skim of snow as fast as he dared. He had posted the letter, the alarm had been sounded.

⤜ CHAPTER 6 ⤛

FROM EVE'S JOURNAL

Jago opened the canvas flap at the back of the wagon and held it for me.

I climbed back in among the dusty props.

'Goodnight,' Jago said. 'Goodnight, Eve.'

'Yes, goodnight Jago,' I said. 'Thank you for saving me.' I burrowed back under the soft dusty cloth; I curled up as small as I could. As I lay listening to the wind among the trees, I couldn't help thinking of poor Jack, who was out there somewhere and would certainly be missing me by now.

Finally I drifted off feeling entirely unreal, alone, cut off from everything I had ever known. Airships throbbed overhead at regular intervals and the familiar drone of their engines as they passed over the park finally sent me to sleep.

I woke suddenly to complete darkness and the sound of dogs barking, and the clanging sounds of metal on metal.

I pulled myself up through the warm covers; the canvas

back flap was tied tight with rope from the outside. I felt a jolt. 'What's happening, what is it?' I called out into the darkness. The sound of dogs yapping and snarling was all very close to the wagon. My heart pounded fast in my chest. The wagon gave a lurch and I was thrown back among the striped poles, hitting my head. I yelled out. The lurch developed into a fast forward movement, bumpy at first as if we were travelling at speed over hummocks of grass, but then it was suddenly smooth – a pathway perhaps – and then came the clatter of hooves and the judder of riding over cobbles. I waited for a while crouched in pain among all the ropes and poles. I held on tight to the edge of the canvas. The snaps and howls of the dogs gradually faded. I pulled myself up on to the driving board of the wagon beside Jago. He was holding the reins and concentrating on the forward rush.

'What is it?' I said breathlessly to Jago, who leaned forward, reins in hand. 'Wild dogs?'

'Oh dogs, of course, but not wild – trained to attack,' he said. 'Nasty dogs, sniffer dogs, Corporation dogs. Something must be up. They only bring them out at night and never anywhere near any paying Gawkers either. That kind of dog is very useful for scaring the poor and the unprotected. That was a Buckland Corp. security patrol unless I miss my guess. We would always rather keep away from them. It was time to move, and fast.'

We clattered on through the dark streets.

I shivered, held my hand to my head and gripped the board with the other. Finally the horse slowed to an amble. 'What were they looking for?' I asked Jago, still in fear, thinking of the horde of fierce dogs, the ragged man who meant me harm, the alarm bells clanging.

'Oh it could be anything. They don't like travellers and illicits being here at all. They don't like them sleeping in the parks and so on. They take every opportunity to harass the unofficial poor. What could be easier or more satisfying than scaring the defenceless? Mummers and players, poor gypsies, illegal immigrants or circus folk, whoever they want to scare with a pack of dogs and vile men with sticks they can. I've no doubt that there are some sick Gawkers in this place who will pay good money to see poor people attacked with a dog and a lead-tipped cudgel.'

It seemed odd to hear Jago talk about such horrors among all the calmly sleeping houses that surrounded us. He said such mysterious things too, it was as if he were living in an entirely different world to me.

'Shall I tell you something, Jago,' I said. 'Today was the first time I have been out on my own ever, as far as I can remember, which is not very far at all.'

'What about your status here?' he asked me, 'Are you on a pass or are you a permanent resident, or do you work for the Corporation officially?'

'I am a resident,' I said.

'Well,' he said, 'I can tell you that the Corporation almost tolerate me and the rest of our circus. They just about put up with us, just,' said Jago. 'We are neither official nor unofficial. We come and go as we please from the forest camps north of here using hidden routes. All visitors of course usually come in on the airships. We are tolerated mainly because the Gawkers like what we do, and we do look so very scummy and and so very authentic, that's the big word in here.' He plucked at his tattered sleeve. 'Authentic. The Buckland Corporation could never train us as well as we've trained ourselves and we don't thieve. Even though we could do it really well, it's not worth the risk, what with the police and the Corporation cadet corps in here, and the old Victorian laws applying.'

'You say such strange things,' I said.

'Such as?' said Jago.

'You keep mentioning the Corporation, and yesterday you said something about cast natives, whatever they are.'

He turned and looked at me. 'Are you serious?'

'Of course! I'm afraid that much of what you say is a riddle to me.'

'Where do you live, Eve?'

'Why here in London,' I said puzzled, 'in rooms above a shop until yesterday.'

'That is partly true,' he said.

'Partly true, what can the full truth be?' I asked.

'The full truth is, Eve, that while you and I are here in London, in the old city of London, this London of ours is no longer a real place, is it?'

'Isn't it? How can that be, what do you mean?' I said, mystified.

'Because some years ago it was made into a museum of itself, a "theme park" it is called. The whole city and every-thing in it, right up to the furthest boundaries is a rebuilt, restored, recreation of its own past. It's really only an illusion now — the memory of a city that once was. People like us live our lives here, and we live them in the manner of the past, and other people pay to come in to see us all living our lives here in the manner of the past, to experience the past for themselves as if thay had travelled in a time machine. You've seen the name Buckland stencilled along the side of the airships?'

'Of course,' I said uneasily, feeling giddy at what I was hearing.

'The Buckland Corporation owns and runs this whole place, and organises all the paying "guests" as they are called, the ones we call Gawkers, the visitors that come in on the airships.'

My head was really spinning now. I was living in an historical anachronism? I had been living in something called a "theme park"?

'This whole city here is known as Pastworld,' he said, 'Pastworld London, and people pay a great deal of money to come in here to experience the beauty and the squalor, the dirt, the danger, the reality of Victorian life exactly as it was lived then.'

My head was still spinning. 'You mean we are not really Victorians?'

'No, Eve, we are living in an era far beyond the 1880s. Outside of Pastworld, beyond this place, outside of the skydome that encloses it, it is 2048 and that world looks and is very, very, different from this one.'

'I really don't understand,' I said. 'Why did all this happen?'

'If it's any comfort to you, Eve, it's not the first time. There are many others like you in this place, people who have been born in here, born into poverty and ignorance, they too were unaware that this is not the real world.

Although in many ways for them and for us too, it is a real world, of a kind.'

'I am not a child,' I said. 'Why did my guardian tell me absoultely nothing about all of this? Why?'

'I have no idea, I expect he had his reasons, Eve. Perhaps he wanted to protect you for some reason from the truth.'

We trotted on across the cobbles and I sat feeling faint, trying to come to terms with what I had just heard. In an odd way it all made sense. The strangeness of my life, my lack of memories. I was an empty person, like an exhibit, a waxwork, with no life of its own, on show in a museum. Why had Jack never told me the truth, what was he scared of?

After a while the fog faded out, simply drifted away, and bright stars were suddenly visible above us, sharp and clear. Jago, to distract me, pointed out the constellations.

'That's Orion, the hunter.'

'I know,' I said, 'those three stars in a line represent his belt, the stars on the outer edge are the tips of his bow, and there you can see Betelgeuse, one of the brightest things you would ever see in the night sky.'

'You know your stars all right,' Jago said. 'If only that was the real night sky, eh?'

'You mean the sky isn't real either?'

'Projections on a huge dome,' he said quietly.

I suddenly realised something strange and troubling.

'So I have never seen the real sky,' I said, 'day or night.'

We watched as the stars appeared and disappeared between all the buildings and the jaggy pointed rooflines. It was cold now and my breath misted.

We passed a sweeper at work brushing away at the thin snow with a besom broom, but otherwise the neat cobbled streets had an empty haunted look about them, something like the blank empty theatre set that they really were. I shivered.

I had so many questions to ask Jago, but could think of nothing to say as my mind raced trying to make sense of everything.

Jago said, 'Those dogs back in the park, it could mean that a crime's been committed, I mean a real one, a big one, a Fantom killing, someone found with their insides spread out, and their head missing. Something like that might set them off all right.'

'A phantom killing,' I said. 'Is that an illusion, a piece of theatre like all the rest?'

'Of course not, the Fantom is . . . wait, you've never heard of the Fantom?'

❧ CHAPTER 7 ❧

The Fantom pushed aside the rags that hung over the low doorway. He bent his head and made his way into a dingy room. He shone his carbide police lantern around the edges of the space. Suddenly it was as if an urgent dance had started up among a group of shadows on the walls. He pulled off his black silk mask and his eyes burned bright behind his clear eyeglasses.

'God,' he said, 'it stinks in here. I had a message, an urgent message. Come on out with it, I'm risking everything even just being here in this room.'

'I saw her,' said one of the ragged men. He stepped forward with some confidence. He walked straight into the bright beam of light while the shadows behind him muttered and stood about, nervously shifting their weight from foot to foot. 'I'm sure it was her. I am one hundred per cent sure it was her,' he added. 'She was just as you said she would be. I couldn't get the message to you at first and in any case I wanted to be certain. She gave me a coin from her purse, you know. I looked up and she smiled at me, so nicely. And then I saw them, it was *her* eyes. I saw those eyes, and I knew it was her because those eyes were just exactly as you said they would be, exactly like . . .'

'Go on,' said the Fantom, placing the police lantern down slowly and deliberately on a messy table in the far corner of the room so that its beam continued to shine directly at the ragged man's face.

'Nothing. I followed her. She went to the big market near my pitch. I managed to grab hold of her, I actually got a grip.' Here the ragged man pulled his jacket from his own shoulder, turned and exposed it directly into the lamp beam. 'Right here on her tender little shoulder.' He paused and cast his eyes down at his feet.

'Go on,' said the Fantom, 'and then what?'

'And then I'm afraid she was spirited away,' he said, 'by a show magician, a dark-skinned man, an Indian. They drove off with her. He did some strange magic which I still can't explain. And then I lost them.'

'How?' said the Fantom, his voice quiet and restrained but dammed up as if with violent anger, waiting for just the right moment to explode.

'I fell over.' The beggar stopped speaking. One or two of the shadows behind him laughed but they soon stopped. The Fantom turned his gaze towards them, and he looked in that instant suddenly as supernatural as his reputation.

'Where are they now, and which group of performers

were they? There are dozens of them plying their trade in this forsaken place,' the Fantom asked, his voice still quiet but bordering on a possible shout or scream, the pressure of restraint now like the low whistling of the steam in the rattling kettle.

'Don't know, I didn't take it in. I could only see her and those eyes.' The beggar raised himself up, taller suddenly, confident. 'There's more though,' he said.

'Is there?' the Fantom said. He was toying with the ragged man like a cat with a mouse.

The ragged man spoke up, a smile clear in his voice, and in his eyes. Now he was the cat. 'I saw the one you said had charge of her.'

'He was more or less blind, with burn-scarred skin across his hands?'

'Yes.'

'Good, go on.'

'I went back to where I had first seen her. When she gave me the coin, the sixpence.'

'Sixpence, the lovely, generous girl! Go on.'

'Her hands touched mine for a moment and they were warm, she hadn't been out in the cold for long.'

'Well reasoned. Go on,' said the Fantom.

'Anyhow, he was looking for her. He was desperate, I could tell. He was asking anyone he could find.'

'And?'

'Then he went off but I waited. I waited in the cold in case she came back. Then he came out to post a letter.'

'A letter?'

'A letter,' the ragged man said and barely suppressing his own glee, he pulled the blind man's letter from his pocket with a flourish. 'I haven't opened it you see. I've kept it for you alone. I've been waiting here for you since,' he said.

The Fantom closed his eyes for a moment. He took the letter and he held it in his hands carefully and with his eyes still closed he brought it up to his face. The room was silent apart from the low rattle and thin whistle of the kettle.

The Fantom opened his eyes and looked down at the address. It was written out in large scrawling childish-looking letters. 'How quaint,' the Fantom said. He read it out slowly.

MR LUCIUS BROWN ESQ.
19 SHELLEY AVENUE
LETCHWORTH
HERTS
1X 3DR

When he had finished reading, he yelped like a dog. The ragged man grinned and turned to the shadows behind him as if to say, 'See, now I'm immune.'

'You haven't opened it, and I should hope not too,' the Fantom said. 'A letter should only be opened by the person it is addressed to.' He walked over to the range and held the envelope in the steam from the wheezing kettle. When the seal had loosened, he gingerly prised open the flap, and unfolded the letter it contained. There was just a single sheet, and one word was scrawled across it in the same big, clumsy letters,

PROMETHEUS

The Fantom read that out too. He read it again; he spelled it out slowly for all the shadows. There was a silence in the room. The Fantom stared at the paper and the envelope, then he laughed quietly. He carefully folded the paper and put the sheet back inside the envelope and, going to the table he swept his arm across it, scattering the cups and saucers and glassware on to the floor, where they smashed and sent glittering fragments up into the lamp beam. The Fantom sat at the table and carefully resealed the envelope. He turned to his ragged minion. 'You have done so well, here take it.' He handed the resealed letter to the ragged man. 'Post it in that very same postbox and then watch and wait. He will come now. He will come to help look for her; he needs to take her back, but we will find them first. Oh yes, our half blind Jack will lead us straight to him and then we will find her as well. It begins. We have the key now. Tell me everything, report to me directly and somebody find that circus or whatever it was.'

He picked up the lamp and he shone it all the way round the low room picking out and looking at each of the tough faces in the shadows.

'Oh,' he said, 'how could I? I nearly forgot, I brought you a little something for your supper, mind how you cook it now, it's quite fresh and needs just to be lightly sautéed, perhaps in a little butter and salt.' He pulled something out from under his cloak. It was wrapped in bloodied grocer's paper. He put it on one of the remaining plates on the table and shone his flickering lamp down on to it. Then he carefully tore the wet paper from around it and peeled it down on all sides. A large human heart sat in the middle of the soggy paper.

'Look at that,' he said quietly. 'It looks as if it could almost still be beating. You can't say I don't think of you.'

Excerpt taken from the Little Planet Guide to Pastworld™ London

Visitors should note the following observations. Inevitably a real underground crime network has developed on the fringes of the theme park itself. Rival criminal overlords exist hidden in the murky 'Dickensian' alleys, coordinating crime in the theme park. Potential visitors (known by the park natives as 'Gawkers') should take careful note. Many will be unfamiliar with the handling of actual 'cash' money, which is the only currency in use in the park. Debit or credit cards and e-money do not work in Pastworld London.

Despite the compulsory training and costuming days before admission to the park, and despite the presence of very cleverly disguised CCTV systems and single-frame still security camera coverage, many visitors are still being ripped off, and unfortunately in some cases mugged and, even worse, murdered by members of the criminal fringe.

⇒ CHAPTER 8 ⇐

Caleb Brown, a slender young man of seventeen with dark hair and sea-blue eyes, stood shaded from the suburban sun by a festive, striped Victorian-style awning. It was decorated in the livery colours of the Buckland Corporation. He stood next to his father, Lucius. They were waiting patiently in line along with many others, to board a Buckland Corporation passenger airship.

Finally their seat numbers were called forward. Costume authentication inspectors lined the route from the departure lounge. It was their job to carry out mandatory spot checks on any travellers going to Pastworld. One of the inspectors stepped forward and with a nod and a sweeping gesture of his uniformed arm, politely ushered Caleb and his father Lucius into an inspection cubicle. These were small areas sectioned off with that same gaily striped fabric as the sun awning and the welcome banners.

'Good morning to both of you gentlemen on behalf of the Buckland Corporation,' said the inspector. 'It is our policy to carry out authenticity checks as far as costuming and other items are concerned before your journey. I am sorry if you have been examined once already today but we like to be thorough here at Buckland.' He looked both of them up and down, muttering and nodding his head, as if mentally checking certain items off on a list. He tugged the flap of Caleb's long frock coat open and looked at his tie and then at the tiepin. He pulled at Caleb's waistcoat. At that point Caleb's father reached across and stayed the authentication inspector's hand. He handed over a card from his own waistcoat pocket. The costume authentication inspector looked at the card, read it quickly, bowed a little and then gave it straight back to him. He straightened then, saluted smartly and pulled aside the cubicle curtain.

'No need for any further inspection at all, Messrs Brown,' he nodded to them one after the other, still smiling.

'Glad to have both of you travelling as guests with us today. A rare privilege indeed.'

'I passed through this very same system only a month or so ago,' said Lucius, 'on my last visit, and you are all to be commended for your thoroughness. It is appreciated, I assure you.'

The inspector saluted once more.

'You see,' said Caleb's father as they walked away. 'One flick of that card and look what happened – no more fuss. Perhaps your poor old father is not such a useless old duffer after all?' he said.

'No,' said Caleb with a half smile. He hefted the weight of his Gladstone bag and paused to look up at the looming bulk of the airship above them. It had the word 'Buckland' picked out in friendly letters all the way down its soft, bulging flank. He pulled a rueful face, a brief rebellious grimace. *Buckand*, he thought, *always that word, it seems to pursue us.*

His father was distracted by the sheer scale of the airship as it hovered above them.

'Airships,' he said, 'they were all my idea you know,' and nodded to himself.

They walked up the steps with a group of excited fellow passengers who were all, like them, dressed to the nines in their Victorian Sunday best. Some waved scarves or bright parasols back at the crowd of onlookers who were lined up to watch, as on every launch. They seemed a long way down below them at the base fence of the docking bay. Caleb noticed the luggage trolley being unloaded into the cabin hold. There were steamer trunks and big brass-cornered campaign cases. There were sets of vintage leather suitcases and crocodile-skin bags, and all were being carefully placed and ordered in neat stacks in the luggage hold. Caleb had a sudden image of them all falling out of the hold. Somewhere perhaps over the park itself, tumbling from the sky and spilling all of their expensive 'authentic' contents across the dirty roofs and smoky chimneys of Pastworld.

They were soon ushered into the airship's gondola. A barman in a dark waistcoat and a long white apron stood behind a polished mahogany bar at one end of the corridor, and a viewing chamber with a huge panoramic window, was at the other end near their cabin. A servant in Buckland Corp. livery stepped forward and took their topcoats and hung them carefully on wooden hangers on a coat rack. Their cabin was fitted out as a gentleman's club. There were a few button-backed armchairs and a leather chesterfield sofa. Hand block-printed paper covered the walls. Chairs were arranged beside the large porthole windows.

A voice on the loudspeaker outside announced the imminent departure of their flight. Many could never afford a trip to Pastworld London, and many would have liked to be sitting where Caleb was now, having that chance to escape the sanitised present even if only for a few weeks. They would have willingly paid the enormous sum if they had it for just the chance to sail so elegantly back into another time.

———⧫———

The airship cabin smelled faintly of leather and cologne and there were traces of cigar smoke. Once in the cabin they were already on Pastworld rules. Here the universal smoking ban no longer applied. Caleb settled himself down, embraced by the softness of the cabin chair. He had to admit to himself a rising sense of excitement, of curiosity. His father, sat himself down opposite Caleb, close to the porthole. He politely refused a glass of champagne which was offered by a smiling animatronic steward. Caleb quickly took a glass though and raised the fluted stem and watched the bubbles in the refracted light from the porthole. The champagne fizzed on his tongue. He drank the whole glass quickly and held it out to the robo steward for a top-up.

'That's enough I think, Caleb,' his father said not unkindly.

'I thought we were on holiday,' Caleb said, sipping at the second glass more slowly. His father shook his head and turned his attention to his *Pastworld Gazetteer*. This was an early original edition which he had brought with him. 'I feel I should remind you, Caleb, that all of the old, harsh Victorian criminal laws in Pastworld apply. Being drunk and disorderly would be a very serious matter.'

'Two glasses of champagne are hardly going to make me drunk and disoderly, are they?' Caleb said, his sea-blue eyes flashing and a winning smile on his face.

'Well some of your so called "friends" back in Letchworth wouldn't fare too well in Pastworld. Victorian prisons were not holiday camps, and never forget one thing, they have the death penalty here as well.'

'Not for drinking this, surely,' Caleb said, holding out the glass, and laughed.

The airship lifted off, and while it rose majestically up from its mooring pylon soothing music was played into the cabin from an old-fashioned acoustical gramophone. The ghostly, scratchy playing of long dead musicians filled the cabin with soothing salon waltzes and tangos. The authentic experience, the immersion in the life of the past had begun.

Lucius conducted the music from his cabin chair, while Caleb, feeling relaxed from the champagne, just looked out of the porthole at the passing constant blue of the sky.

After an hour or so of smooth, steady flight an announcement was made over the speaker sytem.

'This Buckland Corporation airship is about to dock at the airlock to the Pastworld skydome. We ask that passengers remain seated during this short procedure. Passengers are reminded that after docking is complete we will be on Pastworld side itself and we would recommend that you make your way then to the panoramic viewing cabin.'

The interior went dark. There was a feeling of suspension, a hiatus. Then after a minute or two the gaslights kicked in, and the cabin was lit differently. It was softer somehow. The sense of forward movement was back too.

'Come on then, my boy. This will be well worth seeing if its anything like my last visit.' Lucius stood up and Caleb followed him down the narrow corridor to the viewing cabin.

The panoramic window curved across the whole back of the gondola cabin. It stretched from the floor to the ceiling as well, so that the effect was of a great glass wall with just a few narrow glazing bars to support it. The sensation it gave was that of simply hanging quietly in the sky. Below was an empty-looking townscape, a buffer zone of old suburbia that had been cleared during the first great construction phase.

While they stood at the wide window a ragged trail of mist drifted across under the belly of the cabin and hid it all.

Caleb looked at the mist, it thickened as they passed over it. He could clearly see a sudden darker shape of spreading grey, like a rolling shadow, a stain below them.

'Worth it now,' said Lucius, noting the reaction of Caleb to the great view spread out below them. 'The famous artificial fog bank. Just look at it, my God.' His father's voice fell to a whisper.

The fog shrouded everything, even the taller landmark buildings. At first, apart from those, there was little else to see but the fog itself. His father, still speaking in a whisper said, 'Think of it all down there, Caleb, underneath the machined fog, no real mechanised vehicles as you would know them, no cars, only old steam-powered trains, and horses, lots of horses, and all the teeming streets below us are lit once again with gas lamps.'

Caleb continued to stare out of the window at the swirling pattern of fog.

'Nothing can prepare you for the moment of actually stepping back into the past,' Lucius said with a sigh.

The airship then drifted lower, until in one sudden movement they were below the thicker fog line, and the whole of the city opened up below them. The other passengers in the cabin burst into spontaneous applause at the sight.

The streets and buildings stretched from one side of the window to the other. Horse-drawn carriages could be seen, crowded pavements, the great dull curve of the river, green squares and parks, and white church spires, grey roofs and dark red railway trains trailing billows of steam. Even Caleb gasped. He hadn't wanted to give his father the satisfaction of seeing how interested he really was in the city below them, didn't want him to see that a great flicker of excitement had just at that moment grown, doubled, trebled, as the airship slipped gracefully through the gloomy fog bank and floated over the dream-like city itself.

⤜ CHAPTER 9 ⤛

Caleb disembarked and waited to collect their luggage. They had a steamer trunk packed with authentically tailored clothes, they had individual bags packed with unlikely toiletries. There were bottles of pomade for their hair and after-shaving balms with printed paper labels, soft shaving brushes made of real badger hair, ivory-handled toothbrushes and round tins of harsh dentifrice paste, silver-backed hairbrushes, open razors for his father (Caleb had yet to shave often enough to warrant the worry). Caleb could not then have guessed that his father carried one extra little piece of baggage. It felt heavier than any packed steamer trunk. It was a simple white envelope, which he had tucked into his inside pocket. The letter inside consisted of just a single word scrawled across a folded piece of paper. A word which carried with it a burden of fear, guilt and knowledge.

They were finally able to claim their stack of luggage from the efficient baggage reclaim system. A smiling porter in a peaked cap and a colourful striped waistcoat trundled their trunk behind them on a trolley, while they carried their own smaller individual Gladstone bags. They took their place in line in an enclosed arcade on the outer edge of the Pastworld arrivals terminal.

THE BUCKLAND CORPORATION

WELCOMES

ALL OF OUR GUESTS TO

PASTWORLD
L O N D O N

was printed in old woodblock type across a large calico banner suspended above the staircase that led to the exit. After their turn had come to climb the elaborate wrought-iron stairs to join the hansom cab queue, the porter manually pushed at the heavily insulated main doors. The doors were made of thick bronze and were decorated in bas reliefs of airships. As the big doors slid apart there was a sudden eruption of noise. The sounds of a wild unknown and ancient foreign clamour – rapidly moving horse carriages, distant chuffing trains, steam engines, close vocal shouts and wild street cries. They were confronted at once not only by the noise itself, but also by strong animal and chemical smells. The warp and texture of the very real dirty and noisy life in the city was opened up right in front of them.

The porter slid the trunk out ready on to the pavement outside, which, in contrast to the immaculate terminal floor, was uneven, grubby and wet. Caleb realised for the first time just how far they had come in their short flight.

'We have truly crossed over,' his father said.

While they waited, the visitors in the queue practised their new rules of politeness on one another. Hats were doffed, men bowed to their partners, who in turn bobbed curtsies back, dissolving into giggles at the unreality of it all. Lucius and Caleb's hansom cab soon clattered up beside them. Caleb found himself looking into the dripping muzzle of a dappled grey cab horse. Their porter moved off to load the trunk and cases and at that point a ragged man stepped forward from among the queue of carriages and offered to help. The porter raised his fist and the man stepped back. Lucius looked nervously over at the beggar and the beggar stared back at him from under his sacking hood. The porter loaded the trunks himself and then he doffed his cap. Lucius modestly tipped the porter with one of the many small coins that jingled in his pocket, then, followed by Caleb, he clambered up into the cab. The whole interior rocked on its springs as they settled into the quilted, horsehair seats.

On the journey from the arrivals terminal to their lodgings Caleb became what the local residents in Pastworld called a 'Gawker', that is an awed tourist, a rubberneck, a simple eye. There was almost too much to see and gawk at.

For a start there was the rain. Caleb had never seen such grey and louring weather; it was never like that back at home. There were rolling, low clouds that morning, as well as a light artificial fog, and a cold, fine, drizzling rain. Everything was blurred and softened. The outlines of the buildings and the people were hazy. There were pungent smells of burning coal and hot steam smuts, acrid soot, and hot oil and working steam engines and, above and over all of that, horse manure, and urine, which caught Caleb unawares, and seemed to linger in the back of his throat.

And no matter how many photographic images of old London and its people he had seen, nothing had prepared him for the experience of actually being there.

He was suddenly immersed in the vivid world of the past.

The images he had seen had been mainly mono-chrome, either old Victorian or Edwardian photographs. Images that looked as if they had been pickled in malt vinegar or tobacco smoke. Faded-looking pictures in soft yellows and sepia browns. No modern cameras were ever allowed into Pastworld, so there was nothing to prepare for the shock of the colours and the bustling movement. The women's clothes seemed to be very bright, floral patterned, or plain velvets and silks and all in strong purples, yellows and reds. This contrasted sharply with the dull tones of the men's clothes. They wore mostly formal black, but there were some local swells wearing checked tweeds and gold-threaded waistcoats. Everyone wore hats. Some of the women wore large creations topped with elaborate swirls of feathers. The men wore shiny top hats, or sombre trilbys and homburgs. There were Buckland Corporation cadets in their red uniforms, and the London policemen, or bobbies, in dark blue, with high, crested helmets.

That morning, during his first immersion, Caleb's eyes darted this way and that. He was confused by so many things at once. The haste and hurry, the constant noise from the heavy traffic. The clattering and clopping hooves of the horses, the metal jingle of harness. There were steaming piles of grimly unhygenic manure in the roadways and it seemed there was a constant wash of horse piss in the gutters. Caleb could almost feel the germs rising in the steam, crawling over everything, the twisted writhing colonies of bacteria spilling from cobbles to shoes, from shoes to clothes, from clothes to flesh, and he shuddered.

Caleb watched the overwhelming crowds of poor people as they moved among the smarter Gawkers and residents. He was surprised by their noise and robust roughness, by their numbers, by the variety of their skin colours, and by their bewildering speed of movement and confidence as they dodged around each other on the pavements. With all the shoving and pushing, Pastworld already looked a dangerous place. For some perhaps even a terrifying one. To a skinny seventeen-year-old boy from a dull, wealthy garden city there was an immediate sense of lawlessness and adventure in the air. It seemed to Caleb that almost anything might and could, and perhaps indeed should, happen.

❧ CHAPTER 10 ❧

The hansom cab pulled up outside a tall Georgian house in Cloudesley Square, Islington, which was just north of the centre of the old city. He noticed his father's anxiety. It became visible just for a moment as they arrived at their lodging house. Another ragged man stepped forward out of the mist and helped the driver down with the steamer trunk. The man then dragged the heavy trunk up the short steps to the front door. After that he stood wringing his hands, waiting to be tipped along with the cab driver. His father looked the beggar up and down, took in his shabby coat, his leaky boots. He gave the beggar a coin; the beggar looked down at the coin and then back at Lucius Brown then, stepping forward close to him, he looked Lucius in the eye.

'That was a heavy case, very heavy,' he said quietly, almost mournfully. Then the beggar pocketed the coin, spat on to the ground and, grumbling under his breath, moved off through the mist.

'Unofficial he was guvn'or, for sure,' said the cab driver, pocketing his fare and his own generous tip, while doffing his hat. 'They're the ones you want to watch out for when you're out and about in the City,' and he clicked his horse forward.

'Unofficial,' Lucius muttered, and he covered his eyes with his hands and stood silently for a moment as if transfixed to the spot. Caleb noticed that his father's hand was trembling, like someone suffering from stage fright. After a moment Lucius braced himself, stepped forward and banged on the front door of the house.

'Mrs Bullock,' said Lucius doffing his hat and bowing slightly.

'Why yes, indeed, Mr Brown and son, is it not?' said the pleasant elderly woman in a long brown dress who had opened the door. She stood aside and ushered them into the hallway. Lucius introduced Caleb, who tried an awkward, shallow bow himself, and smiled as best he could.

'My,' said Mrs Bullock, 'what a handsome young man. You'd best watch out for all the young ladies with him I think, Mr Brown.'

Caleb blushed and looked around at the busy decor of the hallway. The walls were patterned over with dark foliate wallpaper. Pictures in heavy frames hung on gold chains from the picture rail. A white marble bust of Queen Victoria stood on a marbled column beside a fancy hallstand stuffed with umbrellas. There was a smell here too – of lavender overlaid with boiled vegetables.

Mrs Bullock picked up two big cream official envelopes from the post table.

'These were forwarded here and have been waiting for you,' she said, 'and there were two boxes delivered by Carter Patterson. Proper Corporation red wax seal on those envelopes, I noticed. You are clearly important men Mr Brown, Master Brown.'

'Once upon a time perhaps,' Lucius replied, tilting his head.

She nodded at them deferentially, while performing a sort of curtsy.

'It's not every day that I have an esteemed Buckland Corporation official to stay in my lodging house.' She turned and flicked her feather duster over the ornaments above the umbrella stand.

'Thank you for looking after everything so nicely, Mrs Bullock,' Lucius said. 'Now if you'll excuse us, it's been a tiring journey.'

'Where are my manners!' she said. 'Your rooms are on the first floor at the front, straight up the stairs. I've lit a fire for you and there's plenty of hot water. You won't be disturbed.'

Lucius clicked the door shut behind him. He leaned against the tapestry draught curtain and closed his eyes. He stayed like that for a moment with the envelopes tight in his hand.

'What are the letters?' Caleb asked.

'They'll be our invitations, of course,' Lucius said, going over to warm himself at the coal fire. 'The big Halloween fancy dress party to be given by Abel Buckland himself, my old boss and the CEO of the Buckland Corporation, which is tomorrow night.' Lucius proudly displayed the invitations. They had a giant engraved skull and crossbones on one side and the Pastworld logotype on the other. Lucius ran his finger over the engraving, the lines were proud of the surface, raised like a series of bumps.

'Proper engraving you see,' Lucius said before he placed them side by side on the overmantel. Then with his back half turned he took out another letter, but this time from his inner pocket. Caleb watched him open it and read it to himself. A curious expression passed across his father's face in a split second; a pure and sudden wave of anguish. The expression passed quickly, but not quickly enough for Caleb not to notice it. He had caught sight of one word scrawled in big letters across the paper. He could make no sense of it. His father threw the screwed-up letter into the fire, and then he stood, with his head bowed, leaning on the mantel and watched the ball of paper burn through until it was nothing but blackened ash. He picked up a heavy brass poker from the fender and broke the blackened ash down further, thrusting the fragments deep down among the glowing embers of the coal.

'What was that all about?' Caleb asked.

'Oh,' said Lucius, 'nothing really – a silly note that was in the pocket of this suit here. You can show some interest then, you do have a tongue when it suits you.'

'What?' Caleb protested.

'We have driven through the streets of this most remarkable city,' said his father, who seemed suddenly and inexplicably cross. His trembling hand held the heavy brass poker out towards Caleb almost like a weapon. 'A great technical achievement, one of the great wonders of the modern world and much of it due in no small measure to my efforts, and you have said what exactly? Nothing or next to nothing, no comment at all. I despair of your generation, my boy, sometimes, I really do.'

'I was looking at everything. You saw me, I was trying my best to take it all in,' said Caleb, puzzled by the clenched fury of the outburst. It was so unlike his father and to Caleb it seemed that he was lashing out in anger because he was upset. What was his father frightened of? What did the letter mean, that one word? And why burn it like that, as if it was diseased, as if it might attack him? Caleb knew instictively that something was up, something connected with the letter. But he said no more about it.

His father switched attention to the boxes. They contained two Halloween costumes, each specially tailored to their measurements. His father's was a formal black Victorian suit except it had the bones of a skeleton printed all over the outside front. It was to be worn under a long cape, so that the white of the bones would only show properly when the cape was swirled open or removed. Caleb's box contained a similar formal suit but without the bones printed on it. Instead, he had been supplied with a skull mask to wear. The crumpled skull grinned back at him, making the box with the neatly folded suit inside look like a miniature coffin.

———•◆•———

Caleb was still getting used to the stiff and awkward Victorian clothes they had to wear. He got undressed in his little bedroom, which was made to feel smaller by the decoration, more foliate-patterned wallpaper, more pictures in gold frames, watercolours of highland cattle, and views of the Pyramids. He was looking forward to a dreamless night in the old-fashioned brass bedstead.

He had been fidgeting with the clothes all day, fussing with the trousers which were worn high up on the waist, held up by tight elastic braces that pressed down on his shoulders. The hard leather ankle boots had hurt his feet. He hung the jacket on a hanger next to the velvet-collared top coat, and the deep buttoned waistcoat. This white shirt had the devilishly difficult to fix, detachable and very stiff collar, which had left a red itchy weal around Caleb's throat, and which was held in place, front and back, with solid gold studs.

He brushed his teeth at the sink, dabbing the brush in the round tin of dentifrice, which tasted strongly medicinal. He looked up at himself in the mirror. His hair was flat with pomade, there were red marks on his shoulders where the braces had rubbed; he hardly knew himself.

———•◆•———

His father woke him early. 'Authentic breakfast,' he said.

The morning papers were laid out in a fan shape on the side table at breakfast. Caleb's father ignored them as he ate his way through a bowl of porridge. Caleb picked up a *London Mercury*. There was a dramatic engraving of a sinister-looking man in a cape, a tall hat, and a black face mask. Caleb held out the picture to his father and read aloud the headline caption. "'*The Fantom is back. New victim found in Shoreditch, with severed limbs and head removed. The head was later recovered from the top of a building scheduled soon for grand public demolition*," it says here.'

His father looked up hurriedly, nervously, and then as if trying to distract Caleb away from the subject. 'The Fantom,' he said, 'will no doubt prove to be an actor like all the others working for the Corporation. It's all a bit cheap really, isn't it.'

'Hanging would be much too good for him,' Mrs Bullock said as she bustled in and acknowledged the image with a shudder. She laid down two full plates of bacon and eggs. 'He used to rob banks, they say, as if that wasn't bad enough, but now it's much worse. They say he takes out their hearts and the like.' She shuddered and then offered them a fresh pot of tea and another round of toast.

⇥ CHAPTER 11 ⇤

Later that afternoon Caleb stood in the window of the upper sitting room of the lodging house. His new, crisply tailored suit clung to his thin frame. He looked elegant, like a young man about town or a 'swell' as they were known. He stood as still as one of the Sunderland china figures lined up along the chimney mantel, watching his father fuss with his own clothes in the bathroom behind him.

'There, I'm ready,' said Lucius, finally bustling in through the connecting door. 'Turn round then, Caleb, let's, have a good look at you.'

Caleb turned from the window and his father gasped. It looked to Caleb as if his father had just seen a real ghost, had a sudden shock of recognition. In his severe black suit and high white collar with his blazing sea-blue eyes clearly lit, Caleb looked suddenly like someone else altogether.

'Well,' Caleb said, 'what, what's the matter?'

'Nothing, my boy, nothing at all,' said his father. 'Sorry but for a moment you reminded me of someone that's all.'

There was a loud knock at the front door and in a moment Mrs Bullock called up the stairs.

'Hansom's here, Mr Brown.'

'Thank you,' Lucius called down. 'Come on now, Caleb, look lively. At least we shall travel on a steam train, you might enjoy that,' and he rubbed his hands together as if delighted at the prospect, but Caleb noticed that there was still a look of anxiety and fear behind his father's eyes.

Outside the local railway station at Highbury Corner Caleb saw close to the day to day realities of a city run on horse power. Cab and dray horses were lined up at the crossing place. Caleb had hardly ever seen a real horse before and now here were dozens of them. They steamed, they stamped, they shook their heads, spraying saliva in sticky gobbets. They pissed and shat where they stood or as they walked. Their lips curled back and showed their big teeth. They weren't even still while they waited, but jerked forward or scraped their hooves on the cobbles. It felt risky just standing close to them.

———◆———

They sat in one of the many retro-furbished suburban steam railway trains. It was Caleb's first such journey. It felt very odd to travel so slowly. The train felt not only noisy, but he thought, thrillingly aggressive. As the houses slipped by, Caleb breathed in and savoured the trails and ribbons of steam, and the flecks of dark soot smuts which flew in through the half-open window.

His father broke through his thoughts. He had seen a glimpse of the murky river through the steamed-over window. He leaned across and rubbed a clear space free in the glass, and pointed it out. 'There,' he said tapping the glass, 'the house we need to get to for the party is some-where south, and near the river down there.'

———— • • ————

While the doors were slammed heavily shut, the train stood like a great creature breathing out chuffs, bursts, and sighs of steam. Caleb turned away reluctantly.

They left the foggy platform and went down some stairs. A slippery, dingily-lit, tiled connecting tunnel linked the twenty or so railway platforms below ground. The great steam trains rumbled overhead. An excited Gawker, who was dressed head to foot in black and wearing a long-flowing opera cloak, waved a silver dagger above his head. He had a black mask all over his face, and was making his way annoyingly and deliberately against the flow of the other passengers. He looked over at Caleb and pointed his fake dagger as he passed and laughed. He called out 'I am the Fantom' and the crowd of Gawkers all laughed. Caleb noticed that Lucius didn't laugh; instead he grimaced and muttered the words 'Idiots! What do they know?' under his breath.

The station exit turnstiles were crowded too. Ahead of them was another Halloween partygoer also dressed in an opera cloak. He gave in his little cardboard ticket to the ticket collector and turned his head as he did so. Caleb saw that he too wore a mask; only this mask was a skull, a death's head, just like the one he had tucked in his pocket. If Caleb had believed in such things, he would have later thought that it was an omen; but then death masks of every kind were two a penny that night.

❧ CHAPTER 12 ❧

Lucius Brown claimed that he carried with him a natural sense of direction, an inner awareness of where he ought to be going, but it was soon clear to Caleb that his father had a very odd idea of where they ought to be going. Once outside the station his father turned to face in what he said he knew was certainly 'the right direction'. They walked on; Caleb dragged his feet a little way behind his father. They were walking down a long and strangely empty road, which seemed a perverse choice. Caleb was uneasy. He didn't like the look of the street. It was underlit, with the gas lamps spaced very far apart. It looked as if no one was expected to walk down it in the first place, as if it was an undesignated route.

He felt distinctly nervous away from all the bustling crowds, just the two of them, walking among dark wet shadows. He was not sure whether it was the loneliness of the route, or the darkness, the idea of Halloween, or the growing wisps and tatters of fog all around them, that made him so uneasy.

'Halloween is an imported festival,' his father said suddenly, turning back to Caleb. 'It has been emphasised here falsely in my view. It is an American celebration, grafted on to our past here. For all their boasts of authenticity the Corporation do get things fundamentally wrong sometimes. I once sent a memo about it to Mr Buckland, told him exactly what I thought. Stick to Guy Fawkes, I said. I sometimes doubt that my memos were ever read.' He turned and walked on. 'I sense in a real old street like this one an essence or memory of the past. The chaos and pain of past lives which has somehow been pressed, and moulded over the years into these very bricks and stones.' He stopped and tapped at the wet wall beside them. 'And I suppose that is one of the main points about the success of Pastworld, of this whole place, the saving of the ghosts of the past.' They walked side by side now. Caleb had allowed himself to catch up. Caleb wonderd if his father did not also feel the threat that he sensed all around them in the murk and the shadows. Lucius turned to Caleb and stopped him, he held on to his arm and said almost in a whisper, 'I know that I have seen complex sophisticated machines which most certainly possessed a soul, and which had more than an inkling of their own existence.' Caleb frowned; he thought that this was a strange thing for his father to say.

'Somewhere a long way beneath our feet is a whole other city, very different to this one full of machinery and systems for controlling the fogs and so on,' Lucius continued.

It was obvious he was distracted and Caleb thought it was no wonder his father was taking them on such a strange route. 'Are you sure this is the right way? This road seems so dark and empty,' Caleb said.

'Bear with me for a moment, Caleb. I have my own reasons for going this way,' his father said.

The sinister road curved now round the arches and the looming Byzantine brickwork embankments that supported the railway lines. Seen from this angle the foundations of the railway station looked like some newly discovered ruin. They were the freshly revealed archaeological layers of another city and civilisation even more ancient and bleak. The walls were covered over in a seemingly haphazard jumble of thickly lettered posters. One advertised stout, others warned pedestrians to stay on designated routes only. Lucius seemed to be willfully ignoring that advice.

They passed a sign post. Old Battersea was indicated by a pointing hand, back down the same long, bleak, empty road along which they had just walked. Caleb stopped his father and pointed to the sign.

'It says here that Old Battersea is back that way?'

'I know what I am doing, Caleb.'

Caleb noticed with a jolt, as he turned to look back once more in exasperation, that a single and very raggedly dressed man was following some way behind them part hidden by the mist.

They walked up the hill on a narrow pavement and then they turned into a wider street and at once found themselves heading against an onward pressure of people. Crowds of the huddled and wet natives of Pastworld streamed past, all going home after the factories and shops and offices had closed, making their way back down the hill towards the railway station. To Caleb they looked like ragged prisoners of war. Some children held begging bowls out to them. Caleb and his father were jostled too by various ruffians, some of whom looked official, some however seemed to Caleb to be more real and more definitely sinister.

His father hesitated and stood still. He looked around him in distraction and frustration and then he pulled out his gazetteer map and appeared to be studying it, but it seemed to Caleb that he was waiting and looking for something else, something not on any map.

They waited at a junction for the traffic to pass. Caleb watched the crowds of people as they passed him, pushing on over to the other side of the road. It was then that the ragged man stepped out suddenly from behind a curtained carriage. Caleb thought to tell his father they were being followed, but before he could say anything Lucius had set off across the road and headed further up the hill. Caleb set off after him but noticed with a rising panic that the beggar followed closer behind them now.

Caleb heard excited voices somewhere behind him calling out 'Trick or Treat'. They passed a green grocer's shop, and Caleb noticed the earthy banks of raw beetroots and carved pumpkin heads and tumbled orange squashes and vegetables which were all piled up in racks and wooden crates outside.

Two children and their mother passed in front of him. There were two little girls, and they were giggling together. They wore Halloween masks and little tattered black witch's costumes and they carried bags for collecting treats. The mother held them both by the shoulders as she anxiously guided them along the crowded pavement. Caleb, in a moment of mischief, pulled the skull mask out of his pocket and put it on over his face. One of the little girls caught sight of him and screamed happily, nudging the other, and they carried on up the hill giggling together and looking back at Caleb. The ragged man still kept a steady pace behind them. Caleb was more and more uneasy, the ragged man definitely seemed to be keeping them in his sights. Caleb, his mask still on his face, finally stopped his father.

'We're being followed,' he mumbled through the mask. 'Look.' He pointed back down the street.

His father turned and looked back briefly into the heaving crowd. He looked at the ragged man for a moment and then closed his eyes and covered them with his hand, 'Oh no, no,' he muttered but then he snapped to, turned and fussed with the map, checked the direction and appeared not to really take in what Caleb had said.

After walking for another few yards his father suddenly said, 'Caleb, I have important business, I am going on ahead for a moment. I will be back after I have consulted someone. It's very important but only to me, don't worry. You must stay here, Caleb, keep out of the wet. I won't be long, I promise.' His father went on further up the hill, and was then lost to sight in the fog and crowd.

Caleb, puzzled, stood sheltered in a shop doorway for a while. A strange sight he made, the young man with the skull head standing lost in the shadows of the doorway. He watched the passing people huddled into their coat collars or under their umbrellas. He thought that his father had just behaved very oddly once again and again it was completely out of his normal character; something was up. He was rattled by something. Perhaps it was that letter? Caleb decided that he would wait no longer. He went after his father instead.

He walked on up the hill into a denser bank of drifting fog. Two people stood together in the murk at a minor road junction on the rise. One was a broad young man, his face partly hidden by an old, tattered umbrella, and the other a scruffily dressed older man with a stick and thick glasses, not yet perhaps a beggar but he didn't look far off it. Caleb noticed then that the older man was blind or at least nearly blind, and that the younger man was holding on lightly to the sleeve of his coat. As Caleb passed he could see that the older man looked very agitated. The young man beside him lifted his umbrella and Caleb saw his face for a moment too and thought that he looked feral and dangerous. He had a down-turned mouth and a shadowed scowl. He was surely just the kind of illicit non-accredited beggar they had all been warned about during their Pastworld induction lessons. The young man spotted him staring and jutted his chin forward and called, 'Got any silver, young skull face? Coins, dosh, come on, you can spare it.'

He held out a ragged mittened hand. Caleb, thinking hurriedly of his induction lessons and not even here in the fogs of the past being able to be impolite, stopped and turned to answer him.

'I am very sorry,' he said, haltingly repeating the official line. 'I have already given out my recommended beggar's allowance for today.'

The blind man fixed his sightless pale eyes in the direction of Caleb's voice. He shuffled himself forward, and at the same time the tough young man let go of the blind man's arm. The young man, as a parting shot, called out 'Skull-faced skinflint bloody Gawker' to Caleb in a coarse rasping voice. Then he stepped back just a little but stayed near, waited and watched them from a shadowy doorway.

'Help,' the blind man said quietly under his breath, 'help me then.'

'I'm sorry I don't think I can,' Caleb replied. But the blind man quickly interrupted him.

'You could help,' he whispered. 'I'm meant to meet someone important you see and it's urgent, and I mean real life and death urgent. You can take me to them perhaps . . . Take me away from here at least; I should be somewhere else instead. You can see; and I can only just about manage, I can hardly see anything at all now. Come on, you can do it as a Christian act. It's somewhere just near here.'

'Sorry,' said Caleb, 'I don't know this area I'm afraid.'

'Take me, *please*, come on, come on. You can see all right, can't you?'

'Yes,' Caleb replied, 'I can, but I don't even know where we are. I wish I could help.' He saw that the skin on the back of the man's hand and wrist was scarred and thickened where it had once perhaps been badly burned. Suddenly Caleb's father suddenly appeared out of the fog. He was out of breath, as if he had been suddenly running. 'There you are at last. I missed you in this damn fog,' he said to the blind man, then he stopped and took in exactly what was happening in front of him, 'Oh it's you, Caleb,' he said, and he reached his hand out and latched on to the blind man's arm.

The blind man rolled his pale eyes. 'Well, well,' he growled. 'At last, I think I know *that* voice, don't I? We need to talk.'

'Leave us for just a moment, Caleb,' his father blustered, while his eyes darted to the young man in the doorway.

Caleb could make no sense of this.

'Come on, it must be after six o'clock,' the blind man lowered his voice. 'Let's go.'

Caleb's father replied calmly. 'I know what you want,' he said, 'but where are you trying to get to?'

'Someone is waiting for us, with a message from Eve,' the blind man whispered in his rasping voice, staring straight ahead. 'Come on,' said the blind man, 'or he'll get me. He'll leave me to rot with my throat cut, and worse, you have no idea.'

'Eve,' Caleb's father said quietly.

'Yes Eve and double yes Eve, the lovely Eve. She's gone, run off – why else would I risk writing? – she's out there somewhere in this place.'

Caleb watched all this from a few feet away, not far from the feral young beggar.

'They are close behind me now, and there's more than one of them, and they come from him, from hell.' Then the blind man flipped up the face of a rusted-looking pocket watch, which was slung on a dirty string around his neck. Caleb saw that the dial was open, that there was no glass cover over the hands, and that touching them with his trembling fingers only seemed to confirm the blind man's panic further.

'It's half past now. She's probably been waiting there for me since six. You don't know how dangerous this is. She won't wait for ever. Come on, come on, it's your chance too. I must get the message. You must save Eve,' the blind man said and turned his face away, his gums working, chewing and mashing.

It was then that Caleb saw the other beggar, the one who had been tracking them all the way from the station. He stood on the other side of the road watching them, then gave a shrill whistle to someone further off in the crowd. The feral young man with the umbrella moved away from the doorway.

'Come on then take my arm and please,' said Lucius, 'be careful near the traffic. Why not let my son take the other arm, and we will take you, to where this woman is?'

The three stood for a moment near the kerbside, as the traffic rattled past. Caleb shivered. Something hovered near him at eye level, something metallic, like an insect or a thin silver needle, and it buzzed around his head for a moment. He looked straight at it and it suddenly dipped out of sight and vanished into the swirls of fog.

The other ragged man crossed the road towards them. He was light on his feet and dodged and skipped between all the carriages and wagons. The younger beggar reached them first and grabbed at the blind man.

'Did you just touch me?' said the blind man. 'What was that?'

Three or more ragged men were suddenly among them like a pack of fierce dogs. Caleb's father moved closer and turned to him, his mouth open, as if to call out. The blind man was struck with something that flashed bright and silver and he crumpled downwards into his overcoat just where he stood, as if he were a building that had been suddenly demolished. The beggar who had been following Caleb and his father threw something in the air over to Caleb. Instinctively Caleb caught it. He felt something warm and sticky. He looked down and saw red all over his hand and a blood-stained knife. He dropped the knife. The blind man went down on to the wet cobbles near the clattering wheels of the passing carriages; and all without a sound. Caleb instinctively reached out to him, and his bloodied hand closed round the pocket watch on the string, which ripped away from the blind man's neck.

Someone held Caleb now, tight from behind.

'Murder!' shouted a coarse voice. 'Look what he's done.'

Caleb struggled while someone wrenched Caleb's mask from his head. He could not believe what had just happened. Now he watched as his father was punched hard too and fell straight down in the dirt and wet.

The cold rain streamed in Caleb's eyes. He struggled against whoever held him, not knowing what else to do. Someone screamed. Caleb saw the shiny silver blade on the ground at his feet. He saw the ground and the blind man's spilled blood, mingling with the rain water. He saw his father in his pathetic skeleton-printed suit sprawled in a puddle. A ragged man bent down to Caleb's father, and lifted him up in a headlock. Then pointed an accusing finger at Caleb. 'Trick or treat tonight, and this young blighter's killed 'em both,' he called out to whoever would listen among the crowd.

Caleb was trapped.

A carriage stopped and then another. Confused voices shouted 'Blood! Look someone's really hurt here.' Caleb struggled harder against the arms that held him. He whipped his head wildly from side to side. He looked for some support among the crowd of people that had gathered round. Then his father shouted out 'Run' and got smashed in the face for it. His father lifted his head to Caleb again. 'Run,' he croaked again, 'run boy, run while you can.'

The broad young man with the umbrella struck his father again and harder this time. In that instant Caleb decided. He swung his boot back hard and it connected with the shadowy figure who was holding him. The figure yelped and for a moment his grip loosened; it was enough. Caleb took his chance. He ran straight out and across the busy road, between all the carriages. He ran fast, sliding and dodging the wheels and horses, and he kept looking straight ahead.

⇢ CHAPTER 13 ⇠

DI Hudson watched the recording of the whole incident as it unfolded in repeat on the Espion feed screens. There was only the one camera, so it was a confused set of images. Once the camera pulled further back from the boy he had a clearer view. Hudson replayed the stabbing part, back and forth, studying the blind man's collapse, looking for the moment the blow was struck and exactly who had struck it. He enlarged and resolved that section of the image in greater detail. Finally he saw the ragged man dig the knife point hard into the blind man's chest. 'Ouch,' he said aloud to the screen. He watched the Gawker being struck in the face, knocked down and held in the arms of the young tough behind him. Then he watched the skull mask ripped from the youth's face, watched him kick out and run off across the road and into the crowd and there the camera lost him. Three of the ragged men ran off after him, two stayed with the body, two more dragged the man in the skeleton suit back along the pavement. The Espion camera had been kept on track until they reached a waiting hansom cab with closed curtains. The door of the cab opened, and the slumped figure of the man in the suit was pushed inside. Hudson glimpsed a masked face through the open door. He froze the image and stored it, one more piece of evidence for the Inspector. One of the ragged men turned and noticed the needle-sized Espion camera. His hand reached out and for a second it filled the bank of screens, and then the image dissolved in a fizzing snow of white and green sparks; the camera was down. The screen went black.

Hudson alerted Charlie Catchpole and when he arrived showed him the attack.

'I already ran a check on the two victims. The man we presume kidnapped is Lucius Brown. Turns out he's on the big A list, an original Buckland imagineer, once a real Corporation bigwig. The knife victim, who looks as if he's blind, we have no match for, not so far anyway. There's no connection we can find. The boy witness, the one you can see running away just there, is Caleb Brown, age seventeen, son of Lucius. Both came in here on personal invitation – Buckland freedom passes, the works.'

'Has anyone picked up the body of the victim yet?'

'Well about ten minutes ago a cab ambulance arrived at the scene,' Hudson said, 'and I quote "the body has gone" and we know what that means.'

'Sold to a bootleg murder tour,' Catchpole said.

'Exactly,' said Hudson, 'and of course no sign of the boy. He's gone to ground if he has any sense. Anyway this is the bit you have to see.' He rolled the sequence with the cab and paused at the glimpse of the masked figure inside.

'Add that to yesterday's incident, the tower leap, the severed head, the missing heart?'

'What would The Fantom's interest be in this man Brown though?' Catchpole said.

'One of us, and maybe if I'm unlucky again, two of us, may soon have the job of finding out,' said Hudson. 'Time to visit Lestrade and show him what we've got.' He fingered his neck, already imagining the stiff collar, the hard stud at the throat, the constricting waistcoat.

⇒ CHAPTER 14 ⇐

FROM EVE'S JOURNAL

'You've never heard of the Fantom?' Jago asked me.

'No, I don't think so,' I replied, but inside an odd memory had stirred. It was of Jack muttering the word 'phantom' as he read, bent close over the newspaper.

'The Fantom comes and goes like a shadow,' said Jago. 'He's our local Pastworld bogey man, a really terrifying figure. He either travels up high among the roofs and chimneys, or he somehow moves out of sight underground. He's an odd mixture, an old time, daring show-off master criminal. He wears a mask and he's as agile as a cat. Now he's a throat cutter, a disemboweller, a tearer-out of hearts, a decapitator as well. They say he controls all the unofficial begging, and much worse that goes on in the city. He's the Roi des pauvres, king of the ragged men and of the wider criminal underclass. He's too clever to get caught, he's the very best at what he does. They even sell ballad sheets about him in the markets.'

I sat listening to Jago in horror, imagining someone tearing out a heart, a human heart. Jago clicked the horse into action, and we were off again. 'There are big rewards out for him but no one has ever claimed them, no one has ever turned him in – he's that elusive. The poor look up to him in a strange sort of way. They have invested him with this legendary folklore status and now even with super-natural powers. He jumps from buildings and high places. He does what in the last century would have been called 'base jumping'. He once fell during a rooftop pursuit and floated down to the ground on a scarlet parachute.'

We were near the river, surrounded by a series of ware-houses and wharf buildings which rose up like bad teeth on either side of us. Jago slowed the horse, and the wagon came to a halt.

'We're going to meet up tomorrow with the rest of our family,' Jago said.

'Family,' I said, trying the sound of the word in my mouth. It was a word I had hardly used before. At least it felt that way.

'We call them our family. They are a tribe of ragtag and bobtails really. Street entertainers like ourselves, a loose collection, Gypsies, poor young runaways, all sorts, we're a very broad family, we don't ask questions and we don't discriminate.'

'Runaways like me,' I said.

'Runaways just like you,' he said. 'You are welcome to stay with us, Eve. We can protect you, if you feel that you need it and looking at you I think you do.' He looked me over, as if inspecting me for the first time. I felt his eyes all

over me. 'Do you know we might even make something of you, if you'd like us to? You have a dancer's physique – you could be useful. We could train you and you could earn your keep while you're with us,' said Jago. 'Or of course I could just take you back to where you came from if you'd prefer.' He reached over and gave me a squeeze on the wrist. His thin hand was cold, but felt very strong.

'I have never danced ever,' I said, and then surprising myself, 'I should very much like to dance. I have never walked on a rope, and I should very much like to walk on a rope.'

'Well, then you shall,' said Jago with a smile, and he clicked the horse into life again.

I sat beside Jago and watched the passing buildings. Everything was in a state of disrepair, was ruined even. The street lights were mostly dark and there was no sign of life.

'It's very dark,' I said.

'We're off the beaten track, on an unsupervised, undesignated route. One of the cracks in the perfect facade, the cracks we like to slip through. This area is awaiting completion or restoration, whatever the Corporation call it. Looks bleak, doesn't it, but don't worry we are safe. I may be slight but I am fit and strong and besides I am well armed.' He patted the seat beneath us and so I presumed he had a weapon hidden there.

'Jack, my guardian, never told me about the reality of this place,' I said. 'He kept me in as much as possible, and we always went outside together. I thought all this time that we were living in London under the reign of Queen Victoria.'

{ 104 }

Jago smiled. 'There are other undesignated places, wild tracts of woodland and deep forest not far from the city where we sometimes go and refresh ourselves in the real open air under real trees.'

None of this explained why Jack never mentioned a word of this to me in all of our quiet attic life together. I had accepted the world I lived in as the only real world, which it was of course for me. But why had Jack kept me hidden? Jago had no answers to that. Jack sounded eccentric to him, perhaps even a little mad. Why would anyone lock a young girl away in an attic and keep her in ignorance of where she really was?

'Come on wake up, sleepy head.' It was Jago's voice.

I had been lost in a dream floating high in the air on a great wave of red silk, a scarf that extended all the way across the night sky. The flap was pulled back. Grey light filtered in. It was cold. I was to meet the 'family'. The warmth from inside the wagon was sucked out like breath into the frosty air. Snow was falling in big white flakes. I climbed out of the wagon. I stood shivering, wondering at the snow, wondering just how it was made, how high was the skydome that covered and surrounded us. We had stayed overnight in a square, something like the big market at Farringdon, but here the buildings were vacant, half destroyed. There was broken glass at the windows and old, tattered curtains flapped in the empty spaces. Our wagon was one of several, which were all drawn up in a loose half circle; the horses steamed in the cold air. Jago had walked over to a group who stood together laughing and holding mugs of what I hoped was some good hot tea.

Among the group I could see a huge woman dressed in bright red, and next to her was an equally large man draped in a leopard-skin tunic, his arms so huge they looked like legs. Between them, standing on a barrel, was a tiny man about a third my height. He wore an enormously long pair of shoes – they measured at least two feet – and as he chatted and laughed with the others he lifted himself up and balanced improbably on tiptoes until he reached above their heads.

'Come over, meet everyone, Eve, and have some breakfast,' said Jago.

I walked over and stood among the group of odd-looking people. One woman had her back turned. She wore an elegant coat with a big fur collar. I was surprised when her collar moved independently and a bright pair of eyes looked back at me. The collar was a living animal – a familiar little spotted cat. It was the cat lady. The very one that Jack and I used to meet on our evening walks. I wasn't anxious for her to notice me up close. She would surely tell Jack where I was and then I would be brought back and he would be in danger all over again. She was talking to another perfectly ordinary-looking woman; ordinary-looking in everyway, except that she had a big dark beard. Nearly everybody was dressed in some exotic or eccentric costume.

Jago gave me a mug of tea, and it felt good to wrap my cold hands round it.

'This is the whole circus. This is our part of the city and so far it is mercifully free of Corporation interference or any spy cameras, for now anyway. It's a welcome sort of no-man's-land, that's what we call it.'

'No-man's—land.' I rolled the words round in my mind, no—man's-land. I looked around. There were clowns and harlequins, Pierrots and tumblers, acrobats and freaks of all kinds, not very much like the lithographed circus pictures in the books at home, with all the lions and tigers and bears.

'Look no Gawkers here either,' Jago said. 'Never seen one yet anyway. Only our people, our family.'

'Family,' I said, holding the mug of hot tea against my cold cheek. 'Family.'

'All of us,' said Jago, 'the big ones, the little ones, the strong ones, the weak ones, why even little Malcy over there on the barrel, we all look out for each other, like brothers and sisters, just like your Jack tried to look out for you, Eve. It's horrible being on your own in here – it's an old-fashioned dog-eat-dog kind of a place, but at least you can rely on us.'

I looked around at the friendly-looking crowd and nodded and then Jago grabbed me by the shoulders and pulled me into the very middle of the group. I stood there wrapped in the blanket, very nervous of them all gathered round me.

'This is Eve,' said Jago. 'I rescued her from a ragged man and the streets. She hopes to be trained in the myster-ies of our arts.'

They laughed and one cheery voice called out, 'Good luck, love.'

The woman in red put her huge arm round my shoulder.

'Welcome,' she said, and squeezed me, which made me instinctively draw free, the blanket fell from my shoulders and I shivered. The cat woman was next to her and she put her head on one side and said, 'I've seen you somewhere before my love. I wouldn't forget a pretty face like yours.'

'I don't think so,' I said.

The strongman interrupted. 'She's got the build for it, Jago. Dainty little feet, ain't they?'

There was some more good-natured laughter at this. The strongman crouched down in the snow in front of me. 'Don't mind me, miss,' he said. He held my arms tight squeezing at my muscles then patted me down, pressing at my body as he went, at my thighs and calves, he shaped my ankles with his fingers and thumbs as if I were a horse. I had never been touched like that before by anyone. I felt a flush of anger, of shame even, and something else, a spark, a thrill. Then he stopped and drew his hands away. He hesitated and looked at me a little oddly. If I had not known better, I would swear that a moment of doubt, almost of fear had crossed his face as he held my gaze. Then he grabbed me again around my waist and lifted me off my feet and straight up into the air, as if I weighed no more than a feather. He hoisted me up into the gently spinning snowflakes above his head. I wobbled and waved my arms to steady myself. Jago was watching me intently and with a serious expression on his face, while the others around us were smiling.

Later Jago set up the poles and strung the rope between them. The strongman helped him to secure the guy-ropes so that the poles were steady. I watched him practise walking across the rope, back and forth over and over. It still looked like something I wanted to do.

'Could I try the rope please?' I said.

'You can't just start on the rope,' Jago said. 'There is more to it than just running and dancing along a straight line. It's dangerous for one thing.'

'Just let me try once please.'

Jago looked at me seriously with his big dark eyes. 'You really want to try it?'

'Oh please,' I said.

The strongman encouraged him.

'Go on then, Jago,' he said. 'Why not give her a go? She's got the shape for it and she felt strong to me. I'll catch 'er for you if she falls. Ha ha, pretty little thing like that.'

So Jago put a leather safety harness around my middle. He tested the buckles and the rope. The strongman lifted me up and I stood as straight as I could. I was high up on a tiny wooden platform at one end of the tightrope, at least fifteen feet up over the square. I was cold, and I nervously flexed my toes while Jago lifted me a little off the platform to test the support rope.

'Remember, try not to look down,' he said. 'If you feel wobbly, just stand still and breathe slowly, and remember you're safe, there is the harness and if you fall you'll just swing on the safety rope, so don't panic.'

By the time I was ready, some of the wagons had left, trailed off into another part of the city. The strongman had stayed to help Jago, and I could see him below warming himself round a brazier. It was my own fault; I had begged to try the tightrope, I had wanted to try it, but it meant I *must learn the hard way.*

I stepped out on to the rope. I kept my feet close together, one behind the other in a straight line. I felt an instinctive need to curl my toes over and around the rope, but the rope felt too thick.

I swayed and I raised my arms straight out from my body, parallel to my shoulders, and I looked straight ahead to the other pole, twenty feet in front of me. I raised my leg and felt my weight shift suddenly on to the other leg. At first I couldn't bring the other down in front of it and I began to wobble. I flailed my arms to keep my balance. Suddenly I was swinging free on the safety rope and my breath had been pushed out of me in a visible cloudy rush as the harness pulled up on my chest. I swung past Jago, who was standing at the top of the ladder, and he smiled at me as if to say 'I told you so.' I felt a fresh determination and a little lurch in my stomach as I was lifted up and dumped back on to the platform.

'Don't panic,' said Jago. 'Just walk forward slowly, confidently, as if you were on a pavement, and you had to walk only on the cracks, one foot behind the other. Didn't you play that as a child?'

'Not that I remember,' I said.

I stood for a moment hunched forward, breathing hard, with my hands on my knees. I straightened myself, and I tried again.

This time, emboldened by the smile from Jago and an appreciative whistle from the strongman I launched myself at speed. I walked forward without thought, with my arms outstretched. I imagined that the rope at my feet was like a wide road opening up on either side of me. I would show Jago. I crossed the rope, and this time the sky didn't turn over and the harness didn't tighten.

'That's better, good, amazing in fact,' Jago said. 'Try again but don't try and run before you can walk.'

I spent the rest of that cold morning trying the tightrope over and over. The strongman watched me from below, huddled by the brazier, warming himself as Jago paid out the line. My tenacity and Jago's patience had impressed him. Despite the cold, and the dangerous height, I was gaining confidence with every one of my simple walks along the rope. I lost count of the number of times I crossed it. Then Jago had a try. He climbed up the support rope and stood bouncing in the middle of the tightrope; he balanced on one leg and twisted his hips so that his body faced outwards. In one hand he held his brightly patched parasol. He flung the parasol up in the air so it turned over and over. He caught the parasol on his head as it fell and held it there, so that he stood balanced on one leg and with the parasol upside down on his upturned head. I was on the platform, shivering but impressed all over again by Jago's skills. If I could only master a little of that skill, I thought, I might be allowed to stay with them, to hide for ever. Anything but go back to living a pretend life in fear in that little attic room. I had discovered something that I could do, and do well and perhaps it would be my ticket to freedom and a new life?

Jago seemed pleased, and surprised enough with my progress as we packed the stuff into the wagon. He allowed me to help harness up the skinny horse. 'Where did you learn to do that, you've obviously done it before?' he said.

'I've never done it before, I told you so,' I said. 'I just somehow felt that I could.'

'Well,' he said, 'I really think that we might make something of you.'

'What's the name of the horse?' I asked.

'She's called Pelaw,' said Jack. 'She's the same colour as Pelaw wax shoe polish, so that's what I chose to call her.'

'Pelaw,' I said, and the horse snorted a little and showed her teeth, shook her mane from side to side. 'She knows her name,' I said.

'Oh yes,' said Jack, 'she knows her name.'

The woman with the cat collar was warming herself at the brazier. She walked over to me.

'I know just who you are now, dear, I've worked it out. You're the girl that sometimes walks with poor Jack, near my lodgings,' she said. 'You're his daughter surely?'

'I think you are confusing me with someone else,' I said brazenly, blushing in the cold air.

'Sorry dear but I could've sworn,' she said and looked at me hard for a moment while she stroked her cat's neck.

She knew that I was lying.

I stayed happily with Jago and the family of other travelling players. For Jago my mystery was not where I had come from and why, but my mysterious ability and balance on the rope. Where had that come from?

I began to perform with the harlequin troupe in market places and on street corners. We travelled together on our routes around the fringes of the city and I began to recognise the extent of the gulf between the 'official' beggars and the hordes of pinched-looking illicits that we passed and played to every day. I knew I had to continue my new life, my real adventure. I had a strange natural instinct for the tightrope. Within a few short days I could run and skip the narrow rope, for it now really did feel as wide as a road to me. My inner confidence was complete and Jago was pleased.

A few days later the woman with the cat found me again. 'It is you, my dear, isn't it? I was right before,' she said. 'I know it is you because I saw poor Jack in the street and he said you had gone, run away and he was in a terrible state worrying about you.'

I had no reason to treat Jack cruelly, even if he had hidden me away and hidden the truth of my situation from me as well.

'You are right,' I said. 'I did run away. I can't tell you why, but I am happy and safe and want to stay here with Jago. Perhaps I might write a note that you could give to Jack from me to reassure him?'

'I think that's the least you could do. It would be a nice thing dear for poor Jack.'

So I wrote him a note of reassurance and gave it to the lady with the cat, and she said she would deliver it to Jack. I felt a clear conscience. Jack had brought me up in ignorance. He had never spoken of my father and mother once and for whatever reason of his own had denied me almost any truth, as well as letting me live in the belief that the world around me was all there was, when it was an *illusion, an imitation of life.*

Soon I was performing in front of bigger crowds. I remember one afternoon I was wearing a flowing white dress. I often felt moments of real fear standing at the top of the support pole. The crowd all gathered below me. Jago was at the bottom of the ladder wearing his one-man-band kit, banging on the bass drum with a foot pedal and playing his quivery little tune on the cornet. That afternoon a harlequin from one of the other wagons was balanced half way up the ladder looking up at me, and holding the balancing parasol in case I felt I should need it. As usual I wanted to show Jago that I could dazzle on the rope. My feet just fitted neatly on to the little platform at the top of the striped pole. There was no safety harness now, no net, no second chance, I was on my own. The strongman was somewhere in the crowd too, waiting in case I should fall. The cornet music stopped, and Jago started playing a sharp roll on the snare drum, which rattled and echoed in the cold air. I knew that when it stopped I would walk forward to the other side of the rope, and no turning back. I looked down at Jago and he nodded. The tumbler held the parasol up to me but I shook my head. Finally the drum roll stopped.

Down among the colourfully dressed crowd were a group of people, who were there just to keep the braziers going. They wore leather gloves and aprons, and poked at the brazier coals with long iron rods. This sent bright orange sparks up into the frosted air like fireworks. I could see jolly muffin sellers, and pork-pie sellers, and standing at the front of the crowd there was one particular boy of about my own age. I had seen him before at our other shows, and there was something about him I liked. Something about him attracted me. It was a very odd feeling, something I had never experienced before.

He was looking up and watching me closely. It's hard to put it into words, but I liked seeing him and my heart lifted a little. He had such a nice smile across his face. Our eyes met, but in that split, silent moment with the crowd hushed and expectant it unnerved me and I wobbled just a fraction on the rope. A gasp went up from the crowd. I recovered myself quickly but the silence from below was deafening. I moved forward very deliberately, and Jago started the drum roll again. I skipped out across half the length of the rope. The rope dipped down in the middle, and despite the fact that I was as slim as Jago, and as light as a feather, the rope still swayed from side to side in the cold air. I shivered and felt goose pimples on my arms. I was halfway across and almost swinging back and forth on the rope, from side to side. The wind loosened my hair and it blew across my face. I was cold. The drum roll rattled on, and I found myself for a moment glued to the spot. I could neither move forwards nor back. Some of the Gawkers in the crowd shouted up at me. I couldn't hear clearly what they said, but every shout was followed by laughter. Some part of my mind thought about the balance parasol, and for a split second I wished I had taken it, and I craned my neck and looked back. The harlequin was now near the top of the striped pole, and held out the opened parasol for me just in case. I reached out for it but it was caught by a sudden flurry of wind and snow flakes, and was wrenched out of his

{ 115 }

hand. We both watched as it sailed out high over the heads of the crowd.

The drum roll stopped. The crowd seemed so intent on watching the bright little parasol spinning and floating over their heads that I went almost unnoticed for a moment. It was time to act; I ran across the rope. I ran all the way back the way I had come, my arms flung out, as if in pursuit of the lost balance parasol. I was so fast that the crowd thought I would fall. A huge roar came up from below, and then I turned and skipped back again the way I had come but even faster. A burst of applause followed. I danced on the rope, I leaped and twirled in the air. I invented moves for myself. I improvised, and the crowd went wild. I went furiously up and down the rope, danced, leaped, and twirled over and over. I had such a sudden surety of balance, such confidence.

I knew that I would not fall, could not fall, I had suddenly, in that moment of athletic showmanship found not only my true vocation, but my salvation too.

The crowd could see that I had no support, and that no hidden wire was holding me and that no safety net protected me. The drum rolls stopped and the cornet tune faded out.

I danced alone on the high rope in the falling snow. I danced with the snowflakes and among the snowflakes. I felt their coldness as they landed on me. It seemed almost as if I had slowed down time itself, so that I actually saw the snow fall slowly all around me. I finished, I stopped, and stood perfectly still in the centre of the dipping rope. I raised my arms high above my head and bowed. There was a sudden crash of applause and roars and shouts from the crowd. Clearly I had astonished them. I had astonished Jago too. He looked up at me, the drumsticks in one hand, his face slack and his mouth wide open. I think he had suddenly seen his fortune made.

⇥ CHAPTER 15 ⇤

The blind man's body lay sprawled, half in the gutter, half up on the pavement. An armed ragged man stood guard over it while the rain washed the blood in marbled swirls down the nearest drain. A crowd of spectral figures had gathered to stare. They huddled under a variety of umbrellas and parasols or else held evening papers over their heads. Some just suffered the wet, regardless. A bobby in a rain cape soon made his way among them. He cleared a path by holding his truncheon out in front of him, nudging and poking people aside. The ragged man turned to face him. The policeman shone his lamp down on to the body.

'Well?' he said.

'A lad knifed him, a young lad in a black suit, he had a skull mask on, ended up round his neck, black hair, skinny thing, he got away.'

The policeman turned back to the crowd, 'nothing to

see here, now move along please, you are in violation,' and he cleared them away pushing his truncheon out at them again, until muttering and mumbling they gradually dispersed, and melted away into the wet fog.

'I suppose you're going to tell me now that this will be a "useful" body,' said the policeman quietly.

'Very useful,' said the ragged man, and he produced a little bundle of white bank notes tied round with red string.

'That useful?' said the policeman.

'That useful,' said the ragged man.

The policeman took the notes. 'In that case I shall report the body already missing when I arrived. We will have a description of the criminal printed and organise Wanted posters which will be circulated at once.'

'That would be the best thing,' said the ragged man. 'You need to catch young killers like that. Only one punishment they understand.' He reached his big mittened hands up to his own throat and bulged his eyes out. The policeman nodded, adjusted his cape, slipping the roll of notes into an inside pocket and set off, away from the body, back down the hill.

Within seconds of his departure the remaining ragged men appeared as if out of nowhere. Together they hefted the sodden body of the blind man up out of the gutter. An old hospital hand cart was wheeled out of a dark doorway and they dropped the body on to the scuffed wooden surface with a heavy wet thump. One of them threw a length of sacking cloth across the body, then put a white hospital orderly's coat over his rags and set to wheeling the hand cart off down a narrow cobbled side street while the others went their separate ways.

⇺ CHAPTER 16 ⇻

Caleb ran across the road and into the confusion of people on the other pavement. He heard a ragged man's voice call out from behind him. 'Stop 'im, 'e's a murderer! 'E's got blood on 'is hands.' Caleb dared to look back and saw that yet another ragged man was coming after him. He ran on regardless.

Caleb had been accused of murder, and that was surely subject to the death penalty. He might be hanged and failing that the ragged men would be after him in any case, and if they caught up with him they would finally shut him up. He could feel the rope around his neck, the knife at his heart as he ran.

He ran on hard pushing his way through the tidal flow of pedestrian traffic. He ran back down the hill in the rain. He ran back to that long empty curving road with the caverns and the dark spaces and the railway arches. He turned, looked back again for an instant, and saw that his pursuers hadn't yet turned the corner. He skidded to a sudden halt, sliding on the wet pavement. Stumbling forward, he turned and squeezed himself into one of the deep, dark brick archways. He caught his breath. Three ragged men soon appeared. He watched them pass, his hands on his knees, drawing breath as quietly as he could. Two of them ran past his hiding place, without as much as a glance at where he crouched. One other following, stopped and turned. He peered into the dark archway. Then he came forward and crouching under the entrance way he crossed through into the wet darkness. Caleb saw him for an instant outlined against the faint light at the entrance, and then the figure entered the gloom, walking straight in towards where Caleb stood with his breath held and his fists clenched. Caleb moved backwards lifting his feet very carefully, lightly, and placing them back down as gently as he could on the wet cobbles. The space opened out behind him into some sort of access tunnel with a low arched ceiling of mossy, dank brick. He felt beside him and by touching the slippery wall he slowly guided himself backwards. He held his head down as he went deeper into the darkness. He felt an open niche in the tunnel wall beside him and he slipped into it and crouched down.

He waited then; his heart pounding. He gathered his thoughts with his eyes shut. He counted in his head and then he counted again. He heard the grunts and kicks of whoever was exploring the shallow space of the archway. Heard something being scraped and smacked on to the walls.

'Come on out, you little skull-faced shit. It'll be better for you to give yourself up now. Don't make me find you.' It was the voice of the broad, young ragged man with the umbrella.

Caleb's breathing finally slowed. He listened to the drops of condensation as they fell from the low arched ceiling above him. He kept his eyes closed; he had the strong feeling that if he opened them he would see the ragged young man standing right in front of him under his tattered umbrella just waiting patiently, like a cat with a mouse, to kill him. If he kept his eyes tight shut, he would neither be seen nor found. It was a crazy irrational thought but he clung to it as tightly and as foolishly as his poor father had clung to the belief that he always knew the right way to anywhere with his inner compass. He heard what he realised was the umbrella being scraped, struck and poked at the walls close to him. Heard the harsh metal tip scraaaatch in long, flashing strokes against the bricks close to his head. He was saved by being tucked into the recess. He heard the footsteps scraping and dragging over the cobbles moving away. Then there was silence.

Caleb stayed still squatted down against the damp bricks for a very long time. He had nowhere to go now, nowhere to make for. He had no friends to turn to anywhere in the whole huge, dark, filthy crowded phony city. Caleb realised in horror that he didn't even know the address of the Halloween party. He had taken no real notice of that engraved invitation or of his father's boasting about it to Mrs Bullock. Their lodgings were miles away in Islington. He had only the vaguest idea of how he might get back to them, and that meant the train. The station was not that far away but he knew that the ragged men would be looking for him by the station entrance. It would be an obvious place for him to go, so he ruled it out.

He stood up and stretched himself. His head was full of conflicting thoughts and emotions. He thought of criminals like 'the Fantom'. Pastworld had a reputation for the razor and the knife. Even his father, a once important Buckland Corp. employee, a so-called 'imagineer' couldn't protect himself. His father was now just another brutal Pastworld statistic. Was most likely dead, sprawled on his back, his pockets plucked empty.

No one on earth knew now where Caleb was. He felt a sudden cruel and insane freedom, as if a heavy burden had been lifted from him.

He gasped out loud, as if expelling all of the held-in breath and emotion of the last hour. He leaned back against the brick arch. He was free to escape from himself if he wanted to. He had finally and properly run away from his over planned, over protected and over regulated life. He could live here, hide in all the dark foggy disorder around him, escape as many others had allegedly done before. He was free to reinvent himself as he wished. No longer just a boy from the suburbs. He could be an adventurer, a soldier, a thief, a secret killer bent on revenge. These were stirring and startling thoughts, and they took place at very high speed, somewhere deep in the back of his whirling head, and not even at a conscious level, they just welled there, competing with all the shock and the horror at what he had seen.

All he had left in this particular version of the real world were the clothes on his back, the mixed pile of heavy coins in his pocket and the poor blind man's rusted pocket watch. It was still attached to its length of dirty string, and he found he was still holding it, gripped tightly in his hand. He moved nearer to the entrance where there was a little light. He stared down at it. The glass cover had been removed, so that the blind man could feel the hands of the watch, to tell the time. Caleb held the watch out in the thin light. He listened, it still ticked; and then he turned it over. Something was cut into the back of the watch case. Caleb tried to make it out in the gloom. He licked his finger, and smeared it across the silvery metal. Words were engraved in a fine copperplate script:

Presented to Lucius Brown,
With the grateful thanks of the
Buckland Corporation,
19th February 2032

It had once been his father's watch.

❧ CHAPTER 17 ❧

The Fantom looked at the corpse laid out on the big round enamel table. The body had been hastily stripped and vaguely washed in some sort of disinfectant. The limbs were outstretched and arranged as he had ordered in the manner of Vitruvian man, the celebrated image by Leonardo da Vinci. He approached the table almost nervously. He was half expecting Jack, such a very familiar figure to him, to sit up and say something, to remind him of his oh-so-carefully-learned numbers perhaps.

'Is it really you, Jack?' he said quietly. He went and stood directly over the body, close to the head. 'What a mess you've let yourself get into. Haven't been seeing too well lately, I hear.' He stopped, paused in his flow as if the corpse might reply in that familiar gruff voice. 'Supposing you were to say something.' He looked down at the stubbled throat. He quickly produced a straight razor. He slashed right through the throat almost severing the head.

There was a little blood.

Now there could only be silence.

He put down the razor. His Gladstone bag, full of all his other instruments, was on a side table, and a bright oil lamp was hooked on to a pole and shone down clearly on the pale dead flesh like moonlight. He noted the burn scars visible on the hands and the lower arms and all across the bloated torso. The skin looked dark and toughened like the outside of some over-roasted leg of lamb.

'Tut tut,' he said, 'that'll teach you to play with fire. This won't take long, Jack old friend, I promise. Just a quick look, I owe you that at least. I'm only after the heart of the matter, I have to be sure you see. Not that you *do* see,' and he coughed and made a little suppressed laugh.

He used a surgeon's scalpel to make the necessary Y incision from the shoulders down to the pubic bone. Soon the rib cage was exposed and the body looked more like something from a Smithfield market wagon. He looked down at the sad, mushy face and the staring eyes. 'No point in closing them now, eh Jack?' he said.

Eventually he removed Jack's heart and weighed it on a butcher's scale. 'The weight of the human heart, thirteen ounces,' he said. 'You have a heavy heart and so you should after what you did to me, sorry, tried to do to me, to *us.*' He lifted the slippery heart and put it to one side on the zinc-topped table.

The Fantom stitched up the autopsy wounds as well as he could, the stitches were not neat but they would do. He straightened the figure and finally, in a sudden and unlikely act of sympathy, or perhaps of some misplaced sense of mercy, he shut Jack's staring pale eyes, pressing them lightly with his fingers. He went out into a dingy, long tiled corridor. An armed ragged man stood guard under a hanging oil lamp. The empty hospital hand cart stood against the wall draped in bloodied sacking. The Fantom pulled a folded piece of paper from his pocket and handed it over. 'This ad will run in the early morning edition of the *London Mercury*. It's all arranged, and paid for, and this is the place, take it. Just dress him as we discussed and go.'

They returned to the room and the ragged man transferred the body on to the hand cart and wheeled it away back down the long corridor.

The Fantom went back into the light and looked long and hard at the heart sitting on its own under the glare of the oil lamp.

⇾⚹ CHAPTER 18 ⚹⇽

Caleb watched the water as it dripped off the bricks and down in to the dank puddles at his feet. He had been silent for so long. His mouth would hardly open.

'They'll kill me if they find me,' he said quietly.

There was no answer.

He had to go, and go now. He went and peered out of the dark archway and into the bleak street. There were no signs of any of the ragged men. There were some street sellers on the other side of the road. He stepped back into the shadow of the arch. He closed his eyes and waited. He heard footsteps pass close to him. He stood stock-still, with his eyes closed. He counted in his head, and tried to be exact in his seconds. One one thousand, two one thousand. Someone had once told him that this was the way to measure a proper second. It had been his father of course, being a precise man. The image of his father's punched face swam back to him again. Three, one thousand, four, one thousand. He calmed himself, then opened his eyes and walked straight out from under the wet arch and back into the street.

CHAPTER 19

Bible J, the dip, was to some by outward appearance perfectly respectable. He was the personal assistant to Mr William Leighton, aesthete, dealer and collector, who lived in an historic house in Fournier Street, Spitalfields. In truth Bible J was also a hardened little thief, a common pickpocket. He was a magician with his hands, a virtuoso conjuror with his fingers. He could lift a wallet, or a coin purse, without the victim discovering the loss until it was much too late. He had lived rough on the streets of Pastworld for a good half of his eighteen years. However, inside of him there was at least a kernel of sympathy. There were also traces of a warm, almost sentimental heart, and above all there was a sense of humour and a winning charm. He was not like the other feral boys he had run with on the streets when he was younger. They had been hard-faced, ruthless, swift to beat or kick, or to use a knife, who made ideal recruits when they were older as the Fantom's ragged men. There was some tenderness about Bible J. He could spot someone in real trouble; he recognised anguish, and he would act accordingly. He had brought the odd waif and stray back to the Fournier Street house, where they had been fed, given a little money, helped on their way.

He had waved loaded revolvers at bank tellers during robberies. He had fired at the Fantom's ragged men high among the tangle of rooftops and chimneys. He had been pursued many times by Buckland Corps Cadets and police officers. He had been listed as Wanted, and been the subject of posters and proclamations, but had never yet actually killed anyone, and had never yet been caught. Being caught after all was a serious matter in Pastworld.

On Halloween night he was to be seen walking purposefully among the late groups of partygoers and stragglers. He was often dressed as a smart and personable young man about town, but tonight he was wearing his butcher boy cap and 'raggy' dip's clothes that he had worn for a day or two now. Indeed had been wearing them since he had narrowly missed being recognised and sliced up by the Fantom, who, for some reason, had not registered who Bible J was. He would surely dine out on that one soon, and just wait till Mr Leighton found out that the Fantom was back on the streets. He wouldn't like that at all.

There were some drunks heading, or staggering rather, down the hill towards the big railway station junction at Clapham. Bible J lost himself among them with intent, like a wolf among a fold of sheep. He slipped through the jolly groups, assessing them, rattling pockets, slipping off watches and rings, stuffing them all into his poacher's pockets. He padded through them, light on his feet, and then quickly turned off on to a quiet side road. It was dark and empty, and had a string of wan, flickery gas lamps, which were spaced so far apart that there were long stretches of darkness between the pools of light. This was a perfect escape route. He set off walking quickly with his head down. Another figure was walking ahead of him. A youth of about his own age, nicely dressed too. Bible J walked behind him for a few paces as quietly as he could. He didn't much like dipping off someone as young as himself. A boy who might be fitter and run faster than him. He drew alongside him. He studied him from the side. *Black hair, white face*, he thought. The boy made no acknowledgement of Bible J, just kept walking, his face as pale as one of the Halloween skull masks he had seen everywhere on the streets. Bible J leaned over and tapped him on the arm. The boy stopped, frozen on the spot. He kept his eyes down, and his head tucked under his collar.

'Got a copper or two for us, mate?' Bible J said in his best cheerful-sounding voice.

The boy stared back at Bible J in silence.

'You all right, mate?' Bible J said. 'You look like you've seen a bleeding ghost. Mind you that's not hard tonight though eh, whole place is groaning with 'em.' Bible J looked around the street, and as if to confirm the idea, and he waved his arms up and down, imitating the movements that ghosts were supposed to make.

The boy nodded; nodding, it seemed, was all he could manage.

'About those few little coins then, smudger,' said Bible J brightly.

'Coins?' the boy answered.

'Looks to me like you must have some on you, mate.' He reached forward and shook the boy's fine top coat. The boy stepped back as if he had been shot.

'Ooh, steady on, no harm meant,' and Bible J advanced again smiling, his arms raised, his palms outwards, empty.

'You must be a Gawker?' he said. 'All dressed up like that,' he added quizzically.

The boy nodded, casting his eyes down once again.

'Got lost on a murder trail did you, or what?' Bible J asked, walking backwards now down the hill keeping pace in front of the boy who had set off again.

The boy shook his head, and stopped dead again on the pavement. Bible J stopped too.

'Coppers, tanners, any coins left at all, any moolah, splosh, dosh, shillings?' Bible J asked, keeping his big, friendly, winning smile on his face.

The boy suddenly pushed his hand into his trouser pocket, like someone in a trance. He pulled out a big handful of coins. They sat in the palm of his hand, a mound of heavy copper and silver.

Bible J let out a low whistle. 'That's the stuff,' he said. 'How much you got there? You and me, we could live like kings on that for a good while.' He poked around among the coins held out on the boy's trembling palm.

'You're nervous, ain't you?' Bible J said. 'Let's see how much you got altogether then.'

Bible J took a handful of the coins and counted them fast, skimming through them, muttering the names and amounts under his breath. After a while he looked up still smiling. 'There's more than enough there for a nice big fat lamb chop and gravy dinner for two, and plenty of change left after, if you know the right place.'

The boy nodded. 'Could you help me?' he said quietly.

'Good idea, mate,' said Bible J. 'Thank you, I will join you. I don't mind if I do. First sensible thing you've said to me all night,' he laughed and added, 'I'm starving, follow me, come on, I won't bite, I promise.'

'I need help,' the boy said more insistently.

The smile faded from Bible J's face, his posture slumped a little. 'You in trouble?' he said with a sigh.

'Yes,' said the boy, lifting his head high for the first time his eyes bright, his face pale and wet.

'Big trouble, little trouble?' Bible J asked, knowing what the answer would be.

'Big trouble,' said the boy.

'Very big?'

'Very big.'

Bible J resigned himself. Here was another waif and stray to look after for a while. Why did he allow himself to get involved. He seemed to seek them out by some special process, as if he was drawn to them.

The boy let himself be taken around the base of the station mound, through the last throngs of laughing partygoers in their Halloween costumes. Bible J said, 'Tell me all about it later. Stick with me and you'll be all right,' and he carried on, jingling the coins in anticipation of the meal they would soon be able to eat.

Figures rushed past them on the pavement, shoved against them, and the boy just let them buffet him, slip past him, turn him this way and that, as if all the strangely dressed teeming people were just another part of the weather.

Further along on a dimly lit street far from the station, the boy stood and watched while Bible J chose a cigar from a glass case at a tobacconist's kiosk.

'Want one?' he asked turning to the boy and smiling.

'No,' the boy said.

Then later still, on a more brightly lit street they stopped in front of a white and gold fronted Lyons Corner House restaurant. It glowed with warm and friendly amber light, which blurred out into the chilly fog from the steamed-over windows. Bible J nodded to the boy. 'Here we go.' He pushed hard against the spring and opened the restaurant doors.

⇸ CHAPTER 20 ⇷

Inspector Lestrade of Scotland Yard changed out of his ridiculous costume, and refreshed himself. He had not enjoyed the Corporation Halloween party. He washed in his private washroom, and then shaved his cheeks, using a freshly stropped razor. He felt better now, cleaner. He studied his face in the glass over the sink, while the suds and water ran out. He was tired, and he looked it. It had been a long day. His office was calm and quiet now, which was just as he liked it, and it was late enough for him not to be bothered by anyone. A single foolscap-sized brown envelope lay on his desk. It was labelled as confidential and was fastened with a wax seal and a loop of string. He sat at the desk, broke the official seal, and unwound the string from the brass nub in the flap. Some file entries, two or three full-plate photographs, mostly of startled looking young adults and children with dirty faces, the usual thing – slates with numbers chalked on.

'Blessed are the poor,' he muttered. He looked through the file pictures with care, just as he looked through dozens of similar files almost every day. There was always a chance that he would see that unique and beautiful face. The lost girl, the one one he had seen only once or twice but had never forgotten. There was, however, nothing among the pictures to detain him. He replaced the file, relooped the string. There was a knock at the door.

'Come,' he said.

———◆———

DI Hudson, as a tough professional detective, had little use for the imagination and even less for the dream of the past. He was a company man to his fingertips, just as Sgt Catchpole was, but Hudson found Pastworld police work insanely inefficient, and maddening. It was hampered by what were to him artificial constraints. He looked out of the porthole and felt depressed at the sight of the city at night – the yellow lamplight and the fog. He never wanted to spend any time there, had never allowed himself to really understand its appeal or get the feel of it.

His colleague, Sgt Catchpole, on the other hand, felt a sense of rising excitement and a sort of secret home-coming relief every time they were flown across to the Pastworld side. He was a romantic. The sight of the lights blurred and softened by fog, even machined fog, struck him as beautiful in a way that Hudson would never under-stand. Sgt Catchpole welcomed the exhilarating feeling of being immersed in history. The sensation of actually stepping back in time. He felt changed by it, and he was changed a little more each time he went in.

When they crossed into Pastworld by airship, any information or files that they carried with them had to be meticulously authentic. Photographs were permitted, but only in a correct period format, there could be no emailing of images, no computers, no moving images at all, and no telephones. There was a form of telegraph, and occasional pockets of electricity in Pastworld, but most of it was hidden 'below stairs' with all the rest of the enabling technology. All of the police methods, once on the Pastworld side had to be authentic to the time and place as well. There was a network of security cameras, but they were very well hidden. The Buckland Corporation restricted such security matters and devices as much as they possibly could. Authenticity of experience was everything. A year or so ago Hudson had managed, through fierce lobbying, to introduce the tiny flying Espion transmitter security cameras. They were the size of a sewing needle, and in appearance much like the body of a dragonfly. They were more or less invisible in the London fogs. They could be remotely controlled from Buckland Security, and were triggered by 'exceptional activity'. They transmitted their images back direct to the Comms Centre but nothing at all to Scotland Yard itself. The images would be analysed, and acted on if serious enough.

Hudson and Catchpole cleared arrivals quickly and were soon climbing the stairs to the office. Hudson knocked on the door feeling self-conscious as usual in costume.

For Inspector Lestrade it was sometimes worth the strain, the frustration and the sheer oddness of living and working in Pastworld to see the discomfiture of his support staff and detective officers from the Outside, when they had to cross over to Pastworld side. The Inspector ushered Hudson and Catchpole in with an amused and surprised smile on his face. The fact that they were both here, so late and with no prior appointment or letter of arrangement gave the inspector a little shift inside, a lurch of excitement in the pit of his stomach. Why were they here – perhaps, perhaps . . . ?

'Well this is a surprise. Do sit down, gentlemen, make yourselves comfortable,' the Inspector said, maintaining the formal manners appropriate to the illusion that he lived in.

They took their seats. Hudson dropped a large brown paper envelope on to the desk.

'He's back,' Hudson said, reaching up and pulling at the collar at his throat.

Before he opened the envelope the Inspector said, 'You are sure?'

'Sure as we can be. There was the body found in Shoreditch. Severed limbs, missing heart, he left the head at the top of Tower 42,' Catchpole said. 'These are pictures from the Espion cameras in here. Looks like it's him, not a copycat.'

The Inspector opened the envelope and pulled out the first sheaf of pictures and flicked through the images of the tower, the masked figure, his sudden death-defying jump.

'So it would seem then,' the Inspector said, not looking up but laying the pictures out in sequence across his desk. He picked out a large reading glass from his desk drawer and looked closely, comparing. 'It looks like our gentleman all right,' he said.

'There's more,' said Catchpole, and he indicated the envelope where there were other photographs, the ones that showed the murder of the blind man and the abduction of Lucius Brown.

'The figure you see there in the dark frock coat, the one printed over with the skeleton pattern, has been positively identified.'

'I can see exactly who it is Sergeant, thank you,' the Inspector raised his free hand and continued to study the pictures. 'It is Lucius Brown, one of our first imagineers, a very senior and founding executive of the Buckland Corporation.'

'That's right,' said Hudson, surprised. 'The knife victim is so far unidentified. We think he may be an illicit, perhaps he was robbing them, and they fought back? The boy that you can see here, and here.' Hudson pointed his stubby fingers across the sheaf of pictures. 'We identified him as Caleb Brown, only son of same Lucius Brown. At present he has been listed by a local Pastworld station as the prime suspect.' He indicated the knife in the boy's hand, the dark stain on his fingers. 'You can see why.' There was no response from the Inspector.

'Well, sir?' Hudson asked, as ever frustrated by the

lack of urgency, the sense that there was another, slower time zone in operation, as indeed there was.

'Well,' said the Inspector, not wishing to show either the rising excitement or the sudden chill and dread in his heart, 'I think you are right in your assumption. You did the right thing in bringing me all of this and so promptly. This sighting changes everything. No doubt someone has already issued Wanted posters of the boy. If we manage to bring him in, it will be for his own protection. If the locals find him, we will get him out safely, obviously the boy is no killer. You can clearly see the scum around them are responsible. I intend to finish them for good at the earliest opportunity. I will need someone to work for me, someone I can trust absolutely on this case. I want them undercover right here in Pastworld from tonight. Things have just got serious. I need someone who can pass as authentic, who looks right in this place.' He smiled at Hudson. 'You'll be glad to hear that you will be spared this time, DI Hudson.' Hudson let out a quiet but relieved sigh. 'You will go back on the next available transport, if you hurry there shoud be one out of the port in about twenty minutes. You will liaise with Catchpole here by post and carry out any research as necessary.'

After Hudson had taken his leave the Inspector said, 'Right, Sergeant Catchpole, I cannot overemphasise how confidential this case has just become. I was here at the founding of this place, at its very inception you might say. Abel Buckland is a personal friend of mine, as was our poor missing victim Lucius Brown. Abel saw a way of saving the sharp and salty, the savoury life of old London.

And he succeeded, perhaps a little too well in founding this place. Just look around us. Millions live here, some rich, most poor. The past has become a sort of new frontier, a place which not only allows opportunies for a new class of entrepreneur but also for the return of bogey men like our friend the Fantom.'

Catchpole said, 'He seems almost supernatural.'

'Perhaps he is,' the Inspector said, with a smile, 'and in a very odd way, there is more to him than mere criminality. Since his first mysterious appearances and his daring crimes the Fantom has assumed a special place in the mythology of Pastworld. But he has an Achilles' heel. I know more about him than I can tell you here. He feels a strong attraction toward a young girl. He senses a close bond, sundered somewhere in the past. The Fantom seeks this girl above all things and will stop at nothing to find her. The history of the girl will be found in another dossier altogether. Her guardian, another important early employee of the Buckland Corporation, is this dead victim. His body will at present most likely be hidden somewhere on an illicit murder trail, as it was not left at the scene in Clapham. You must find it and confirm the identity. Since her disappearance, it has been the greatest and express wish of the Corporation at the highest level that she should be found and retrieved safely. We must get to her before the Fantom does. Now I must add Mr Lucius Brown and his young son, Caleb to that list; they are central to our case. Nothing must get in the way of our finding them. As far as I am concerned you must feel free to deal with the Fantom with extreme prejudice.

Lestrade went to the heavy compact iron safe that was bolted to the floor inside his coat cupboard. He dialled the combination, opened the thick door and pulled out a file and some envelopes. He tucked one of the envelopes into the back of the file, and took it to his desk.

'Read this dossier for a full background, strictly for your eyes only, digest, understand, read between the lines then go and find Lucius, and his son.' The Inspector reached out and shook Catchpole's hand. 'It is an important case, so don't fail me, Sergeant Catchpole.'

———•◆•———

After Catchpole had taken himself and the file off to his lodgings, the Inspector readied himself for another meeting, somewhere quite different, and with a far more difficult and demanding night-time audience.

⇥ CHAPTER 21 ⇤

The heavy stained-glass panels rattled as Bible J pushed against the doors of Lyons, and he and Caleb entered a world of warmth and food smells: fried bacon, sausages, potatoes and lamb chops, and beer and dark coffee, and damp woollen overcoats. There were noises too: the sound of sizzling fat, the clattering of plates, the calling out of orders, the hum of lively conversation and the raucous laughter of the Halloween partygoers, Gawkers and residents. Brisk waitresses in black with white aprons and caps dashed to and fro. Bible J and Caleb had walked in as far as a line of bentwood coat racks when a waitress barred their way.

'Not in here, you don't,' she said looking at them both up and down, but Bible J quickly said, 'It's all right I'm with this fine young gentleman here. I'm his guest, you can see he's a respectable Gawker all dressed up. Look at him, isn't that right?' The waitress looked at Bible J in his rough clothes, and then she looked at the pale and shocked boy, with his mass of dark hair and his bright aqua blue eyes, his smart coat and his good boots. She shook her head. Bible J held out some of the silver coins and she reluctantly stepped aside, but before they could take another step forward she said, 'Where are your manners young man, hats off indoors,' and she snatched the cap from Bible J's head and pushed it at him as if it were something diseased. Bible J smiled back at her good-naturedly. He carried his hat carefully in both hands over to a table by the window. He politely pulled out a chair for the pale boy, and nodded at the seat. 'Old cow,' he said under his breath, grinning.

Bible J stretched out his legs, and then reached somewhere inside his coat, and from the inside pocket, he pulled out the cigar he had bought. He lit it, and blew out a cloud of heavily perfumed cigar smoke, then he coughed and spluttered. He smiled across at the boy and winked. 'Not used to luxury,' he said.

The boy looked back at him. He had a regular face; it would be nondescript, if it were not for his eyes, bright and greeny blue. They reminded Bible J of someone. The main thing was that, sitting lost in the sudden warmth and confusion of the restaurant, he looked to Bible J like someone who needed help badly. He also looked like someone he would have wanted as a friend.

He would soon take him to meet Mr Leighton.

'I've been up and about on the dip, for my boss,' Bible J said, 'or trying to be, since first light,' he added, trying to blow out another proud stream of smoke. 'And I've eaten nothing much at all today and I doubt you have by the look of you either.' A young waitress came over to the table. She pulled a notepad from her apron pocket, and took a stub of pencil from behind her ear ready for their order. 'Now then, Miss,' Bible J said, affably, enjoying his moment and his cigar, 'I would like two Halloween specials, double meat platters, one of those big pork chops, some fried back rashers, a sausage, pumpkin and potato mash, nice big mushrooms, make that two rounds of fried potatoes, nice and salted, and proper platefuls please, I'm no Gawker, I'm a resident.' He smiled up at her and the girl wrote it all down carefully on her pad. She glanced across at the pale boy and smiled at him. 'Oh,' said Bible J, 'and a big tankard of porter beer, and bring one for him while you're at it.'

'Thank you,' she said and nodded to Caleb, who sat staring blankly after her as she walked away. Bible J said, 'Do you know something, a while ago I would have made a play for that nippy, not now though. I think she likes you. You could be in with a chance there, smudger.' He waited for a response from the boy – nothing.

Bible J took his cap off the back of the chair and sat idly spinning it on his finger. He finally managed to blow a wobbly ring of cigar smoke, which hovered in the air between them. Caleb watched the smoke as it grew gradually ragged at the edges until finally it faded out altogether. Bible J smiled and put the cap back on to the chair.

'Right,' he said, 'bull by the horns, first things first. Tell me your name at least, mate?'

'My name is Caleb, Caleb Brown.'

'I get the picture,' said Bible J. 'Post finance crash, parents scared shitless, back to the fundamentals, big religion, new puritans, see I know all about that on account of my own given name.'

Caleb nodded his head, not really paying much attention to what Bible J was saying. The waitress brought the two tankards of beer. Bible J pushed one of the foaming tankards across the white table cloth.

'Thirsty?' he said.

Caleb took the tankard with both hands. He felt a sudden sensation in his fingers, a prickling on his skin from the cold glass.

'Seeings as we're on names,' said Bible J. 'I'm called Bible J, also known as J the dip.' He put his tankard down and mimed taking something out of a pocket. He looked around for a moment as if half expecting someone to notice this mime. 'Yeah, Bible J, that's me and I'm the best at it,' he said quietly. 'I am quite well known. You've really lucked in asking me for help, and standing me a meat dinner too, mate. I am a "tea leaf" about town and at your service. I never forget a bloke that's done me a good turn,' and he smiled his very friendly smile and reached across the table to shake Caleb's hand. Caleb brought his own hand up and then nodded his head. Bible J nodded back at Caleb and they shook hands.

The waitress brought the food, and the table was soon full of plates. 'Tuck in. I hope you're hungry?' Bible J said. Caleb looked up and smiled nervously at Bible J for the first time.

Bible J looked round the busy restaurant, and under

the cover of all the noise he said very quietly. 'Something really bad has happened to you tonight then?'

Caleb said, 'Yes,' and nodded, and opened his mouth. Bible J watched a bobby walk in through the heavy door trailing in some wisps and tatters of fog. Bible J held his finger up against his lips. 'Ssh,' he said. 'I see trouble, heads down, eat up and you tell me in a minute.'

Bible J drank some more of his beer. Caleb looked over at the bobby in his blue uniform and his crested helmet. The bobby was mopping his red face with a hand-kerchief and chatting and smiling to one of the wait-resses.

'Here, have some of these.' Bible J passed a plate of the fried potatoes across the table, and added a generous dollop of brown sauce.

Caleb speared one with his fork and ate it automat-ically.

'That's better, that's the way,' Bible J said. 'I know you're on the run, so no need to say anything just nod. Do you need somewhere to go, a safe place?'

Caleb nodded.

'Good,' said Bible J quietly, 'then perhaps you would do me the honour of accompanying me to my own very special place of refuge.'

Caleb nodded and then suddenly stood up as if they were to go at once. He pushed his chair back which squealed loudly on the tiled floor like a fingernail on a blackboard. The restaurant went suddenly quiet. The bobby looked over at Caleb and frowned. After a moment someone laughed and the clattering and the conversations quickly resumed. Caleb sat down again.

Bible J beamed at Caleb across the table, 'I should leave the old bill out of it if I was you. Can't trust 'em. God you're that pale though, smudger. What's happened to you to make you into such a ghost? You'd better tell me now and be quick.' Caleb leaned forward on his elbows, shielding himself from the view of the bobby.

'Well first,' he said quickly. 'I saw a man killed, stabbed right in front of me in the street when we were robbed. They killed the blind man and then they blamed me, accused me, pointed me out to people in the street. They hit my father, they punched him and he fell, and I ran away,' he added, and then he slumped back in his seat and looked across the table at the greasy plates and the fresh, harsh hot tears burst from his face, and his nose ran with snot.

Bible J said, 'It's serious that, blaming you. Did anybody else hear them?'

'Everybody heard,' Caleb said. 'The whole street.'

Bible J let out a low whistle. 'That is serious. If they think you killed someone in here you know what can happen.' Bible J put his hands round his neck and mimed a hanging action.

'I know,' said Caleb quietly, 'I know.'

He turned to face the pretty waitress, who had come up to the table.

'Is he all right,' she said concerned, 'your friend?' and she put a piece of paper down on to the table.

'He's all right, miss. A bit too much to drink at the Halloween party tonight, that's his trouble see,' he said, nodding over at Caleb. 'Told him to line his stomach first, but he wouldn't listen to me, would he.'

'It's a shame,' the waitress said, 'tell him to come back sometime if he feels like it, when he's better.'

Caleb had put his head down on his arms.

The bobby finished his drink, called out a cheery, 'Good night all,' and left.

'Come on then,' Bible J said, 'time to go.' They stood up to go and Bible J paid the bill. It came to one shilling and sixpence, in old cash money, for the both of them. They pushed open the door and went out into the cold night.

The night streets were still busy with late Gawkers drifting back to their lodging houses and hotels. They were mostly drunk, with their Halloween masks slipped halfway down their faces, or dangling loose around their necks, their costumes all over the place.

Bible J knew, every twist and alley, every twitten. Caleb hardly noticed where he was going; he just allowed himself to be led. He walked with his head tucked down. The snow had almost melted, but the fog remained, and with it a heavy wetness in the air. Bible J sized up the stragglers pretty well. He tapped some of them for a few pennies, engaged their attention, diverted them, and then rifled their coat pockets with the skills of a conjuror. Caleb watched in a daze. Bits of jewellery, scarves, wallets, even a roll of expensive Pastworld authentic bank notes, were all extracted with a flick of the wrist and ended stuffed inside Bible J's or Caleb's coat pockets.

'My father told me to run,' Caleb suddenly said out loud to Bible J.

'What?' Bible J replied.

'I said my father told me to run.' Caleb stumbled forward, turned and then he suddenly broke away and ran off. Bible J called out after him to stop, but Caleb ran headlong straight into the fog and the darkness. Bible J hesitated. He should just let the boy run off, but he knew he couldn't and he set off after him.

He ran across the cobbles and down some steps. He could hear Caleb's boots clattering ahead of him. The steps followed the wall of a church and ran beside the churchyard. A string of wet paper lanterns in the shape of skulls hung from the railings, their candles extinguished. Bible J caught up with Caleb. He reached out, and grabbed Caleb's jacket so hard, that he slowed him down. Caleb twisted round suddenly and they almost fell together across the cobbles.

'Where are you going?' Bible J said, out of breath.

'My father said I should run and I ran. I left him lying in the dirt with his face punched in.'

'He told you to run because he didn't want you to get hurt. It's not your fault. If anyone believes that you killed the other bloke, then you are in real trouble like I said. It'll do you no good running off like this, you need protection. You won't get any help or justice from the police, so you'd best stick with me for now.'

'Where will we go?' Caleb asked.

'My guvn'ors gaff, like I said before. It's a walk from here so we'd best get a move on.'

They walked on through the still busy streets as the sky lightened just a little; a winter dawn was being faded up. There was the occasional street sweeper among the revellers.

Two men had their arms across each other's shoulders and were singing something raucous about 'ghosties'. Bible J lowered his head and slid between them as if to join in. He adjusted to their rolling drunken walk. He momentarily reached his hand into the nearest coat pocket and felt a cold leather wallet against his finger tips, but drunk number two noticed him and, in the way of drunks, lurched suddenly and grabbed tight hold of Bible J's collar. The Gawker shouted out, his speech slurred with too much cheap Pastworld gin.

'Officer hey, officers, wherever you are. Over here. I've got a thief, a bloody little thief!'

Bible J pulled hard and tugged himself free. He felt the collar of his coat split as he spun himself round. He called out to Caleb and they set off together fast, putting some distance between themselves and the drunken Gawkers. He heard them call out 'Stop' but no one made much of an effort. The straggling crowds dressed up in their fancy halloween costumes were all in too good a mood to stop any running boys. The street was soon full of shouting as one set of well-off drunks called out to another.

'Must be losing my touch,' Bible J called out as they ran.

They turned a corner down a walled alley near the Strand and the next thing they knew two red-faced bobbies were standing in front of them looming out of the mist, blocking their way.

The boys slid to a halt. 'Now, now, you two, stay right where you are.' One of the officers said. 'We have had a report of a series of robberies, dips off of Gawkers in fact, and there has been a killing, a murder. A boy of about your age has been reported as a suspect. We shall need to see your papers lads.' Caleb looked blankly back at the policemen. He shuffled himself back a little way and pressed against the alley wall. He reached out to it for support. He heard the distinct jingle and rattle from his coat pockets which had been filled with jewellery and other stuff by Bible J.

'You all right, son?' said the policeman.

Caleb looked distressed. The policeman unhooked his lamp and held it closer to Caleb's face.

'You've got your papers then?' the other policeman said.

'Of course we have,' Bible J said, brushing himself down. 'We're legitimate visitors, give us a chance; they're just here in my pocket.'

'With respect, all of you lot try that one. If you really are innocent Gawkers, then I need to see the proof.'

'I'm just trying to find the proof.'

'You don't look very like visitors, especially you. Gawker's are always clean, with respect,' the other constable said.

Caleb watched the exchange between them.

'Wait on,' said the nearest policeman, 'don't I know you?'and he shone his lantern directly at Bible J.

'How would you make that out?' Bible J said, drawing himself up straighter, as if that might confer a little more respectability. Then suddenly he kicked out straight at the nearest policeman and caught him hard in his plump stomach. The constable dropped his iron lamp and doubled over.

'Come on,' Bible J shouted and he ran straight out into the road, among all the early morning traffic and horses. Caleb froze. 'Run you idiot. They'll lock us up and throw away the key. Come on.'

'That was a serious assault,' the other policeman said unhooking his truncheon and aiming a swift blow at Caleb.

Caleb ran.

⇥ CHAPTER 22 ⇤

He followed Bible J and they ducked and dived through the clattering traffic. They ran on together, hidden by the bulk of a horse-drawn omnibus. They heard a police whistle, a piercing shriek. Bible J seemed to take that as his cue and he called out for Caleb to jump and they leaped for the platform by the outside staircase of the omnibus. They landed and clung on to the stair rail. Caleb balanced himself, breathing fast as the omnibus bumped over cobbles and potholes. The policeman blew his whistle over and over, as he pushed his way through the crowds of pedestrians looking for them.

The bus conductor made his way out to the platform. 'Hold on very tightly now please.' He noticed the two boys, and the pursuing policeman's whistle and said in a quieter, and much less friendly voice, 'You've got five minutes to work this lot, and then you're off. You can do the downstairs, then hop it, quick.'

The early morning passengers either stood, bumping against one another with the unsteady movement of the bus or sat on the slatted wooden seats. Bible J pushed between the standing passengers, a fixed, smiling expression on his face.

'Please, sir,' he said, to a red-faced man in a tweed cape, 'could you spare a poor lad a penny?'

One of the other passengers groaned. 'Oh no, not more of them,' but the red-faced man fished in his pocket and then held out a great meaty handful of coins. He spoke through his beaming smile in an American accent. Caleb looked back nervously through the window for signs of a police pursuit.

'Now, which of these things is a penny, my lad? I never can seem to get used to your money here,' he said and he laughed.

Bible J pulled a bright new penny out of the cluster of coins, and held it up for the man to see.

'Ok, so that's a penny. Help yourself kid. Maybe you can buy yourself a little soap.'

The woman sitting next to him muttered, 'He don't smell too good.'

'That's the idea,' said another passenger. 'It's authentic,' and they all laughed. The boys made their way further between the seats. Bible J collected coins from two more of the Gawkers. Caleb turned to go back to the platform when a hand grabbed at his wrist.

'Hey you,' said a man wearing a black suit and a high white shirt collar. Caleb tried to pull his hand away but the man gripped him harder.

Bible J recognised the plain clothes copper and stepped back and hid himself among the standing passengers. The man's great round moon face came close to Caleb's and he breathed sickly sweet minted breath at him as he spoke.

'I've seen you. I know all about you and your sort. Perhaps you might show me your accreditation?'

The omnibus slowed and stopped. 'Farringdon Road,' the conductor shouted and rang a bell. The man stood up abruptly and pulled Caleb after him towards the platform. One or two of the passengers applauded.

'I've done nothing,' Caleb called out as he was dragged past the conductor.

The conductor raised his hands and rang the bell. The man pulled Caleb with him down onto the pavement. Caleb turned his head and looked up at the windows of the departing omnibus. Bible J looked back at him through the window. Bible J held up his hand palm outwards and showed Caleb that he had hold of the watch, his father's watch. Bible J pointed at the face of the watch and nodded, and mouthed 'Wait' to Caleb as he was led off among the crowd.

Excerpt taken from the Little Planet Guide to Pastworld™ London

People visit Pastworld for a variety of reasons. For most it is a trip into the past to experience a way of life and an atmosphere of free and rumbustious living that had, until Pastworld's completion, all but vanished. The great city of London was chosen, after the apocalyptic financial meltdown at the start of the new century, to be 'reverted'. The city was retro-fitted and restored to the condition of its great Victorian heyday. The opening ceremony took place at the re-dedication of the once vandalised and destroyed Euston Arch, and an emotional day it was for those who cared for the architecture of the old city.

Travellers though should be aware of all the legal anomalies and pitfalls. The Buckland Corporation turned back the legal clock too. Old statutes were brushed off and brought back, forced through in a special Act of Parliament by a panicked government terrified of losing the huge financial patronage of the Buckland Corporation. A man, woman, boy or girl, can be hanged for certain crimes, and this brings a frisson of danger to daily life. It's irresistible to some visitors, risk takers, thrill-seekers or voyeurs.

There are those who would enjoy watching capital punishment carried out in front of them. There are those who would pay to watch the Ripper disembowel a victim or two, or who wish to witness any number of brutal and psychotic events. Look for instance at the popularity of the bootleg murder tours . . .

⇥ CHAPTER 23 ⇤

Sgt Catchpole's spirits lifted. He was back in Pastworld, and this time with a mystery to solve, a proper mission to complete. He left the office at police headquarters and made his way through the night streets to the lodging house he had used many times before. The landlady happily welcomed him back, despite the hour. She fussed over him, made him a nightcap cup of strong tea laced with a little whisky.

He settled himself down in a comfortable button-backed armchair in his rooms by his landlady's good coal fire, and began to read the dossier that the Inspector had given him. While he read, he was comforted by the thought that no telephone would ring, no text alert buzz him. There would be no emails to attend to, no screens to monitor, just the crackling of the fire and the rustle of real sheets of paper as he turned the pages and read the file.

The notes were written in longhand on neat lined pages.

FILE: The Fantom

Strictly Confidential

Subject: The Fantom. AKA The Gentleman.

Age: Indeterminate; early 20s at most.

Known Associates: An affiliation of beggars and petty thieves; a city-wide network colloquially called 'the ragged men'. Mostly ex-convicts or street children kept and nurtured by the Fantom over a number of years. Exact numbers unknown. On numerous occasions Inspector Lestrade has requested forces from the cadet corps to deal with the ragged men problem in a single 'surgical' strike. Permission and funding to this date have been denied by the Buckland Corporation

Biography: The Fantom at once terrifies and uplifts the spirits of the lower populace. The Gawkers see him as an adjunct to all the other entertainments on offer, just another elaborate recreation managed by the Buckland Corporation. Sadly in this they are much deceived. The Fantom is now as unofficial as it is possible to get. Suffice it to say that he must always be approached with the utmost caution. He is protected by his ragged men; these are the key to finding and destroying him. They are for the most part organised as a series of cells, a force to protect and supply the Fantom.

Once the Fantom was content to carry out violent and showy bank robberies. This enabled him to both comfortably control and hide his empire. His later public appearances – those open street battles with rival criminals, those jumps to certain doom from roofs and towers, those resurrections, and those redistributions of wealth – are but the tip of a very large iceberg. He deals with those who try to find, thwart, or betray him with a vicious and mechanical psychotic violence. It is never enough for him to kill an enemy or perceived enemy. He also mutilates in emulation and parody perhaps of the famous Ripper of the East London murders. It is as if he were handing The Corporation a series of historically styled murders to add to the authenticity of their dream city.

Sgt Catchpole looked up from the notes. He felt at the back of the folder and pulled out an envelope sealed with a wax seal and stamped in red officious letters, *Strictly Confidential.* He broke open the seal. Inside was a type-written fragment cut from a longer document.

SUBJECT: Dr Jack Mulhearn.

After initial Biology master's degree trained in the USA at MIT and came back to London just before the financial crash. Sought employment from the Buckland Corporation after his tenure at the Bio-Med research institute was cancelled. Assisted Lucius Brown on various classified projects for Buckland Corp., including the haunted house initiative, seance and ghost manifestations and finally the Prometheus project, which was terminated by the Corporation after an accidental fire destroyed the experimental site. Missing since the fire and officially recorded as dead. He is actually believed to be living somewhere quietly and well hidden in the Pastworld complex, sheltering Subject B. There have been no official sightings and in any case his appearance is likely to be much changed after fire injuries etc. He was marked with a small security biometric tattoo on his inner right wrist, a mark shared by few but carrying high corporate significance.

⇥ CHAPTER 24 ⇤

Inspector Lestrade arrived at the head offices of the Buckland Corporation. The building stood close to the restored fruit and vegetable market at Covent Garden and had once been a club for actors and lawyers. He was shown into a magnificent first floor room, with a desk at one end dominated by an antique globe of the world. The centre of the huge room was completely filled with an enormous scale model of Pastworld London. It was complete with toy airships on wires which hovered over the miniature buildings and streets. Mr Abel Buckland stood in an elaborate quilted dressing gown adjusting something on one of the model buildings. He looked up and smiled at the inspector.

'I have this whole model running on a very fine and elaborate system of steam and clockwork,' he said. 'It even has its own underground railway running beneath it. If you look in the cutaway section you can see it all. The most perfect miniature clockwork imaginable. I want to put a big skydome over the model eventually, just like the real thing, right up to the ceiling in here. I'll run it both night and day and show all the constellations seasonally just as they would appear.'

Lestrade cleared his throat. 'This is not a social visit, Abel. A severed head was retrieved from a girder on top of Tower 42, and Lucius Brown has been abducted. He was violently lifted in the street on his way to the Corporation Halloween Party. I need your permission to strike at the ragged men now.'

Abel Buckland set a little airship moving on its wire across the city. 'Your proposal for solving all of this is to kill all the ragged men?'

The Inspector watched the little machine whirr for a moment, and then he said, 'I have some photographs I think you should see.' He walked over and tipped the photographs out among the bric-a-brac and toys on the desk.

Buckland came and sat in his chair. He put on a pair of glasses and peered down at the pictures. He picked one up. 'I suppose this is from one of those wretched little spy cameras,' he said. 'You'll be asking me to approve a whole slew more of them in a moment if I know you.'

'No, I won't,' said the Inspector. 'Just look very carefully.'

Buckland flicked through the pictures. He paused, studied one picture in particular, and then another.

'So,' Buckland said eventually, 'it was not just Lucius then, but Jack as well.'

'Oh yes, him as well, and they killed him, straight away.'

'He was blinded then by the fire, or nearly by the look of it. Why didn't he just come in, come back to us?'

'He was protecting her.'

'Our clever friend the Gentleman seems to have arranged it all somehow?'

'It certainly looks that way.'

'What are you doing about it?' Buckland looked up, pale in the lamplight. He let the photograph fall to the desk.

'I have two prongs. First I sent in a good man. He will be on the trail and will report to me on whatever he finds. He is looking for Lucius and the boy, Lucius Brown's son. My other prong is the cadet corps, a crack team. Give me the word and we can sweep away the ragged men in an hour.'

'And this man you have sent, he is reliable?' Abel said, ignoring the Inspector's request.

'Perfectly reliable. Sergeant Catchpole is a romantic like you, and perhaps like I once was. He is someone very much in tune with the dream of this place, I assure you.'

'Good, good. We must keep this dream alive at all costs. The dream is all.' Buckland stared wistfully across the room at the huge whirring model, at its twinkling lights. 'Find him, find the Gentleman. It's been too long. I would save him if I could. And of course you must find her too, the girl. That goes without saying, it was never more important,' he said. 'The big demolition is planned as a real spectacular. The last of the wretched old modern buildings is scheduled to come down in a beautiful and contolled explosion. I want it all solved by then. That will be a good moment for your "solution" to the ragged men problem. Use your cadets by all means, but leave the Fantom, he is mine.'

The Inspector said, 'Well it was all our fault in the first place. If we had listened to . . .'

Buckland interrupted him.'What we did was in the interests of science and pure research, and that is that. We have nothing to reproach ourselves for. I feel no guilt, rather pride. Yes, Lestrade, pride.'

The Inspector went to pick up the photographs, but Buckland stayed his hand. 'No, leave them with me,' he said. 'Do you know that visitor and resident applications numbers are predicted to double in five years? We will have to open new induction centres, and commission a new fleet of airships. The past, with all its rough and ready crudity, its dirt and its rock solid certainties, is going to mean so much to so many people in the future. He gestured at the huge twinkling model with wide open arms. 'Find them please, Lestrade. You and I are the only ones left who know the truth about them. Find them, and try your best to save them both.'

⇥ CHAPTER 25 ⇤

Catchpole hovered among the crowd near the rendezvous point for the bootleg murder tour at Spitalfields market. It was conveniently placed for the mortuary. Here there was a properly festive atmosphere. One of Pastworld's regular Dickensian Christmas days, Catchpole thought. A group of early carol singers were gathered below the great porch of Christchurch, and Catchpole listened to them as the snow fell gently on the crowds. It was a pretty picture if you didn't know any better.

Catchpole observed that a line had formed behind a shifty-looking plump man dressed as a policeman. He was holding his truncheon up in the air. The policeman blew lightly on his whistle and started to talk to the group around him in a low insistent voice, a voice imparting confidential information, dark secrets. Catchpole was too far away to hear, but he knew the excited Gawkers were here to see all the gruesome evidence at a terrible murder scene.

Catchpole strolled over, one hand behind his back, his face fixed and serious. The fake policeman watched him suspiciously as he approached. Catchpole quickly pulled a five-pound note out from his coat pocket, much more than the normal fee for an illicit murder tour. He slipped it to the constable, who tipped his helmet, as Catchpole joined the group.

'Glad to have you with us, sir,' the guide said quietly. Then to the line of excited Gawkers: 'We can't stand here all day chit-chatting, there's murder afoot. This way now.'

The group moved off in an orderly crocodile, the guide at the front, Catchpole a few paces behind him. The guide stopped near the pub on the corner and raised his truncheon again.

'In a moment we shall all go through this public bar and out into the backyard. A man was found dead this morning. I am told that he had been beaten, he was also mutilated, cut open and the internal organs disturbed. It may well be the work of a madman, but if this is anything like some similar cases that have occurred over the years then he is a madman of some medical skill. No doubt you have all read about these cases and the criminal known as the Fantom. You will have seen the engravings in the newspapers, and on the Wanted posters, and perhaps even the pictures of the victims of his crimes? Of course that will be nothing like the sight that will greet us today. Be prepared to be shocked and disgusted. You must not touch anything nor disturb the site in any way.' They were led into the noisy public bar.

The pub had a low ceiling and the interior was stuffy

and dark. The people crowded in the bar were for the most part men, dressed in dirty work clothes. One or two women sat on the benches around the walls, holding flagons of beer, and laughing with the groups of the men. One of them called out 'Happy Christmas' to the Gawkers as they walked nervously through the bar.

They all went out into a dingy little yard, where the festive snowfall had hardly penetrated. The light was squeezed between the back of the pub and the nearby spire of the great church, and although the little patch of sky that could be seen was a bright picture-book blue, by the time the light reached the yard it had somehow clocked in as grey and dismal.

The group of Gawkers were formed up by the fake constable in a line against the far wall of the yard. Even on a cold frosted morning the bricks smelled of stale urine.

Something was bunched up under a blanket against the outside wall of the yard. Catchpole, having paid the most, was at the front with the guide near the blanket. The other Gawkers settled into an expectant silence. This is what they had paid their money for, the real gruesome authentic thing.

'This body, this poor individual,' said the guide, 'is more than likely another victim of the famous criminal known popularly as the Fantom.'

With a flourish the constable pulled back the blanket.

There was a sudden gasp from the Gawkers. Someone put their hand up to their mouth and stifled a scream, another turned away to face the back wall. The guide knelt down and tugged at the lifeless head which was twisted away towards the bricks. He pulled it up by the hair.

'See here,' he said, 'you will notice that the throat is cut through so deeply as to almost sever the head from the body.'

Catchpole watched the faces of the Gawkers as they craned forward for a better look. Although they seemed genuinely horrified, they kept looking. He turned his attention back to the guide. He was holding the head up, his gloved finger pointing at the gaping wound in the throat which flapped open like a second mouth, edged with dried blood. The victim on such a tour was usually some poor, worthless illicit, who somehow was supposed to deserve all he or she had got, or if the victim was female, a so-called common prostitute. The guide looked round the dismal yard, into the furthest corners where one or two of the more squeamish Gawkers had taken themselves. They stood staring, shocked and fearful, looking like trapped animals. The guide then laid the murder victim's head down with some gentleness on to the cobbles. With another flourish he pulled the blanket down to reveal the hastily stitched up abdomen. Other Gawkers looked more alarmed now. One of them suddenly let out a piercing scream. At the same time there was a burst of laughter from inside the pub.

Catchpole crouched down beside the body. He noticed the sticky trail of thick brownish red fluid which had seeped from under the blanket. It was dark and oily-looking and he could smell the telltale tang of iron, the iron of pooled blood, the iron in the soul. The body had been simply dumped on a murder tour site, an act of provocation that looked like nothing more than an advertisement for what the Fantom could do and get away with if he wished. Gawkers pressed against Catchpole and the guide, trying to get close. The guide held out his hand in a stop gesture, and motioned the group back again to the far wall.

'Please, ladies and gentlemen,' the guide said, 'you are damaging the integrity of a crime scene, the clues are being trampled, and may be lost. Please stay well back.'

'How come he's allowed close?' one Gawker called out pointing at Catchpole.

'He paid more,' said the guide matter of factly.

Catchpole looked down at the neat gash in the blind man's throat. He felt suddenly nauseous and very hot despite the snowfall. It was rare now for anyone from the Outside to see the result of savage violence of this sort. This was a very dead, very sad person, as real and as dead as that head left on the ruins of Tower 42. Catchpole's whole bearing changed, now he was a modern professional police detective. He elbowed the guide aside and produced his warrant card and held it close to the guide's face.

'Get them out,' Catchpole said under his breath. 'I'm sealing this crime scene now, take them somewhere else, go on quickly.' The guide whispered, 'Bastard copper,' and then said loudly, 'Ladies and gentlemen, this visit will have to be cancelled at once I'm afraid.'

The guide ushered the complaining Gawkers back through the dark and noisy pub. They were confused.

Some offered to pay more or started to demand a turn to look at the body. The guide silenced them and at the mention of 'an unfortunate official police interest' the Gawkers dispersed, grumbling, into the surrounding crowd.

Catchpole replaced the blanket and walked back through the dismal pub. He found a bobby on routine patrol outside. He showed his warrant card, and the bobby saluted him.

'Go for an ambulance,' Catchpole said, 'at once please.' The constable set off.

Catchpole did not have to wait long. A horse ambulance arrived in minutes. Two uniformed men climbed out of the back, they carried a stretcher with them as they crossed over to the pub. A crowd soon gathered outside the pub in Commercial Street. More police arrived to empty the pub and form a line barring entry. A muffin man walked straight through the line of policemen, as if they weren't even there.

Catchpole turned his back on the Gawkers. What he had seen had indeed been horrible; he wouldn't wish it on anyone. The thought that this was one of the reasons that some Gawkers visited Pastworld in the first place made him feel disgusted. He tried not to think of his churning stomach. The police emerged from the pub along with a stretcher with the covered body on it. A path was cleared through the groups of Gawkers. For a moment he looked at the empty place where some children had been playing snowballs. They were all busy now watching the ambulance as it crossed the piazza in a flurry of snow.

Catchpole looked around at the crowd. The ghoulish Gawkers had all but melted away. The rest of the street was on the move, bustling and busy, hurrying about their business. All except one, a lone woman stood motionless on the busy pavement. Everything and everyone flowed past her but she stayed still like a statue. She seemed to be scanning the street. It looked as if she were waiting for someone. Catchpole, curious, walked over to her.

'Takes me back to my own childhood,' he said, indicating the boys back at their snowball fight, and speaking in what he hoped was a friendly voice, 'except that there never was this much snow and it was never so clean.'

The woman turned to him with a distracted face. She wore a wide battered hat in black felt, and had a spotted fur tippet tucked round her throat. The fur around her neck suddenly moved, a spotted leg stretched out and the head of a cat emerged and looked at him.

'Down then, Kitty,' said the woman. The cat jumped down on the end of a black leash and rubbed itself against her legs.

'A very tame animal,' Catchpole said.

'What happened in there?' she asked. 'Did they find someone? Was it a man or a woman?' She gestured at the pub with her gloved hand.

'As a matter of fact it was a man,' said Catchpole.

'Can you describe him for me?' she asked. 'Only it's really very urgent, you see?'

Catchpole spoke quietly. 'He was a shabby man, seemed to have almost no teeth, and very pale eyes, most likely blind.'

The woman looked down at her spotted cat. 'Oh no,' she said. 'I fear I might know who it is. I have been looking out for him for a few days now.'

She bent down and scooped up her little spotted cat in her arms. She buried her face in its fur for an instant, and then she raised herself to her full height. She spoke to the cat. 'I fear it's Jack, Kitty, isn't it? Poor old Jack.'

'You knew him well then,' said Catchpole. 'You could identify him perhaps?'

'Oh yes, we knew him, not well, but we knew him, didn't we, Kitty? We called him blind Jack, not quite true because he could see, just not well.'

'The body will be taken to the morgue. I wonder if we might walk there and I could ask you to make a formal identification?'

'I don't really fancy it much, but if I can be of help then, I will do what I can. Poor old Jack . . .'

'If it is him,' Catchpole said.

They walked off together through the busy, jovial winter streets.

⇥ CHAPTER 26 ⇤

Caleb was prodded up the steps of a large red-brick building and through an arched doorway. A policeman and a cadet in a red uniform stood together inside the entrance. They both saluted, while the cadet held the door open.

The large entrance had a tiled floor all scattered with sawdust, as if it were a butcher's shop. A gasolier hung over a tall sloping reception desk. From somewhere deep in the building, a drunk was singing. His ragged voice rising and falling along with all sorts of other shouts and screams. A simple wooden bench ran the length of the tiled wall, and one or two people sat slumped on it, waiting. A group of Gawkers sat on along the opposite wall behind a red rope looped on brass supports; they were watching everything.

The pale man pulled Caleb up to the high reception desk. The police clerk behind the desk sat up straighter, tugged at his uniform jacket, adjusted himself. 'Morning, Inspector Prinsep,' he said. He held a pen ready in his hand, as if he had been waiting for just this moment. He inclined his head slightly and put the pen to the ledger.

Caleb stared at him.

'First we need to record your name, as you have no papers of identification,' said the pale-faced man. 'Just tell him the name you go by.'

'My name is Caleb.'

'Aha, Puritan name,' said the police clerk, 'and have you a surname to go with it?' he added pompously but with a friendly smile.

Caleb looked back at him blankly, narrowing his weary eyes. 'Brown,' Caleb replied.

The police clerk scratched the pen across the ledger.

'Poetry and prose in the one name, age,' he said. 'How old are you?'

'Seventeen,' Caleb said.

'Record between fourteen to seventeen years approximately,' said Inspector Prinsep impatiently.

'I know exactly how old I am,' Caleb said.

The clerk scratched the pen across the paper.

'Have you ever attended a place of learning? Do you go, or have you ever gone to a school or similar institution?' Prinsep asked.

'Of course,' Caleb said.

'Can you read?'

The police clerk looked at Caleb with the pen poised.

'Yes,' Caleb said, almost spitting out the reply.

'Are you Corporation accredited and official?' the

clerk asked.

Before Caleb could answer, Prinsep said, 'I think not'. 'He claims he is a visitor, a Gawker, and that he has tickets, permissions, and accreditation. But look at this.' The man plunged his hand into Caleb's coat pocket and pulled out a whole string of pearls and coins and jewellery. He flung them all down in a jingling heap on the open ledger.

The clerk let out a low whistle. Then he wrote something else into the ledger and as he wrote he said, 'There's been a report in already this morning, Inspector, a serious assault, a murder last night.' The clerk blotted the paper with a rocking blotter. Caleb looked up, and over at the opposite wall. A set of wanted posters hung in long glass-fronted frames. A cadet was adding a new one to the end of the line.

An engraved image of an all-purpose young man's face was centred below the word 'Murder'. It was not a good enough attempt at a likeness to identify Caleb positively, but it gave him enough of a scare to realise that he was definitley being hunted. Now there was no question of any attempt to give himself up, to seek official protection.

The clerk looked up and announced briskly, 'Description, height?' Prinsep pulled Caleb roughly over to the back wall, and stood him where a height chart was painted, the feet and inches marked off in dark green.

'Five feet ten inches,' Prinsep read off. The clerk wrote; the nib scratched.

'Hair colour?' Prinsep looked at Caleb with contempt.

WANTED

FOR

MURDER

A
YOUTH
ANSWERING
TO THE
FOLLOWING
DESCRIPTION:

AGED
BETWEEN 16
& 19 YEARS
HAIR *DARK*,
COMPLEXION
LIGHT

**POSSIBLY ARMED
AND DANGEROUS**

'Dark,' he called out.

'Eye colour?'

'Blue,' he said, and the clerk wrote again.

'Complexion?'

'Light,' he called out.

'Place of birth?' the clerk asked.

Caleb looked at the floor.

'Put unknown, London district,' Prinsep said.

'Trade or occupation?'

Prinsep answered again. 'Unlicensed or illicit beggar, certainly a thief.'

'I'm not,' Caleb said intently, quietly.

'I saw you. You were clearly working in tandem with another felon. Wear those pearls often, do you?'

'Poor boy, beggar boy, thief,' said the police clerk, peering over his glasses at him. 'Distinguishing marks?'

'None visible.' The man looked Caleb up and down.

'Address at time of apprehension?'

'Safest to put no fixed abode,' said Prinsep.

Caleb let this go. At first he thought he should have mentioned the lodgings in Islington but something stopped him – some new fear even of the connection with his own father, with that reported killing. *It might be better*, he thought, *to confess robbery*.

'Offence for which apprehended,' said the clerk.

'Pickpocketing with another,' Caleb said.

'Ah, a confession suddenly,' said Prinsep. 'Add in unlicensed begging, as well as thieving, and illicit entry.'

The clerk looked over at Prinsep. He rested his pen on the desk and then wiped at the nib carefully with a piece of cloth. 'I can only put the one official charge, sir,' he said quietly. 'Being an illicit here is unfortunate, but not actually criminal, yet.' There was a pause; Caleb looked from one to the other. He heard the singing start up again, from the cells. Some of the watching Gawkers laughed. Caleb thought of dark brick cells full of rats somewhere below, deep in the building.

'Well, sir?' said the clerk

'Put down pickpocket for now. Empty your coat

pockets fully, young man.'

Caleb pulled everything he could find from his deep jacket pockets and scattered them on the desk.

'Bag and log that lot,' Prinsep said to the desk clerk.

The clerk sighed and dipped his pen back into the brass inkwell at the top of his desk, and wrote slowly across the paper.

'Place and time of apprehension?'

'Farringdon Road, London, Pastworld City, district one, eight forty-five a.m. on November 1st the year of our lord etc.' said the man.

The clerk pushed the ledger across to Prinsep who took the pen and wrote something across the page. The clerk said, 'signed and witnessed by arresting officer in the presence of, etc.' He blotted the signature.

'Come with me.' Prinsep called over a uniformed cadet and together they led Caleb through a door behind the reception area. They walked along a dark corridor lined with doors. The drunken singing was louder now, the gaslights were turned lower. There were worrying noises, apart from the wild singing. There were unexplained scuffles and thumps. The cadet knocked on a door at the end of the corridor. A woman in a starched apron and white cap opened the door.

'Take him, and get him photographed,' Prinsep said.

'Yes, Inspector,' the woman replied.

⇥ CHAPTER 27 ⇤

Catchpole and the lady with the cat walked eastwards through the city making their way towards the big hospital near Aldersgate, and the morgue. Figures were being taken out on stretchers from ambulances drawn up in lines. Sgt Catchpole approached a porter, who stood at the rear entrance wiping his bloodied hands on a leather apron. The woman with the cat turned away to face the busy road.

'Bit of a ruck this morning,' the porter said. 'Railway accident in a tunnel.' The porter showed his brown teeth in a grin. 'Four dead, others with limbs gone or going, and some say it was all started deliberate like. A cowardly act of terror, they said. They're trying to blame the Fantom. Just a story, I expect, told to excite *them*,' and he nodded across at a line of waiting Gawkers. 'Still it's what they pay for after all and if they're lucky, they might even see an amputation or two.'

Catchpole produced a white five-pound note from his waistcoat pocket. 'I'm interested in another kind of victim altogether,' he said. 'I'm talking about a murder victim, a man brought in here beaten, dead, and cut open, a *real* victim of the Fantom. Would have been brought in an hour ago.'

'Oh yes,' said the Porter his eyes firmly on the note. 'They brought him in all right, proper Fantom victim.'

'That'll be the one.'

'Would you be wishing to see the deceased?' the Porter added in a slight mockery of an undertaker's solemn tone and voice. 'The lady friend want a personal little peep, does she?'

'Something like that,' Catchpole said. He flicked out the note with a practised snap.

The porter reached out with two bloodied fingers and slipped it straight under his apron.

'In that case, you'd better come with me,' he said and led the way into the hospital.

Once inside they made their way down a dim corridor with a shiny marble floor, which was already streaked with blood. They crossed the entrance lobby where the victims of the railway accident were laid out on stretchers. At the foot of the stairs they passed a line of Gawkers waiting to be let into the surgery wards to watch the operations. The Gawkers were being held back by a line of uniformed policemen. A doctor in a white coat pushed between them. He called out to the porter, 'Follow me at once.'

'I have to go,' said the porter. 'Basement corridor's what you want, the end room, just follow your nose.'

They followed the low lights along the basement corridor. There were tall double doors at the end, each door bearing a porcelain plaque with the word *MORGUE* impressed upon it in heavy black lettering. Catchpole turned to the woman with the cat. 'Will you be all right? This will not be a nice experience.'

'We'll manage, won't we, Kitty.'

Catchpole pushed the doors open. Once inside it took their eyes a moment to adjust to the raised brightness of the gaslit white-tiled interior after the flickering, dim amber lights of the corridor. There was a series of white enamel tables draped with sheets, and a line of enamel buckets and a weighing scale. He saw clearly the shapes of bodies shadowed under the sheets.

Another porter in a dirty leather apron sat slumped in a chair near one of the draped tables. He was reading a newspaper and turned as they came in. He stumbled to his feet, brushing his hands down the floor-length apron.

'Secure area,' he said.

'Really,' said Catchpole. He sauntered over to the nearest table.

'You'd better leave,' said the porter nodding his head towards the cat lady. 'Both of you. No animals allowed.'

'Nice clean room,' Catchpole, running his finger along the crisp edge of the sheeted table, ruffling the crisp sheet, and pulling at it. 'I have a problem to solve you see,' said Catchpole, lifting the sheet and peering underneath and then quickly holding out his warrant card. 'We are looking for someone, a missing person.'

'Well I doubt they're under there. They're coming for this one later. I'd make yourself scarce,' said the porter.

'They?' said Catchpole.

'The Corporation, high-ups,' said the porter. 'All sorts of alarm bells set off.'

'Really,' said Catchpole.

'Can't say why,' said the porter. 'Lips sealed. Nothing I know anything about. Only it was when we took his clothes off and we found . . .'

'Found,' said Catchpole, looking up from the table. 'Found what?'

'I've said too much,' said the porter.

'Look,' said Catchpole, 'I'll make this very simple. You read your paper, let me just show this lady here. She needs to make an identification. And then we'll be out of your hair.' He waved the warrant again and then tucked it back into his waistcoat pocket.

'Just a minute then, and that's it.'

Catchpole pulled the sheet fully away from the man's upper body, bunching it at his waist. The blind man lay there as pale as a merman. He would almost have looked asleep were it not for the deep wounds spreading down from his shoulders, the neat entry cut over his heart, the slashed throat and his crudely stitched abdomen.

'Very nasty,' he said, and he tucked the cloth back up above the gaping throat. 'Please look now,' he said quietly to the lady. She approached the enamel table. She hesitated with her eyes closed, stroking the head of her spotted cat. Then she opened her eyes and looked down at the peaceful head.

'That's Jack, isn't it, Kitty?' she said. 'That's poor blind Jack. He was a clever man you know and he was kind and he was harmless. He was always out with his daughter for walks. He'd been in this place,' she looked at the bright white windowless room, 'not *here* of course, you know what I mean, Pastworld, as long as I have, ever since it opened.'

Catchpole covered the face once more.

'There's more,' said the porter. 'When they cut him open in here, what do you think?'

'Let me guess,' said Catchpole. 'No heart.'

'Got it in one, and you know what that means?'

The woman with the cat crossed herself. Her cat jumped down and mewed at the bloodied enamel bucket of waste under the table. She pulled the lead tight, tugged the cat nearer to her button boots and moved away from the table again.

Catchpole lifted the sheet and looked at the corpse a last time. The blind man's arms were tight by his side, his hands resting palm up to either side of his waist. Catchpole lifted one of the hands. It was heavy and ice-cold to the touch. He noticed, there on the inner skin of the forearm, the tattoo. It was a series of numbers and blue black vertical lines; an old-fashioned bar code.

'Oh, I see you've spotted it,' said the porter with impatience rising in his voice. He glanced at the double doors. 'Well, I didn't tell you. They can't blame me. You'd think he was just a pathetic old wino, wouldn't you, by the look

of him? But no, very few were ever allowed that mark. Security clearance see, for the real secret high-ups from a few years back. Wouldn't need it now. Someone from Buckland head office is due here any minute to look for himself. I think you'd better clear off now.' He pulled the rest of the coarse sheet over the blind man's head, smoothing it at the sides. 'I'll be for the high jump if they catch you in here with her, snooping around.'

Catchpole took the cat lady's arm and together they slipped quietly back into the gloomy corridor.

When they reached the bottom of the staircase, there were voices from the corridor above. Catchpole kept his head down. As they climbed up the stairs a small delegation came down them. It consisted of two junior cadets flanking a black-suited Buckland Corp. officer.

Catchpole took his companion into a busy public bar.

'I should think you might need a stiff drink after that?'

'A brandy and water, dear, if I could.'

They sat together, tucked in a corner. The cat was motionless on her lap.

'So you are a resident yourself then, not a Gawker?'

'Yes, I came in on the single mother work scheme, but that was no good in the end. I lost my poor baby, to diphtheria. I went unofficial after that, worked with street entertainers. You from the outside then? What's it like back there now? It's been so long, hasn't it, Kitty?'

'Well you know the Outside is the Outside. I doubt it's

{ 187 }

changed much since you were there to be honest. Except perhaps there are even more regulations now. More control, more interference. More of that sense of 'sameness'. The feeling of everyone doing the right thing at the right time. Of doing the same thing at the same time. Liberal enough, but a stifling, narrow conformity. Life without any risks at all. Colourless if you understand what I mean. No wonder this place is so popular.'

She looked round the crowded noisy bar and nodded. 'It's poor Eve I feel sorry for now.'

'Eve?'

'Jack's daughter, Eve. She ran off one morning just like that,' she snapped her gloved fingers, 'and never came back. Cruel that was and she seemed such a nice girl too. Jack was finished by it. I don't think the girl realised quite how he took her running off like that. He was desperate to find that silly girl. I thought that I spotted her once, but she denied it was her. Then I saw her again, a bit later, dancing up on the high rope, and very good she was too. That time I just knew it was her. I had a nice little talk to her and she wrote a note for me to give to Jack, to reassure him. I couldn't simply pop the note through his door, I wanted to give it to him personal instead. I thought I could reassure him better in person, say that I had actually seen her, spoken to her. He was in that much of a state. I left a message in the shop below his flat, gave him a time and place to meet me. He'll never get her note now, poor Jack.'

'Was there any connection between him and the Fantom that you know of?'

She shook her head. 'He did say to me once that someone was out to get him, finish him and that if he ever disappeared I was to check those awful murder tours. He said that's where they'd dump his body. Looks like he was right. Don't know anything about the Fantom and Jack though. I always thought the Fantom was a bogey man just put there to scare us, and keep us in our place. Can't imagine poor old Jack having anything to do with something like the Fantom.' She fumbled in her bag and pulled out an envelope. 'When he didn't return home, I remembered what he said. "They'll hide my body on a murder tour." There I've said enough now. Your best bet is to find Eve and talk to her yourself.'

'Could I see the note?'

She hesitated and looked down at the folded envelope in her gloved hand.

'I suppose it can do no harm now that poor Jack's dead.' She shook her head. She handed Catchpole the envelope, and as he went to take it from her he felt her resistance to let it go.

'You can trust me,' he said kindly, and she released the letter.

'Where can I find you if I need to again?' Catchpole asked. 'It's important that I find this girl, this Eve. I think she is in danger too after what's happened.'

She didn't answer, she just stared up at him with her dark eyes. Catchpole took one of his official visitor's cards with his lodging address details and pressed it on her.

'If you see her, ask her to find me here, and if you

need to speak to me or to contact me in any way then this is where you will find me.'

'All right,' she said in a distracted voice. She took the card, finished her brandy and water, and stood up. 'I'll be off home now. I can't say its been a pleasure, but at least I know what's happened to him now.'

Her coat made a sharp black shape against the snow, and the tail of her spotted cat swished as she walked away. Catchpole walked back to his lodgings, head down, staring at the once pure snow, which was now all scuffed over with boot and shoe tracks.

———◆◆———

Later Catchpole sat in a pool of soft light in the sitting room of his lodgings. He opened the envelope. It was brief and touchingly naive; the letters were large and perfectly formed on the page. He supposed it was to make them easier to read for someone with very little sight.

Dearest Jack,

Don't worry about me. I am safe. I have found lodgings, and am embarked on a new life. Please don't look for me. Stay safe too, as I promise I shall.

Your loving Eve

The official Buckland Corporation file on Lucius Brown had been sent across by Hudson. He turned to it. The file was marked:

Two documents were of particular interest to him. The
first was a paper on the Prometheus Project. He started
to read.

ATTACHED REPORT 1.

Prometheus Project

Dr Brown has requested an increase in
funding for the above named project for
another two-year period. The recent
results of his and Dr Mulhearn's work
were demonstrated recently in the private
facility to both Mr Buckland and myself,
and it was an extraordinary experience.
My personal view is that the funding
should certainly be continued at the
level requested by Brown and Mulhearn but
on the proviso that personal secrecy
clauses are added to the contracts. There
is a definite need for a renewed exclu-
sivity contract to cover the outcome of
all the results of this line of research.

APPROVED

He turned to the second document that had caught his attention.

Profile

Dr Lucius Brown studied Biological and Physical sciences at university, where he also received a Master's degree in Architectural History. It was here that he met and studied alongside Mr Abel Buckland. Dr Brown's particular brilliance can be seen in various places throughout the Pastworld complex. It was his genius that came up with the scheme to make the ghosts and apparitions for the haunted spaces of the city which caused such a sensation during the opening night celebrations. This success gave Brown founder status within the Corporation.

Dr Brown and Dr Jack Mulhearn continued their collaboration on another special project which had absorbed an enormous amount of funding. The interim results were spectacular and very well received and a second and larger funding round was approved.

However, both Mr Brown and Dr Mulhearn reversed their opinion on the merits of the project, and near the end of the

second phase lobbied to have the
experiment closed down. The request was
denied at the highest level. Shortly
after there was an apparently accidental
fire which destroyed the entire labora-
tory area and facility. Dr Mulhearn was
officially listed as dead in the fire,
along with all final experimental
results. Now he is believed to have fled
and is in hiding. Dr Lucius Brown
retired shortly after these sad losses.

See Confidential Appendix A.

Appendix A was missing from the file. Catchpole looked
up. There was a strange story unfolding, odd connections,
secret experiments, experiments with what though? He
made a note to ask Hudson to send over anything more
to do with Dr Mulhearn and if possible a copy of
Appendix A.

⇴ CHAPTER 28 ⇴

FROM EVE'S JOURNAL

'The last place these people who are looking for you will expect you to be is walking and dancing on a rope in full view high above the heads of a crowd. We shall hide you in plain sight like a leaf on a tree. It's an old trick. We'll say you're from Russia.'

I didn't mind being 'from Russia' and so Jago began to introduce me after his trumpet tune as, 'All the way from Russia, the dazzling Eve.'

Jago spent one afternoon working inside the wagon, sawing and hammering. He showed me later what he had done.

'It's an escape trap, a false floor, like the ones we use in conjuring,' he said. 'You can roll out of the wagon from here, and escape if you have to. You never know when this might be useful to you or perhaps to any of us. With the ragged men after you, we can't be too careful.'

Every time I performed, every time I danced and spun

on the rope in my white muslin dress, I noticed that the boy was there. He seemed to position himself at the front of the crowd every time. I would look for him and I could spot him easily enough. I always knew it was him and where he was in the crowd. I could sense his eyes following me across the rope. For some reason it was always his eyes out of all of the crowd that seemed to bore into me.

Jago said, 'I think you are developing a following, Eve. There's a young man who comes to see you again and again and I'm not sure that I would trust him.'

Out of all the people who came to watch me dance the high rope, he was the only one that I really noticed, the friendly looking boy, with the wide smile and the dark eyes.

Finally one afternoon the boy came round after the show. He was hanging around near the horse, Pelaw, stroking her ears. He was trying to appear indifferent. He avoided looking at me when I went up the steps of the caravan. He didn't try to speak to me, but I noticed him all the same and then Jago sent him away. He was very protective of me always.

'Don't worry Jago,' I said. 'Let him come and talk to me next time.'

The boy came round to the caravans again. Jago looked over at me with his friendly brown eyes as if to say 'Shall I get rid of him?' I shook my head. I gestured for the boy to come nearer.

Close to he had such a friendly face, smiling eyes, a tousled mop of hair. He was an average-looking boy really, neither fair nor dark, neither tall nor short. He seemed shy standing there with his cap.

'I think you are so clever on that rope, miss. I don't know how you do it,' he said awkwardly, looking down at my feet.

'Thank you,' I said. 'It's practice, I think'

'I'm . . .' He hesitated and then said his name with a grin. 'I am Japhet McCreddie at least where I work, but I'm Bible J to my friends.' He extended his hand and I took it.

So the boy Bible J took to coming to see me (and also I think to pet the horse) after my shows. He came at least two or three times in one week. He said he was always 'out and about' for his employer, a Mr William Leighton, running errands and the like.

Jago knew of Mr Leighton. 'He runs seances in his house, charges a fortune too. He's a crook on the quiet, a thief,' he said. 'I should watch out for Bible J and Leighton.'

→≫ CHAPTER 29 ≪←

A long sheet of white cloth was hung against one wall, opposite a window with an iron grille over it. Caleb saw a brass clamp on a stand behind a high stool in front of the cloth. A policeman stood holding something square. The woman called out a series of numbers.

'One, nine, two, four, eight.'

The police officer chalked the numbers on to a slate framed in wood, with a loop of rope attached. When he had finished, he held it up.

The woman peered at it and then nodded. The police officer put the slate placard around Caleb's neck so that it hung down on his chest. The starched nurse took her sharp metal comb and tugged at his thick hair, forcing it back from his forehead.

'No nits at least,' she said brusquely.

Caleb found himself staring eye to eye with an old-fashioned box camera which stood close by. 'This won't take a moment,' said the man in the white coat.

Caleb was placed on the high stool. His neck was fixed into the brass bracket so that he couldn't move it. He could feel his leg trembling. A group of Gawkers sat discreetly along the other side wall.

The slate placard was surprisingly heavy and he could feel the rope cut into his neck. The man in the white coat tucked his own head under a black shroud behind the camera.

'Hold still,' said the police officer, 'the light.'

There was a sudden rise in the light levels.

'And, one, two, three, all finished,' said the man from under the cloth. The police officer placed a large brass disc over the blank glass eye of the camera. There was a loud click and the bright light faded down again.

Caleb blinked once and squirmed, tried to move his head, but the brass bracket held him firm. The woman eased his head out of the bracket. She took the placard from around his neck, and rubbed the number off the slate.

'Follow me,' she said. They went back down the noisy, dingy corridor, and out to the reception area. The bench along the tiled wall was filled now with beggars, swells, Gawkers and all sorts. Caleb was told to sit near the desk. He stared down at the scattered sawdust, heaped in a pile under the bench. Some of it was stained blood red. He half expected to see someone's teeth mixed up in it. He was careful not to look up, not to catch the eye of any of the Gawkers, or indeed of anyone on the bench. He thought about his poor father. He would have given anything to hear him going on about anything. And yet he had run away from him. Caleb began to doubt himself now. When the ragged man stood and threw the knife, when he looked down and saw the blood, had his father really shouted 'Run'? Or had he just imagined he said it and then set off in fear?

Inspector Prinsep walked past the bench. He laid his hand briefly on Caleb's shoulder.

'Remember,' he said, '19248, so-called Brown, Caleb. I'll be looking out for you especially, because I don't like pickpockets and thieves.' Caleb looked up, his blue eyes blazing.

'I'm not a th—' Caleb started to say, but realised he had already confessed to it, so he looked down quickly.

Prinsep swept on past him and out of the main doors. Caleb waited on the bench as the minutes ticked by. He sat staring down trying to count the blood-stained flecks of sawdust. He heard the clock hands 'tock' slowly round. A bell rang somewhere in the building. A uniformed police officer and the clerk at the desk had a quiet, muttered conversation.

Caleb sat alone on the long bench seat and waited in

the gaslit vestibule. After hours of staring into nothing, of enduring the stares of visiting Gawkers, Caleb felt himself falling into a shallow sleep, when the door crashed open, and he woke with a start.

⇢ CHAPTER 30 ⇠

William Leighton was hiding behind the drawing-room door of his historic house in Spitalfields. He had left the door open by a tiny crack, just enough to watch Mrs Boulter his housekeeper. He was sure that she was up to something. The same ragged man had passed the house twice while he had been sitting in his upstairs front room. He had watched the man walk past once, pause and look at the front door, then move off. Then Mrs Boulter had appeared on the step outside. He had watched her scan the street. Then she went back inside, and a minute or so later the same ragged man had walked past again, hesitated near the door, then moved off.

Leighton went quickly, quietly, down the stairs to the ground floor, past the green panelling of his hallway, past the false ancestral portraits, and into his crowded front parlour, his cave of treasures. He waited. Sure enough Mrs Boulter appeared nervously in the hallway; she believed him to be upstairs in his seance room. She opened the front door and Leighton watched. It was then that Bible J burst in. Bible J grabbed Mrs Boulter and swung her out of the way.

'Put me down you little rat,' she said.

'Don't take on, Ma B. Where's his nibs?' Bible J said.

'Upstairs,' Mrs Boulter said, brushing at her pinafore apron, and straightening her black jet necklace.

'Downstairs actually,' said Leighton, poking his head out of the parlour door.

Mrs Boulter started. Her eye went immediately to the front door which stood open, and she shook her head firmly from side to side before she shut it. Leighton was meant to think that the gesture was aimed at Bible J, but he could see that it was sent out somewhere into the street.

'In here, Mr McCreddie,' he said. 'Now!'

Once back in the parlour he put his finger to his lips to silence Bible J and looked out of the window. Sure enough he saw the back of that same ragged man walking back on the other side of the road towards the church.

'She's up to something,' he said under his breath to Bible J.

Bible J looked like a startled rabbit. 'What do you mean?' he said.

'Not now, where have you been anyway and what have you got for me?'

Bible J took out the contents of his poacher's pockets and scattered them across the parlour table. 'There was more,' he said, 'but another boy had some of my stuff in his coat and he got caught by Prinsep and dragged off the bus.'

'What other boy?' said Leighton. 'Oh, wait, let me guess, a new waif and stray.'

'Could say that,' said Bible J. 'He's a presentable lad, about my age, respectable Gawker. Dad got kidnapped. Another bloke got shivved and the ragged men blamed this boy and he took off. I found him wandering in Clapham. He was in a bit of a state.'

'Kidnapped,' said Leighton, his interest stirred. 'Who was kidnapped?'

'His dad. He was taken by ragged men. He told the kid to run.'

'When I hear "kidnap", I hear "ransom", I hear "reward from a grateful Corporation",' said Leighton. 'Where is this waif now?'

'Wherever old Prinsep took him, Farringdon Road police station, I should think.'

'Time to go and get him out. What was he taken away for?'

'We were begging off Gawkers on the bus and Prinsep took him for that, but they'll have found the loot in his pockets by now.'

'Pickpocketing, then. A letter and a bribe should do it.'

Bible J hopped on a late omnibus back to Farringdon. He was dressed in his house uniform. He had bathed and shaved and looked altogether groomed and respectable.

More Mr Japhet McCreddie now rather than good old charmer Bible J. He had money and a Buckland Corporation letter of authority, a genuine one that he'd found with several others in a bank safe in Marylebone once after a particularly good raid. The letters had proved useful many times.

Bible J knew just how to play this. He strode up the steps into the vestibule of the police station. He nodded at the cadet on duty, braced himself and walked forward through the double doors into the reception area.

He spotted Caleb straight away sitting half asleep slumped on his own on a wooden bench. A group of Gawkers were studying the Wanted poster gallery, and Bible J saw that one of the posters referred to Caleb.

The desk Clerk looked up at Bible J with a weary expression. 'Gawker side is over against that wall,' he said gesturing with his pen. 'Kindly do not approach the desk here except on business.'

'I am not a Gawker, and I am on business,' said Bible J, handing over the letter. The clerk scanned the contents. Bible J leaned over the edge of the desk and slipped four crisp white five-pound notes on to the clerk's ledger. The desk clerk pushed the ledger across the desk. Bible J signed slowly across the ledger paper. He stood tall and looked around the room.

'Where is he? Is that him?' The desk clerk nodded and then shut the ledger with a snap, trapping the bank notes.

Bible J strode over and then crouched down near the dirty, bloodied sawdust on the floor in front of Caleb. He looked into Caleb's face and winked deliberately slowly.

'Caleb Brown, is it? My name is Japhet McCreddie, and I am here to take you away. I can only apologise for whatever may have happened to you in here.'

Caleb stood up and swayed unsteadily for a moment, and then collapsed back on to the bench and flopped forward like a broken doll. Bible J, the rescuer, the conjurer of pocket contents supported him before his head struck the wood and then the last thing Caleb Brown heard in the police station was the clock chime out the hour on the wall above the desk.

———◆———

Caleb's photograph with the chalked number clear across his chest was developed, fixed and dry by six o'clock that evening. A clerk carefully noted the details in his best copperplate script on an index card and also transcribed them on to the front of an envelope. A copy was sent to the Office of Security, Pastworld Central, where it lay waiting to be discovered.

⇥ CHAPTER 31 ⇤

It was the kind of town house a young child might automatically draw if asked. The outer woodwork was dressed with dark blue-black paintwork, as were the window frames, the outer shutters and the front door. It stood tall and shadowy, with its four floors and attic rooms which stretched in darkness all along the roof line. Bible J fished out a key from his navy-blue frock coat, unlocked the front door and ushered Caleb in. The hall of the house was panelled and the wood was painted with flat distemper, in a rich green. The house smelled faintly of burnt wax, of snuffed candles and vanilla incense, musty old fabrics, and real history.

Bible J turned as soon as he had clicked shut the door and put his finger to his lips. It seemed the kind of house where, by rights, there ought to have been a footman welcoming them, or a butler, or maid of some sort. However, there seemed to be nobody in the house at all. It ticked and tocked and hummed with a sense of expectant still-ness. There was an air of well-tended luxury. The walls were busy with historic-looking pictures, oil portraits and engraved views of London. It certainly did not seem the sort of place that would normally welcome a character like Bible J, let alone allow him his own key to the door. Bible J led the way up the stairs.

They went into a sitting room on the first floor. It was just a little brighter than the hallway. A single candle burned in a sconce over the mantel. Caleb had never seen such a room before outside of a museum. There was here, as elsewhere in the house, a great profusion of very valuable looking things. The wide floorboards were waxed, with bright patterned oriental rugs over them. There was a long polished oval table in the middle of the room with fine chairs grouped around it, and some other antique chairs were also lined up higgledy-piggeldy against the panelled walls. There was even a black sedan chair tucked in the corner. Bible J sat himself down on a low sofa under the windows, below the closed shutters.

'Don't be shy. Sit down there, that's it. This house is the real thing, eh?' he whispered. 'It's what they call a proper house, authentic enough for anyone. We live well here,' he laughed quietly and shook his head. 'The bloke who owns this gaff is harmless enough, he's a,' Bible J paused and thought for a moment, 'he's a collector, that's the word. He's mad for all the old stuff like this, and old houses, and what he calls his 'salvage', his 'treasures'. He runs an old curiosity shop Holborn way and he lives his life here in this old house as a mostly respectable gent. I run errands for him. I help him find the special stuff, see. What better way could there be for yours truly, Bible J the dip, to live his life?'

He stood and went over to one of several antique cabinets against the wall. He opened the door and pulled out a decanter and glasses. He poured something out of the decanter and handed one of the glasses to Caleb.

'Knock that back,' he said, 'quietly mind.'

Caleb took the glass and drained the contents. His throat was instantly scorched by something which tasted hot and cold at the same time. It was awful. He coughed and spluttered.

'I said quietly,' Bible J, took the glass from Caleb. 'That's his best brandy.'

There was a noise from above them, footsteps across the ceiling.

'Watch out, that's set him off.'

Caleb felt warmth from the brandy spreading through his body.

'Who?' he said.

'Himself, the collector, my boss. He's just sprung you, smudger,' said Bible J, nodding his head up to the ceiling.

It wasn't a moment before the door opened and William Leighton walked in.

'Well, well, Mr McCreddie, what is all this noise? Are you aware of the time?'

Bible J stood up, and he broke out one of his big friendly smiles. 'Sorry, I only just got back from the police station with that poor lad, Mr Leighton.'

Leighton walked further into the room. He was

dressed in a dark waistcoat and had a white shirt with billowing sleeves, a high collar, and a white stock. His once
dark hair was peppered with grey now and he favoured
long sideburns. He peered at Caleb over a pair of gold-
rimmed spectacles.

'Why, I wonder to myself, does this more or less
respectable young man need help from rapscallions like
you and me, Mr Japhet?' he said good naturedly, then he
walked over to a gas mantle and struck a match. After a
popping sound a soft greenish light filled the room.

'I see you have been at the brandy,' Leighton said,
nodding at the decanter on the cabinet.

'Sorry, Mr William, I thought he was going to faint,'
Bible J said.

'Tell me what happened to you,' Mr William said
quietly.

Caleb told him.

It was all horribly true, and the reality of that truth
suddenly hit him again in the stomach like a hammer and
he slumped back on to the sofa, as if winded.

'Pour him another glass, Mr McCreddie.' After a sip or
two of brandy Caleb sat up.

'I was accused of murder by the men who really did
it. There are Wanted posters up now describing me more
or less.'

'True,' said Bible J. 'I saw one at Farringdon.'

'An accusation of murder is a serious business in this
town, and I mean money business. You'll be best off with
us here for now. Interesting, all very interesting,' Leighton
said.

'Thank you for saving me,' Caleb said.

'I can pull strings if I have to,' said Leighton. 'I can grease a few palms when necessary. Bible J here told me of your plight and we hatched our little plan. I am well aware of what it might be like to be lost and alone in this place, and what a state of shock you must be in.'

<hr />

Caleb shut the bedroom door and breathed out a long sigh. It was late now, dark at the window and as he looked over the roofline and the looming church spire he thought, *I'll never find him. Dad's dead by now, as cold as this glass.* He pulled his head back behind the little calico curtain. A lone ragged man was walking slowly past the house, his head covered with a rough sacking hood. He moved off down the street without looking up once.

A night light burned on the mantle. Caleb got into bed.

He couldn't sleep. He lay staring up at the flickering shadows that crossed and recrossed the low ceiling. He imagined more ragged men. Saw them clearly in his mind gathering in the street below, their faces hidden either by identical rough hoods, or by skull masks like his own. He was sure he heard them whispering, plotting.

He got out of bed and looked out of the window again. The street was empty. A light burned in the house opposite, otherwise there was nothing but wet cobbles and fading wisps of fog. He got back into bed and listened to the house around him as it creaked and settled.

He forced his eyes shut and saw at once his father's face and heard him call out clearly, 'Run'. He tried counting in his head, one one thousand, two one thousand, three one thousand, precise seconds as he had been taught. Finally he lost count and dreamed a vivid dream that he was slowly falling. That he was being chased through the air by an airship. That he landed on a steep staircase in a tall tower and ran down and down the spiral stairs giddy with fear until he finally reached the cobbled streets and then he was running, and running faster than he had ever run before. He was being chased by the moon with its big, pale, bone face, like a skull. Tatters of fog trailed out around the moon like a highwayman's cape. The moon came grinning after him, low and fast over the cobbles.

☆ CHAPTER 32 ☆

Two Buckland Corporation cadets flanked Inspector Lestrade as he climbed the steps of the Buckland Corporation headquarters again. The night porter stood to attention as soon as he saw him and made a half-hearted salute. The Inspector swept up the central stair-case and went straight to Abel Buckland's office. He indicated that the cadets should wait outside, and then he opened the double doors.

Mr Buckland was sitting at the top of a very high stepladder looking down on his miniature city. The room was in almost complete darkness except for the tiny lamps and lights all over the model laid out below him. He looked over as the door opened and slammed closed again.

'Well?' he said.

'Good evening, Abel,' said Lestrade. 'I can report that we were correct. The body was indeed that of Dr

Mulhearn. I had it from my man. He took one of Jack's personal acquaintances to identify the body.'

Buckland stayed where he was staring down at the vast toy city below him, at the lines of little airships blinking in formation above the streets, at the little model steam trains chuffing along the tiny suburban routes.

'I am afraid the local police have bettered your man,' Buckland said sadly. 'Look on my desk.'

Lestrade skirted round the huge model and went to the desk. The oil lamp was lit and there was enough light to see the envelopes stacked on a ledger. There was a brown envelope on top with the flap open and the ties loosened.

'Look inside,' said Buckland.

An official arrest photograph and statement were inside.

'Look carefully,' said Buckland.

'*Number 19248*,' read the Inspector, '*a pickpocket, self-confessed, found on an omnibus trying to steal.*'

'He gave his name to the duty clerk.'

'So he did, it's all down here. Oh I see, *Brown, first name, Caleb.*'

'Brown, first name Caleb, yes that's the very one. You have a man out looking for the boy and his father, and guess what, the locals had one of them strapped into a neck brace blinking in front of one of their cameras. Ironic, don't you think?'

'Sorry, Abel, I assumed . . .'

'Never assume. That boy is the son of Lucius Brown, my partner at one time, a founder and pioneer of this place. Need I say more? Caleb Brown is now in very grave danger, as is my precious Gentleman – I need to save him and to save him I must find him. We have a chance, a real chance at last. Your man needs this information and right away. You see in all of their cack-handed incompetence, the local desk clerk signed this young Caleb Brown over to that thumping 'official' crook William Leighton of all people for a 'consideration' of £20. It's down there in black and white in best clerk's copperplate, time of arrest, so-called guarantee bond, address everything. Now get the information over to your man and do it now.'

'I will of course at once, I'm sorry –'

'Let me stop you there, Lestrade. No waffling no excuses. Before you go have a look at the topmost tip of the old Tower 42 on my model beside you.'

The inspector looked closely at the miniature of the threatened building, the last of its kind, complete with tiny demolition notices. A model of a cloaked and masked figure stood on the tallest point. His hands were raised high; he was holding a tiny severed bloodied head.

'The Fantom,' said Buckland. 'Pray that it will not be your head or mine he is holding ready to leave in that high place.'

⇥ CHAPTER 33 ⇤

Caleb was woken early the next morning by someone coming into his room. He thought at first in his bleary half-awake half-dreaming state, that he was at home and it was his father. He quickly sat up in bed. Then reality kicked in and he remembered. It wasn't his father; it would never be his father. It was a sallow-faced woman in a dusty black dress, her hair scraped back tightly from her face in a hard-looking bun, and black glass jewels glittering on her front.

She went to the window and pulled the curtains back roughly, which let the grey morning light into the room. She turned and studied him. She spoke briskly, 'So you're a new one then. What are you called and how'd he find you?'

'I'm Caleb, Caleb Brown,' he said defensively.

'Good morning, Caleb Brown, if that's your name.'

'Oh, it's my name all right,' Caleb said, throwing back

the bedclothes.

'I'm Mrs Boulter, and I run the household here,' she said.

Caleb looked into her hard dark eyes. There was no welcome in her severe, blank face. He could find no warmth, no humour, no expression except one of exasperation.

'Come on then. Get yourself dressed quickly, come down to the kitchen and I suppose I'll give you some breakfast. No dawdling. I'm a busy woman.'

Bible J came in a minute later. 'Morning,' he said cheerily, and draped some clothes across the fireguard. 'Here. Try these, smudger, the house style.'

'Get yourself dressed, and then come down.'

Caleb put the new clothes on, and then he caught sight of himself in the mirror over the washbasin. His hair was plastered down now, and curled across his forehead in dark ringlets. The dark waistcoat and the white linen made him look older. Above the washbasin and the mirror was a black-and-silver tinsel picture which read 'God is Love'. Caleb wished he could believe it.

He clattered down the narrow stairs to the kitchen in the basement. What little light there was came in through some thick squares of dingy glass at street level. Mrs Boulter handed him a china bowl of porridge.

Caleb ate the sticky porridge at the kitchen table while she clattered about at the sink.

'Did he tell you of any duties you would have here?' she asked.

'No one said anything about duties. I don't think I'll

be here for very long.'

She turned from the sink and quickly looked him up and down. 'You've the look of a thief like that other one, and not much healthier. You'd best try and keep your wits about you in this house and jump to it when himself upstairs tells you.'

Bible J swept into the kitchen.

'Good morning, Ma B.' He helped himself to tea from the pot on the table.

'Mr L sends his compliments,' Bible J said, 'and could you send young Mr Caleb here up to the morning room with a breakfast tray.'

'Come.'

Bible J opened the door wide and let Caleb through first with the breakfast tray. Caleb stood for a moment in the middle of the crowded room, which was piled high with more treasures.

Mr Leighton sat on the other side of an oval table.

'Well, good morning, young man. Come in. Just put the tray down here,' he said.

Caleb set the tray down carefully and then just stood.

'The house uniform looks very well on you. First of all, some dull housekeeping matters. Here in this house as a general rule and certainly in this particular room, if there are any clients or visitors I am to be referred to as Mister William, for authenticity's sake. I would like you to refer to me publicly by that name always, do you understand, Caleb?'

'Yes,' Caleb said.

'This is, I hope, an agreeable and welcoming household. It is managed by Mrs Boulter. I strongly believe in charity for young persons from the streets here. I have helped many others like you. Why young Mr McCreddie here, for instance, I have helped since I found him many years ago.'

Bible J smiled and nodded holding his jacket lapels in both hands.

Mr William ate some of the toast and while he chewed he opened a handkerchief to reveal the rusted-looking pocket watch and the length of dirty string. 'Mr McCreddie showed me this watch, which was among his haul from last night.'

'It was the murdered man's,' Caleb said, 'though it says it was presented to my father. It was once my father's watch.'

Leighton turned the watch over. He rubbed at the inscription with the handkerchief.

'It seems that your father was an important person, Caleb. Do you think that's why the ragged men took him?'

Caleb fumbled for an answer. 'I don't know,' he replied hesitantly.

'An important man to the Buckland Corporation at least. When the police talked to you at the station did you give them your real name?'

'Yes.'

'It will take a while, but the message will get through to them. The wheels grind slowly here in Pastworld but they do grind.' He smiled to himself. 'You and your father are something of a mystery then, Mr Brown?'

'Yes, Mr William.'

'Very good, I like mysteries. Now we will say a short prayer for you and for your father's safe deliverance. Let us bow our heads.'

Leighton closed his eyes; Bible J winked at Caleb. Caleb let his head drop forward.

'Oh Lord, look down upon this miserable boy and treat him with mercy, and his father too. If you needs must, then take them to your bosom without pain and suffering and lead them to dwell with you in eternity, amen.'

'Amen,' said Bible J with a smirk. He was working on his teeth with a sharpened matchstick.

Caleb raised his head and Mr William said.

'Yes indeed. You are a mystery, I shall look into it. Meanwhile best see if Mrs Boulter has anything for you to do.'

Then he handed Caleb the pocket watch and dismissed him quickly with his hand. Bible J winked at him again as he closed the door. They went back down to the kitchen where Caleb was given boring chores to do by Mrs Boulter. First he had to clean the stone floor with a stringy mop and a bucket of water. Then polish and buff two pairs of black elastic-sided boots. He biffed the leather uppers of the boots with the polishing brush. It was satisfying enough, if he imagined that he was attacking ragged men, scattering them and pulling his father up from the cold ground. Eventually Bible J came back down, and sat with his feet up on the table.

'Mr William likes what he sees. He's got a sniff of

something big with you. You're a good find. Later he says you can help me to lay out the chairs and prepare the room upstairs for one of his "scientific" meetings tonight. I was forgetting, smudger, do you scare easy? Our man upstairs, he likes to speak to the dead.

⇥ CHAPTER 34 ⇤

At one o'clock exactly, after he had furiously brushed at some more boots and shoes, Caleb reluctantly lugged a heavy and awkward lunch tray – a bowl of hot soup, bread, butter, some mouldy cheese that smelled of staleness and was wrapped in a mouldy rag – up the twisty stairs from the dingy kitchen to the morning room. Leighton was at the table and Bible J was sitting in the window looking out at the street.

'Sit down for a moment, Caleb.'

Bible J stood and shut the door.

'Thing is,' Leighton said, 'We are outlaws and by now you're like us. Not exactly popular with the authorities here. They will have Wanted posters up all over for you. Bible J take young Mr Brown here upstairs, and show him the room. Here.' He threw a key over to Bible J.

Bible J motioned Caleb upstairs. He unlocked a door off the corridor. 'We've got a whole special collection in here, cabinets full. I'll only show you, if you promise you won't touch any of them, at least for now?'

Caleb said, 'I promise.'

It was a small, plainly decorated room, simple and severe compared to the hallway and especially compared the rest of the furniture-crammed and overstuffed rooms. There was a dark green blind pulled down at the single window. A plain school clock ticked on the wall over the simple mantel. Bible J lit an oil lamp on a small side table. A thousand reflections leaped from the walls, each of which was lined with tall glass-fronted oak cabinets. Guns of all sorts were lined up on hooks and brackets behind the glass. There were Mausers, Colts, Berettas, Smith and Wessons, flintlock-action duelling pistols, Winchesters, and various antique military service revolvers and rifles, all laid out in rows. They gleamed darkly around the room.

Bible J unlocked one of the cabinet doors. He took out a heavy revolver with a wooden handle. 'An 1858 Remington.44,' he said, 'from the American Civil War. I shot a ragged man once in the kneecap with this one, right in front of the Fantom himself. He knows me. He's threatened me, and Mr Leighton. We've also got a New Model Army revolver from the same year, and a spiller and Burr.36, and an 1836 Paterson.' He laid the gun across his palm and pointed out the parts to Caleb.

'You load the bullets in the chamber here, that cylindrical bit, then you've got six shots. Round they go, bang, bang.' He spun the chamber and Caleb heard the well-oiled mechanism click as the chamber turned. Then he pulled the trigger and there was a hollow *clack* as the hammer hit the empty chamber.

'What does he want them all for?' Caleb asked.

'Well for a start he just likes 'em as things; he collects them. Then there is the question of what you might call professional uses; he's got another kind of life away from this house and his spiritual experiments. He robs, banks and the like, not for a while now because of the Fantom. The Fantom threatened to cut Mr Leighton open if he carried on with his robberies. Trouble is we were too good at it. I wasn't averse to using one of these now and then either,' he said, and sighted down the barrel.

'Never point it at anyone, though, never,' he said. 'Unless you mean real business of course, that is, and there have been times when Mr Leighton and I have meant real business. Between you and me you should have seen the reaction when I pointed this one at one of the Fantom's ragged men. I shoved it right in his face.' Bible J laughed.

'Here,' he said 'you try it, hold it. Go on, it won't bite. You might have to get used to it one of these days.'

Bible J handed the gun to Caleb.

Caleb took the gun. He felt a surge of confidence, an excitement. This was the sort of thing he needed. A weapon, a defence against the ragged men. The gun was heavy and smelled of oil. He held it by the wooden grip. He lifted the revolver up to arms length. He aimed at the centre of the window and squeezed the trigger. There was the same sharp clack as the hammer fell, and the gun leaped a little in his hand.

'We'll have to give you a proper live practice go sometime,' Bible J said, and pulled out a drawer from below the cabinet. It was full of boxed and loose bullets and cartridges. 'These fit the revolver you see,' he held out a handful of brass and copper bullets.

Bible J loaded one of the bullets and spun the chamber fast. It whirled and clicked, and then he stopped it in an instant with the flat of his palm. He raised the gun with a fixed grin on his face. He levelled the gun barrel to the side of his own head.

'You never point the gun at anyone, ever,' he said again.

Caleb nodded.

'And by the way Caleb, never ever do this.' He slowly squeezed the trigger.

Caleb flinched instinctively; he expected a bang and Bible J's head to explode in a cloud of red.

Instead there was just the hollow clack again.

'Sorry, Caleb, just a trick,' Bible J said, and held out his free hand where the bullet still sat, shining dimly in the hollow of his palm.

'Normally we use crossed holsters with two guns.' He mimed swinging two guns up from his waist with his arms crossed and made a shooting noise with his mouth. 'It might be your job one day to reload fast if we was ever cornered, and in a fight. Mr Leighton might let you practise some loading before you know it. It's all against the Fantom see. The Fantom is Mr Leighton's worst enemy, his worst nightmare, and mine. Mr William'd do anything to get the Fantom off his back. So staying here might be the best thing you could do; you help us we'll help you. The Fantom runs the ragged men. The ragged men took your dad. The best way to find your dad is to stick with us I reckon and follow them.' He locked the gun back in the cabinet, and snuffed out the lamp.

Caleb looked into the smiling eyes of Bible J. He just wasn't sure if he could trust him. He was friendly enough, and somehow he made Caleb feel better. Could he really trust someone who was such a conjuror, a magician at stealing and distraction? Maybe Bible J was setting him up. There was fear and death along every street in the ragged men, waiting, looking for him in every dark corner. He put out his hand like a flag of surrender and Bible J grasped it and shook it hard, threw back a wolfish grin at Caleb and said with a laugh, 'Best thing you've done since you stood me a plate of fried potatoes.'

———◆◆◆———

Mr William pushed away the tray and dabbed at his mouth with a napkin. 'Later on this evening,' he said, 'I am hosting what I like to call a "spiritual and scientific meeting" here in this very room. We hold these things from time to time. I would like to think that you will be willing to help us in the staging? You will welcome our credulous visitors to our soirée, and I would like you to be present and assist at the meeting itself. Powers will appear to present themselves for our visitors. They will see and hear things that may disturb them. Whatsoever these things are, and they cannot be sure what exactly they are, we make sure that they all appear to be part of a great plan and purpose of the new science. I flatter myself that they will believe that I have chanced through that science to the revelation of a mystery that was previously closed to us.' He stopped and chuckled quietly to himself. 'The Gawkers, sorry, our visitors, believe that my science is as a doorway through which they may look briefly in wonder at eternity and contact loved ones who have gone before them. For this the room will only be semi-lit, and if we require it you may have to carefully adjust the light levels by means of the gas taps on the mantles. This is purely to aid certain of our illusions. Do you think you could do that?'

'I could try,' he said. Leighton stood and ushered Caleb over to one of the gas lamp brackets.

'This little tap here at the base of the pipe must be turned this way to brighten and this way to darken. Here, you try it.'

Caleb reached up and turned the little tap and the yellow white light flared higher and brightened. When he turned it the other way the mantel darkened and the glow of light was warmer and Caleb noticed that the shadow of his hand on the wall was suddenly brown.

'There you see, it is a very straightforward task,' said Leighton. 'That is all there is to say about that for now. You may go downstairs, but remember the rules of address, very important this evening, and remember too that whatever you see in this house is our tradecraft, our secrets, not to be spoken of to anybody outside.'

'Yes, Mister William,' Caleb said. He backed out of the

door and made a little bow like the kind of footmen he had seen in old films.

'Good, that's it,' said Leighton with a smile.

Caleb went down to the kitchen. There was no sign of Mrs Boulter. He sat at the table and looked at the dingy light filtering on to the table. His life on the Outside seemed very far away now. No one there would have any idea yet what had happened to him. Soon though the ripple of news would spread out and surely someone would come and look for him?

✹ CHAPTER 35 ✹

Bible J was sent on an errand all kitted out in his smart house uniform. He wore his dip's coat and he had a package to deliver for Mr William.

He dodged between all the Gawkers on the crowded pavements. He even managed to do a little dipping on the way, minor things, a few coins, a silk handkerchief. No one noticed. The package was to be left at a house in one of the smart squares. A butler took it from him at the front door, and an envelope for Mr Leighton was handed over in exchange. It was all very discreetly managed inside the vestibule of the house out of the way of prying eyes.

Bible J tucked the envelope into a secure inner pocket, and then he turned back to the street. He was free for a short while. 'Come on,' he said, his hands crossed over his heart, 'time to go and see her. I haven't seen her for an age it feels like.' He dashed down the steps from the house in sudden high spirits. He made his way through the maze of streets. It was a bright morning, as if someone had suddenly turned the lights on full in a room that was usually dim. The buildings threw razor-sharp shadows across one another. The wet pavements and the cobbled roads dazzled for once like sunlit rivers. Bible J hurried along towards Holborn, and he soon heard the sounds of a drum and an out of tune trumpet being blown very loudly. He pushed foward in his excitement and ran into Lincoln's Inn Fields.

There was a jolly crowd of Gawkers filing into a modest tent with a banner across the entrance which read, *JAGO'S PANDEMONIUM SHOW*. Bible J pushed his way through the line and paid over his few pennies at the booth.

It was warm inside. Some of the Gawkers were eating roast chestnuts bought from a brazier in the square and there was an air of noisy expectancy. A skinny man dressed as a harlequin was playing the trumpet tune and another one was banging loudly on the bass drum. Then Jago came out and bowed to the audience and there was a burst of applause. He raised his arms and the audience fell silent.

'Hello, Jago,' Bible J mouthed, grinning.

'Welcome, ladies and gentlemen, to Jago's Pandemonium Show. I am Jago and I would like to introduce without delay our star turn, all the way from the far frozen wastes of Russia, the very lovely Eve.'

When she danced on the narrow rope, she became something else. She balanced and twirled above their heads. Bible J watched her and the more he watched the more he understood that there was surely something properly mysterious about her. She stood straight on the rope with a parasol in one hand as a balance. She leaped up above the rope and the crowd gasped. She spun in the air it seemed any number of times, and as usual Bible J thought, *Surely impossible*, and when she landed back on the rope, she landed firmly on her feet with no trace of a wobble, her head held high and her body completely still. She was so confident and graceful as she moved. The crowd roared their approval and applauded wildly. This was a close crowd, all pushed together hugger-mugger and all eager to get a view of Eve. At the climax of her act, she picked up Jago, a skinny but nevertheless full-grown man, in her arms and walked across the rope with him as if she had been just carrying a balance stick. And then when finally she floated down off the rope, down to the little stage, she seemed to fall, if this was possible, slowly. She held her parasol open above her head, and as she floated down the crowd were hushed for a moment as if they were watching a kind of miracle. She defied the normal rules of science, or appeared to. Bible J as usual looked in vain for a wire, anything that might be holding her from above, slowing her down, but he could see nothing. *However it's done*, he thought, *it's a very clever trick*.

She landed lightly on the platform and bowed. And then raised her face high and beamed bright-eyed, showed her perfect smile, her perfect teeth. She was indeed beautiful. Her skin was pale and flawless, and her features fine. She had a narrow jaw, a pertly tilted nose, and above all she had those shining turquoise-blue eyes.

Afterwards Bible J pushed through the crowd and ducked under the barrier between the crowd of Gawkers and the circus wagons.

He went round to the other side. The horse stood quietly ignoring all the noise and clamour, munching on some hay. Bible J patted the horse and laid his cheek on its flank. 'All right,' he said, as if expecting an answer. The horse shook its head and made a quiet sound, a sort of approval.

Jago was sitting on the top step of the wagon, rubbing his head and face with a towel. He stood up and looked over at Bible J.

'Hello again,' Jago said. 'How is the mysterious Mr Leighton? You should be careful, it will all end in tears one day.' He smiled good naturedly. 'You should get an honest job in the circus. You'll want to see Eve – you caught the show of course?'

'Of course,' said Bible J, 'and she was even better today.'

'She just goes on getting better,' Jago said and rapped hard on the step. Eve appeared in the doorway. She tripped down with a flicker of her feet and lifted her head to look directly at Bible J.

'Someone to see you,' Jago said.

She reached her hand out and just in time Bible J remembered his manners and bowed a little from the waist. And then he shook her hand awkwardly, and noticed at the same time close up the beautiful sea-blue of her eyes. The perfect sheen of her pale skin.

They both stood awkwardly for a moment.

'I saw you pat the horse,' Eve said.

'It's a nice horse,' said Bible J with a grin, and added, 'I tried to work out how you do the trick at the end.'

'There is no trick,' she said, looking directly back at him, unblinking.

'Your eyes,' Bible J said, 'it's a funny thing, but just the other day I rescued a boy from the streets, from Outside, a Gawker, but he has eyes the same colour as yours.'

'Do you rescue many people from the streets?'

'I have done from time to time. He was just in a bad way and I helped him.'

'You were kind to our horse, you were kind to this boy...'

'Caleb.'

'Caleb. Well you helped him, so you are kind. I knew you were. Shall you come to see the show again?'

'Oh yes,' said Bible J, 'very soon. I'll bring Caleb with me perhaps. Will you still be here?'

Eve turned to Jago. 'Are we performing here for a little longer?'

'If they keep coming then we will be here, unless we are moved on.'

Bible J said, 'I have to get back to the house anyway. I will come again very soon.'

'Yes, come and say hello again,' and then she smiled her full dazzling smile.

On the way back to Fournier Street the fog was back with a vengeance. Bible J thought about Eve. He had known lots of girls but none had been like her. She was special. He had met a beautiful girl and she thought he was kind. He felt closer to her than he ever had felt to anyone, and he didn't really know her at all. What could that mean? It felt like some kind of giddy madness had overtaken him.

⇥ CHAPTER 36 ⇤

Mr William Leighton's drawing room was set out formally. The room was more or less in darkness, very few lamps were lit, and gradually over the course of half an hour a mixed group of solemn, wealthy residents and Gawkers assembled and sat together around the table in the gloom of the November evening. Caleb had taken all of the damp coats, cloaks, hats and scarves and hung them near the drawing room as instructed. Bible J had taken the money at the door, all of it in notes. The pile grew deep on the salver.

The men were in their dark evening jackets, with high white shirt collars, and brocaded waistcoats with gold watch chains. The women mostly wore sombre dresses in dusty-coloured velvets, plum or greengage. One or two of them had paisley shawls wrapped around their shoulders against the cold.

The meeting started promptly. Caleb closed the

double doors, and then pulled the heavy inner draught curtains. The effect of Mr Leighton's entrance was startling. Everyone sat straighter like a group of children when the headmaster comes in unannounced. They seemed ready, eager for anything. Caleb had been told to wait against the wall until such time as he might be needed.

There was no sign of Bible J.

Leighton took his seat. He spoke, with his head bowed, and his hands on the table, fingers spread.

'Oh spirits bless our endeavours,' Mr Leighton said, 'and enable our science. A science which serves only to reveal truth, and help us, all of us here gathered, to come to terms with the mysteries of life and the losses of death, and those border lands that lie between those two worlds. Those of the quick and the dead.'

The room went very quiet. The sound of the fluttering gas filaments could be heard as they hissed and popped, and there was a smell in the room of something sweet and cloying, like a freshly opened hyacinth flower.

'Let us put our hands upon the table and let us join our hands together.'

Caleb watched the visitors make a circle of their hands around the table. The silence extended while all bowed their heads in concentration. The room held its breath. After a moment or two Leighton spoke. 'Are you there?'

There was a long silence.

Leighton spoke again. 'Are you there? If you are with us this evening perhaps you would give us a simple sign, such as a rap on this table, indeed anything that it might please you to do to enlighten us of your presence here in this room.' After a moment and the clearing of a throat, and what Caleb thought was a stifled laugh from somewhere, there was a sharp knock on the table. One of the women let out a yelp of surprise, and then quickly apologised.

'Do not break the circle,' Leighton said, 'or we must start again. Tap once more if you are there.'

There was a sharp knock from somewhere on the table.

'Is that little Miss Burgess? Tap once for yes, tap twice for no.'

Tap.

'Good evening, Miss Burgess, and welcome.'

There was stillness around the table now, lowered heads. The room felt distinctly colder.

'Shall you materialise tonight?'

Tap, tap.

'Shall you speak to us tonight?'

Tap.

There was another silence, which went on for a minute or so, and then came the sound of a young child's voice. It came from nowhere that Caleb could identify. It just floated into and around the room. The texture of the voice was distant, and it was surrounded with a flicker of other unidentifiable sounds.

'Hello, help me. Are you there? Help me, help me.'

Everyone became agitated; Caleb watched as they lifted their heads looking around the darkened room for the source of the crackling, whispered voice.

Leighton spoke again. 'Keep the circle now. How do you require us to help, Miss Burgess?'

Again the scratchy flicker around the voice, the same phrase: 'Help me, help me.'

The audience were disturbed, one woman began crying quietly. A woman in a plum-coloured velvet dress said, 'It sounds like my Amy,' and she too cried quietly. 'It sounds just like my Amy.' A man sitting beside her gave her his handkerchief.

'Do not break the circle. We have the manifestation of a voice, a miracle in our midst,' said Leighton.

'I want my mother,' came the voice distinctly. The woman in the plum velvet broke the circle again and suddenly brought her hands up to her face and sobbed. Leighton spoke then, clearly and slowly, and with a certain weariness of tone, as if this were a familiar occurrence. 'Mr Brown, I wonder if you would raise the light levels for us. Our experiment must now conclude, just for the moment.' Caleb snapped out of his own reverie and raised the flow of the gas jets. The room jumped into semi-brightness. The audience stretched in their seats. There were audible mutterings of disappointment.

'I think we shall take some refreshment now, and we shall attempt another contact. Perhaps our Miss Burgess may even materialise this time,' Leighton said.

Caleb stood by the door and watched the Gawkers wait patiently while Leighton poured glasses of sherry from behind an occasional table. The woman in the plum velvet dress stood apart in obvious distress and finally

Leighton asked Caleb to show her out.

Caleb held her cape for her in the hallway and she shrugged herself into it. She turned to Caleb and said through her tears, 'It's all silly tricks, isn't it?' She held her head high. 'Cruel, nasty conjuring tricks.' Then she stepped out into the street and Caleb shut the door behind her.

The Gawkers were back around the table upstairs. Leighton asked Caleb to dim the gaslight back down. Caleb adjusted the glow until the gloom was established again. They all joined hands in a circle once more, and Leighton cleared his throat and said, 'Are you still with us, Miss Burgess?'

'I am here,' came the crackling voice.

Caleb stood and waited by the gas bracket.

'Shall you materialise?' said Mr William into the gloom.

This time there was a loud *tap* on the table.

A milky white light appeared in front of the door. It flickered on and off, back into darkness for a few seconds then settled as a shifting, white glow like the fogs outside but brighter. A figure appeared, very faintly, in the centre of the light. There were gasps from the table, and audible intakes of breath. Caleb realised at once that this was just the sort of illusion that his father was always boasting about. The very thing he claimed to have developed back in the early days of Pastworld when he had devised ghosts and such things.

'Don't break the circle,' said Leighton. 'Concentrate now on the manifestation. Are you with us, Miss

Burgess?'

The room felt colder. Caleb could clearly see his breath in the air now and the figure in the light raised its arms wide.

'Help me, I want my mummy.' It was the girl's voice again but subtly different this time as if from far away. The figure in the light seemed to be a girl wearing a long white nightdress.

'Miss Burgess, thank you for joining us. We can see you very clearly now. Have you a message of comfort for anyone here?' said Leighton.

'I would like to touch my poor mummy, to feel her kind hand again.'

In the silence that followed the room felt colder still. Caleb knew for sure that what he was watching was something fake – very clever, but fake. He guessed that it was some sort of holograph projection. It was very well done but certainly not a real ghost, and yet the people around the table seemed to have completely fallen for it. There was palpable emotion in the room and Caleb shivered, not just from the cold. Hadn't his father been banging on about ghosts and illusions and machines when they were walking near Clapham Junction station?

'I fear that your mother may not be here,' said Leighton.

'Then I should like to feel any hand at all. I should like to make a contact with someone from your world who has suffered a grievous loss. I want to comfort someone once more before I go back for ever into the darkness.'

There were some sighs and sobs from around the

table at this. Caleb recognised the voice; it was Bible J, either speaking into a special distorting device or cleverly putting on a girl's voice. That broke his own tension and for the first time in days he was tempted to laugh out loud, but he controlled himself.

Leighton replied, 'I will send someone to hold your hand, Miss Burgess. Mr Brown, knowing your sad history as I do, I wonder if you would go and take comfort from our revenant, our lost soul, for you are grieving too I think?'

Caleb looked over at Mr Leighton. Was this a sick joke on his part?

Mr Leighton gestured for him to walk forward. Caleb brushed at the front of his uniform as if to prepare himself. 'It's true but I don't know,' he said quietly, embarrassed, hesitating.

'Go forward please, go to her. No harm will come to you. Take her hand, take comfort from this poor lost child.'

Caleb stayed where he was.

'I'll do it,' said a woman standing up from the table. She squeezed past the chairs and walked nervously towards the light. She reached out nervously toward the ghostly white outstretched hand.

A loud bang came from outside the door and with it a sudden flash of bright light which stabbed its way under and over the closed door, and flicked around the gloomy parlour, like a flash of lightning. There was shouting followed by instant confusion around the table. The image flickered off and the room was plunged into dimness once again, and a wind of cold air swirled in from below.

'Lights, lights, Caleb,' Mr William snapped.

Caleb went over and turned the gas jet up too high, too quickly and the room flooded with bright, greenish light. The Gawkers were caught awkwardly holding hands and blinking, fearful of another thunderflash.

The door burst open and Bible J was pushed hard into the room. Caleb saw that one of his arms was covered in a white sleeve and white glove. A ragged man, his face mostly hidden by a tattered scarf, had Bible J by the throat, and held a pistol to his temple. Behind him came another ragged man who strode right into the middle of the room, stretched his arm out straight and levelled his own gun directly at Mr Leighton's head.

⟶ CHAPTER 37 ⟵

The ragged man stood in the centre of the room with an army revolver held straight out in his hand.

'Nobody move. Stay just where you are. Now, very slowly, all put your hands up in the air where I can see them.'

The Gawkers raised their arms, as did Caleb and Leighton.

Bible J was pushed further forward and he stumbled across the floor. Another ragged man came in, carrying a large carpet bag held wide open. The man with the gun said, 'All of you are to put any valuables – cash money, jewellery watches anything and everything – into the bag, and you are to do it slowly. Leighton, you will put all of the entrance money in this bag now.'

'I haven't got it here. My houseboy will have to fetch it.'

'Send him to fetch it then.'

'Would you be so good as to go to the room upstairs young man and bring down the cash box? Mr Japhet has the key.'

Bible J stood with his arms in the air as Caleb fished the key out of his waistcoat pocket. He nodded his head almost imperceptibly as Caleb took the key.

'Hurry,' said the ragged man.

Caleb went to the stairs. Another armed man stood guard outside the door and watched him as he went up to the next landing and as he unlocked and opened the door. It was the gun room. The cash box was on the table. He looked at the cabinets and the rows of darkly gleaming guns. He quickly opened one of the cabinets and took out a Remington revolver. It was already loaded. *What am I doing?* he thought, but he was suddenly too nervous to answer his own question. He tucked the gun into the waistband of his trousers and draped his waistcoat over the bulge. He took the cash box with him and locked the door, then went back down to the seance room.

The ragged man emptied the box contents into the bag, which was now stuffed full of jewellery and cash. Then he spoke to the assembled Gawkers. 'Ladies, gen-tlemen, Gawkers and thieves, you have contributed tonight to the funds of the mighty Fantom, and you can be sure those funds will be put to a very good use.' There were mutterings and murmurings from the Gawkers.

Mr Leighton said, 'Your employer will pay dearly for this.'

'I doubt that, mate,' said the ragged man. 'You'll have to find him first, now he really is supernatural. He comes from a "no where" and he goes to a "no place".' The ragged man picked up the carpet bag and backed towards the door. He looked at Caleb, reached forward and pulled the revolver out of his waistband. 'Nice try,' he said, 'brave lad.' He pocketed the gun, and backed out of the door, slammed it shut and turned the key.

Mr Leighton kept his hands in the air after the door had shut.

'Stay as you are,' he counselled. 'Don't move anyone, wait. I don't trust them.' There was the sound of a door slamming below and the sound of hooves and wheels on cobbles.

'They've gone,' he said, lowering his arms.

He was at once surrounded by querulous Gawkers, demanding he send for the police. They were outraged, and they were embarrased for allowing themselves to be robbed so easily. Angry and disillusioned; they jostled around him, some of the women were in tears, their voices broken with fear.

Bible J had slipped the white sleeve and glove from his hand and hidden it under the table.

'Their object was to frighten you,' said Leighton. 'I will see that you are all financially recompensed. Caleb, see that everyone has their coats and show them out of the house. I too am in distress; my aura has been damaged. Leave me until next time, my friends, when all shall be well.'

The confused and angry Gawkers eventually left and Leighton ran up the staircase to the gun room.

'Key,' he snapped out.

He stepped into the gun room, lit the lamp and pulled Caleb and Bible J in with him.

'I'm not blaming you, it's not your fault. I should have explained about the Fantom and myself and the danger that he represents to me personally. Caleb, that was a good idea taking one of the guns. We might have had a chance of taking one of the bastards with it or getting one on the way out. Shame there was no time.'

He looked around at all of the precious guns. 'It's a good job you didn't use it. They would have finished you off like that.' He snapped his fingers. 'It will soon be time to rally to the cause properly. That was an act of provocation. One of these days, and soon, we will load up and go and find him and deal with him once and for all.'

⇥ CHAPTER 38 ⇤

The Fantom made his way quickly down the dark brick tunnel. The low light did not bother him; he could see perfectly in any light and his feet found their way automatically beside the rail tracks. A rat scuttled towards him, not a real one, which he would have expected, but a straying mech. It stopped in front of him barring the way. It looked up at him, its eyes seemed to glow red. It lifted its head and opened its mouth and showed two rows of even, sharp teeth set in a fixed grimace, and then the rat said menacingly, 'No entry. Restricted area. Restricted.' The Fantom looked down at the rat, at its spiky, greasy fur standing on end. 'Hello, brother rat,' he said, and there was even a trace of sympathy in his voice. He lifted his foot high in its shiny black boot, and brought it down hard on the little creature's back. He felt the sad and detailed crunch of its destruction through the sole of his boot. He moved his foot away and knelt down and looked at the rat, peering with curiosity into its shattered little eyes as the red light dimmed and faded out. *That would have alerted them*, he thought, *but it's too deep – too far underground for a signal.*

The Fantom's cloak swished out behind him as he turned the last curve. At this point the tunnel went straight for the last few hundred yards and the old disused station soon swam into view. Oil lamps were hung on wires above the platform and their light showed disembodied fragments from the old advertising posters pasted over the curved walls. Smiling faces showed off their once whiter than white teeth, or proudly brandished their toothpaste tubes, or their swirls and spirals of oiled hair, as they loomed out of the darkness and grinned down on to the silent tracks.

A ragged man sat guard on the edge of the platform with a rifle across his knees. He leaped up when the Fantom appeared out of the mouth of the tunnel.

'Asleep again then, Mr James?' the Fantom asked.

'No, sir,' said the ragged man, standing as much to attention as he could. 'Are the others with you?'

'No. They have been out rattling punters somewhere. They'll be here soon enough.' The Fantom hopped up on to the platform and made his way quickly into the staircase hall. More oil lamps were strung on wires above the escalator steps. The metal treads were rusted and thick with dust. He heard a noise behind him: the sound of echoing laughter and little whoops from his gang of ragged men some way away down a tunnel.

The Fantom went through a door into the old ticket

hall. The light was stronger here from a concentration of oil lamps. A couple of armed men sat on a battered chaise longue against the wall while Lucius Brown sat upright, tied with rope to a hard chair in the middle of the space. A tray of food and scattered cutlery lay at his feet.

Lucius watched the Fantom as he crossed the floor into the circle of lights. The Fantom doffed his hat and threw it at one of the ragged men who caught it clumsily. The Fantom peeled away the black face mask and took off his silvered glasses. His features were pale, his skin smooth and his eyes a bright sea-blue.

'I understand that one of my teams put paid to an example of your handiwork tonight,' the Fantom said.

Lucius stiffened visibly in the chair. He tugged at the ropes.

'Relax, Lucius, it wasn't what or who you think. It was just one of your ghost-effect machines, the projection of a spectral little girl, a cheap seance apparition. One of your own illusions I am told. They got a good haul from the rich Gawkers and suckers who all fell for it too.'

'You must be very proud of yourself,' Lucius replied in a measured voice.

'Surely it is you who should be proud,' the Fantom replied. 'Imagine making such a thing and seeing it work. It's just like magic really, but then you are something of a magician, aren't you? Well it apparently fooled them well enough until my men went in and burst their bubble.' The Fantom smiled a rare smile. His face was pleasant enough when he smiled, except perhaps for his very white wolfish teeth.

'You must be tired,' he said to Lucius. 'I see that they have offered to feed you and yet you have not eaten. Was it not to your taste? Sadly, I know so little about you. What do you normally eat? Do you have a favourite dish?'

'I was not hungry. A man in my position does not think of food. Where is my son?'

'Now that is quite a question, and an ironic one too given our circumstances. I have no idea where that boy is, but I wish I did, for I have every intention of meeting him. You and your son would have been here together if my minions had not bungled things so badly. I have so long wanted to meet you both. And of course there is just that one other.'

'What about Jack?'

The Fantom spread his hands and shrugged. 'Another crime statistic I am afraid. I examined him you know, after death. I took the opportunity and looked right inside him. Poor old Dr Jack, he was not long for this world in any case. He had a weak heart.'

Lucius looked at the vicious young man standing opposite him with his arms folded proudly across his chest. 'You will please leave my son alone,' he said, 'should you find him. He at least is innocent in all of this.'

'No one is an innocent, not to me. Look at all those hordes of people, who come crowding in here paying their pathetic shillings to Mr Buckland and co. They eat the cheap food. Smoke the cheap cigars. "Ooh let's watch a hanging", "Oh a terrible accident", "Oh look, George, the brutal arrest of a tiny child felon", "Ooh a real amputation and with such a dirty-looking authentic old rusty-toothed saw too." Then there are the other ones, aren't there? The ones who come here just to see my special work.' The Fantom's face was fixed on Lucius and his eyes seemed even brighter as he delivered his mounting outburst.

'Is that all you see here?' Lucius said quietly. 'No achievements, other than base criminality, squalor and profit?'

The Fantom changed tack, a different kind of light came into his eyes. 'She ran away from your old friend Dr Jack, her keeper, didn't she? He sent you a letter after she broke cover and took off out into the world, that brave, beautiful girl. She's out there now somewhere, you know trailing round with some travelling acrobats. All very authentic, I am sure, but hardly what she was meant for, wouldn't you say?'

'I personally couldn't say anything about what she was meant for. That was not my idea.'

'No, I doubt you would. I doubt you have much to say about either of us. It's quite something, you know, for me to actually have you here, sitting in front of me, powerless and tied with a real, authentic rope, to a real authentic chair. I wonder if you have ever feared this moment. If you have ever woken from your blameless sleep out there, wherever it is you live? Shelley Avenue, is it not? Have you lain in a cold sweat in Shelley Avenue, in quaint old Poet's Corner, remembering me and my face, and what I might be up to while you listen to the sound of the sweetly twittering mech birds or whatever they are in your clean and tidy garden, and have you feared this very moment?'

'No I haven't. You're not that important to me.'

'I wish I could believe that of you. I think I am *very* important. I am sure that they are all out there looking for me right now. Trailing me the best they can, which is not very well. On the Outside they would find me in an instant, but not in here. I think that they never want to find me at all. I am a major attraction in this benighted city of yours, am I not? If what was supposed to happen actually happened as it was meant to, I would be the biggest attraction in this place, and I am sure your Mr Buckland would just love it.'

A group of ragged men had gradually assembled at the back of the ticket hall. They watched the exchange between the Fantom and his mysterious prisoner for a minute or so, and then one of their number stepped forward into the brighter light. The Fantom turned and looked the man up and down.

'Are you standing so near me for a bet? Well, I am afraid you have lost, I'm busy.'

'No, sir, I've something to tell you.'

'It had better be worth the risk you're taking,' the Fantom replied, moving closer to the shivering man.

'I've found out where Jago's Pandemonium Show caravans are parked up.' His sudden smile showed his crooked yellow teeth.

→» CHAPTER 39 «←

Inspector Lestrade arrived at the lodging house and asked for Sgt Catchpole. The landlady showed him into the cosy drawing room where Catchpole was reading. He looked up.

'Good evening, Inspector,' Catchpole said. 'What brings you here at this hour?'

'Good evening, Sergeant Catchpole,' Lestrade said. 'Mr Buckland himself asked me to bring this over to you at once.' He handed over the envelope. 'It seems a local station picked up a particular felon, the very youth that you are looking for as part of your investigation. The youth was signed out on a corrupt surety bond, all the details and the address and so on are in there.'

'You bring this now at this hour?'

'Yes, I am sorry for the lateness. In this case I am simply the messenger,' said Lestrade.

'Does Buckland have police records delivered to him

regularly?' Catchpole said, puzzled.

'Buckland has a whole roster of tame policemen. Did you read the files?'

'Of course,' Catchpole said. 'Is there any more you want to tell me?'

'I wish I could take you into my confidence, but I report only to Abel Buckland. I cannot divulge more. You will eventually find out everything, I have no doubt. I will say only that I have been given permission at last to move against the ragged men. Now, if you'll excuse me, I have a cab waiting. Good night.'

'Good night, Inspector.'

After he had gone Catchpole opened the envelope. Inside was a bleak little arrest photograph of a frightened-looking youth with a shock of dark hair. An arrest record number was chalked on a slate around his neck: *19248.*

The arrest card's scant details were all filled in neat copperplate. Caleb Brown. It was him all right; the running boy. There was a release sheet giving an address of a Mr William Leighton at 31 Fournier Street, signed for by Japhet McCreddie of the same address.

⇥ CHAPTER 40 ⇤

The next morning Catchpole was out early. He walked through the crowds and made his way over to Fournier Street. He banged on the door of Number 31. A woman in an apron answered.

'Sergeant Catchpole of Scotland Yard,' Catchpole said with a smile. 'I have come to see Mr Leighton.'

There was no returning smile from Mrs Boulter. 'Just wait in here if you would, sir.'

Catchpole was shown into a lavishly furnished drawing room. Mr Leighton was plainly either a wealthy man who enjoyed all the tax privileges that residency allowed, or some sort of master thief. The table in the centre of the room was piled with guns and holsters and ammunition belts. He picked up one of the guns, an authentic service revolver. He was turning it in his hands when William Leighton swept into the room, his white shirt billowing.

'We are expecting trouble, officer. I suppose one of those damn fools from last night has reported our little robbery problem.'

Catchpole inclined his head, while Leighton stuck out his elegant hand to be shaken. 'William Leighton,' he said with a firm grip.

Catchpole decided to play along with the confusion. 'So, sir, about last night then?'

'I was giving a scientific demonstration when we were invaded and attacked, inside this very house, and robbed, all of us.'

'They seem to have left quite a lot behind, sir?' said Catchpole, indicating to the precious-looking contents of the room.

'They were in and out very quickly. They took the small stuff, cash, and jewellery, straight from the pockets and from round the necks of my guests. There was nothing I could do despite having arms in the house, and before you say anything about that they are all strictly under licence.'

'I don't doubt it, sir, but why didn't you raise the alarm yourself?' Catchpole asked.

'I would have reported it but I reasoned, what would be the point? I know who did this. I intend to protect myself and my future clients in my own way. I shall not be relying on the incompetence and corruption of your Scotland Yard, no offence.'

'None taken, sir,' said Catchpole with a friendly smile. 'Who was in the house at the time, sir? Apart from your guests that is?'

'My housekeeper, Mrs Boulter, who admitted you, my assistant, Mr McCreddie, and my houseboy, nobody else.'

'Could I speak to them?'

'Mr McCreddie and the houseboy are out at present. They will only confirm what I just told you.'

'Even so, I think I will come back later and speak to them.'

'That is your choice, sergeant. Look, all I can tell you is that there were three or four of them, the Fantom's stooges, the ragged men as they are known. They were armed and dangerous. One of them had a heavy revolver pointed between my eyes. I hardly saw the others. They robbed me and my guests and left quickly using a hansom cab.'

'Nothing else?' said Catchpole.

'There was the woman who left early,' said Leighton dismissively, 'a woman who got upset, a typical Gawker. She left my scientific meeting just before the raid. My houseboy showed her to the door, but that was all. I am a very busy man and I am in a hurry. I really can't add anything to what I have already said.'

'So do you think this guest, the woman who left early, was working for the ragged men?'

'I have no reason to suppose that. It is odd that the ragged men knew exactly when our meeting was to take place, admittedly. The meetings are very private and very discreetly arranged only for the best clients, but I have my own theory as to how they knew.'

'Do you want to add anything else?'

Leighton said nothing. He just shook his head, then

he rang a hand bell and the housekeeper appeared. 'This gentleman is leaving now, Mrs Boulter. Be so good as to show him out.'

'As you wish, sir,' she said, and so Catchpole took his leave and allowed himself to be shown out of the house.

———◆———

It had not been possible to see the boy Caleb yet. He had at least been mentioned indirectly. Catchpole decided he would watch the house and wait for the boy and any other developments. The ragged men had moved against Leighton, robbed him, and just last night. Catchpole was getting a sense of a bigger picture. Perhaps something was happening. Were any of these things linked to the boy and Brown?

After a while he saw the housekeeper leave carrying a provisions basket on the crook of her arm. A ragged man stopped her and they had a conversation which went on for a while. Eventually, he saw the ragged man put a package, something wrapped in sacking, in her shopping basket very discreetly. Then the ragged man moved off. Catchpole decided to follow him.

He walked fast and purposefully. He stuck mostly to the main streets, the ones most loaded with visitors and Gawkers. Yet he didn't bother any of them for money. He slipped between them, so fast that Catchpole had a job to keep up with him.

They were heading towards the river, south of the cathedral, when Catchpole turned a corner and the ragged man was suddenly gone, vanished. The street was empty. It was just a road with no cuts or alleys or other ways out. Catchpole walked slowly up and down the street looking at all the buildings and entrances carefully. One of them had the markings of an old twentieth-century Underground station exit sign still just visible on the stone work. These ghostly echoes of the old system had mostly been thoroughly removed, but sometimes traces remained. Had the beggar gone underground? Catchpole walked up to the entrance way which was all boarded over. The boards themselves were densely covered with a variety of posters, mostly advertising the 'Grand Demolition' only a few days away now. Catchpole didn't want to test the boards covering the entrance way, didn't want to draw attention to himself but he noted the possibility. He walked to the end of the street and then turned to go back and wait for Caleb.

❊ CHAPTER 41 ❊

FROM EVE'S JOURNAL

Bible J came round to see me after the performance this afternoon and several strange things happened. Linked things, and in a way inexplicable things. Firstly, he had someone with him. They were both dressed in what Bible J called the 'house uniform'. Long navy frock coats with metal buttons, waistcoats and white shirts. He was with Caleb, the boy he had found on the street.

Caleb put his hand out and I took it, and looked at his face properly for the first time. I shook suddenly, my arm jerked upwards, and when I let his hand go it was as if I had been stung. I looked at him intently.

'Have we ever met before?' I said.

'No, I've never seen you before today,' Caleb said. 'I'm sure . . .'

'Only I felt something very strange then,' I said. 'When I shook your hand, there was something odd, a connection between us. I feel those things sometimes. And your eyes are

like mine.'

Caleb shrugged awkwardly as if he was not sure what to say, but I wondered if he had felt something too. It looked to me as if he might have?

'Now stop that talk, you two, or you'll make me all jealous,' Bible J said. 'Much more of that spooky stuff and Mr William will put you into one of his scientific meetings.'

'I'm not sure I like the sound of those meetings of his,' I said.

'You wouldn't have liked it last night, would she Caleb?' Caleb shook his head.

'What happened,' I said, still wondering about Caleb. There was something.

'The house was raided by armed ragged men halfway through the meeting. They robbed everyone, took all the Gawkers' entrance money and jewellery.'

I felt suddenly protective of Bible J. I wanted to put my arms around him and hold him close, make him safe. My heart beat a little faster. The thought of guns pointing at Bible J made me cold suddenly, and it all seemed personal too. If they had attacked the home of Bible J, someone known to me, it seemed that they might just have been trying to get to me, even though there was such a small connection between Mr Leighton's house and myself. I was troubled by the thought and also by the presence of the boy Caleb, with his eyes that were so like mine.

Jago came over and Bible J introduced Caleb to him. Bible J told Jago all about the robbery.

'Mr Leighton's packing all the house up, putting every-thing into boxes. It's all going into a warehouse. He's not taking any chances. He thinks Caleb should lose himself somewhere else for a few days too.'

'I am intending to go out of Pastworld, for a day or two,' Jago said. 'I have been planning to go out of the city altogether to spend some quiet time in the big forest.'

My mind suddenly filled with orange and yellow leaves, and I smelled a particular burning smell, in memory. The forest. I remembered a forest . . . I wanted badly to go there.

Bible J said, 'You could take my friend Caleb here with you, Mr Jago. Mr Leighton wants him safe. I've got to help pack the house away.'

'Yes,' said Jago, 'I imagine there must be quite a lot to pack away. I've heard about your Mr Leighton and his collections. I don't know about taking your friend here. No offence but I don't know him. Can I trust him?'

'Thing is,' said Bible J, 'they've got a warrant out for him, a Wanted poster and everything. He's an innocent Gawker, see, but they think he shivved an old bloke. It was the ragged men that did it. They blamed him in front of witnesses that's all.'

I said, 'I think we can trust him, Jago. I just know we can.'

'You seem very sure, Eve,' Jago said.

'I am.'

So the boy Caleb and myself were to be taken out to the forest. Bible J was anxious for me. He looked once at Caleb and at me standing together and I saw a troubled concern cross his usual happy face, a look I had never seen on him before. In that moment I felt something for him, something so strong that I wanted to throw myself in his arms and kiss him.

⇥ CHAPTER 42 ⇤

They travelled out through no-man's-land. They passed whole suburban streets of abandoned houses. Their windows were all blocked off with special grey construction boards pierced with ventilation holes. Weeds and buddleia grew in profusion from the cracked roofs and chimneys. This, Jago said, was the dead zone, the area between the edges of Pastworld itself and the forest buffer areas. The dismal streets stretched all along the northern route. They waited until it was dark and then they set off towards an old construction site entry barrier which was covered over in faded signs and notices that read *NO ENTRY*, and *BUCKLAND CONTSTRUC-TION ONLY*. Jago got down and raised the barrier using a hand winch. The barrier itself was camouflaged with a carefully arranged tangle of briars and weeds. After driving the wagon through, Jago got down again and winched the barrier closed, tucking the weeds and thorns carefully back into place.

'This,' Jago said, 'is the secret route out. No surveillance, but we can't be too careful.' They travelled for a while along a bleak road until they came to a very different kind of barrier. A solid wall of once sleek silver metal. It rose up at least a hundred feet into the air. As they neared it, Jago became nervous. 'This is the dangerous place. We never know if they will discover that this area of the perimeter is in need of maintenance, or that the security camera is broken.' He pointed at a small silver box mounted on a support pole. 'Smile,' he said, 'we might be on camera. Look up when we pass the barrier and you'll see the edge of the skydome.' It was true, a huge wall of darkened glass stretched up above the barrier. It went hundreds of feet up into the air and it was impossible to see where it stopped. The surface just reflected the sky and so as it went higher it became less visible until it faded out altogether.

Jago drove the wagon down a slope and into a long maintenance tunnel. The tunnel was lit with a series of overhead strip lights that gave off a dim, bluish glow. Caleb noticed that Eve looked up at the lights above them in astonishment, her mouth open.

'What is it, Eve?' he said, wondering if he was missing something obvious about the roof of the tunnel.

'Those lights,' she said.

'Those, you mean?' Caleb said, pointing up. 'They look like low-level halogen security lights.'

'Oh yes,' said Eve, 'they are *so* beautiful, aren't they?'

'Before you answer, young Caleb,' Jago whispered, 'it

is worth bearing in mind that Eve has never been beyond the barriers of Pastworld in her life. Pastworld is all she knows, and has ever known.' He raised his voice again. 'There's a lot more to see, Eve, believe me. Wait until you see the forest.'

<hr />

Eve and Jago slept in their usual places in the wagon. Caleb tried to sleep in the seat tucked under a velvet drape. He thought about Eve. She was a strange girl, properly old-fashioned, polite, and as far as he could see, really sweet-natured. He did feel something when he first met her. Her eyes really were like his, and he was struck by her beauty too. She reminded him of one of those perfect Victorian porcelain dolls that you might see in a museum or an antique shop.

Jago had said it was best to wait out the night rain and leave it until it was almost first light to negotiate the main road. With no traffic, there would be less chance of being seen. Caleb drifted off finally, listening to the rain, just beyond the tunnel exit, a sound he hadn't heard for a while.

Jago was up just before dawn. He brewed some tea. There was a milky light now at the end of the tunnel. He said, 'I've just realised something, Eve. This will be the first natural outdoor sunrise you have ever seen in your life.'

Eve stood up suddenly in her fine white dress, looking not so different from how she did when walking on the rope in the circus.

'You're right,' she said, 'I want to see it. Come on,' and she set off running down the tunnel.

'See if you can catch her?' Jago said to Caleb.

'She's mad,' said Caleb.

Jago answered, 'I know.'

Caleb trotted after her down the dank service tunnel. He found her eventually standing in the middle of what was once a motorway. Four lanes wide and all empty. The smooth tarmac was still wet, glistening from the over-night rain. The sky was lightening above them. Eve looked up and saw a high blue colour, and a sprinkling of white clouds. A breeze ruffled her hair.

'No cobbles, Caleb,' she said, her face still raised upwards. 'Why?

'The roads outside are smooth. The only place that still has cobbled roads is Pastworld.'

They stood together, both looking up into the sky, which was growing lighter every second.

'It's beautiful,' Eve said.

Caleb said, 'Look over there.' He turned her to face east as the breeze passed over them again, and then she saw it. Across the flat, scrubby plain a pinkness in the sky, and bursting up through from below the pink a bright gold, a fire which caught on the undersides of the clouds and gilded them.

'Sunrise,' Caleb said.

Eve spread her arms wide and pulled herself from Caleb and twirled around on the spot in a perfect circle, her dress lifting above her ankles.

'My first real sunrise,' Eve said, smiling.

'That's my girl,' said Jago, walking Pelaw and the wagon out from the tunnel. 'Look at her, look how she moves. She's the best girl there is.'

* * *

After a half hour or so of trotting they turned off the straight, wet, empty road and travelled down a rutted and earthy side road towards a green horizon. Once they had passed under the branches of the first trees everything closed in around them. Jago clicked the horse to a halt and they just sat under the canopy of branches.

'Oh it smells so wonderful and it looks so wonderful, it is so wonderful and I think I shall burst,' Eve said.

* * *

Eve jumped down off the wagon, pulling Caleb with her, and they ran right across the wet grass into the denser part of the wood under the canopy of huge interlocked branches. The wind lifted her hair. She could hear the rustling of millions of leaves. Leaves blew around her as she ran. They ran on far under the trees until they lost sight of Jago and the wagon. Then they stood laughing together, catching their breath.

Jago sprinted up and, infected by their high spirits, he leaped up into a tree and sat on a branch and showered orange leaves down on them. Pelaw arrived with the wagon and stopped a little way away. Jago jumped down and unhitched the horse from the shafts and was soon unpacking things from the caravan. Eve went to help but Caleb stayed where he was.

Jago said to her, 'It's funny you should have run all the way to exactly this spot in the forest. It's where I always end up. That's why Pelaw walked the wagon here on her own. The trees are tall and numerous enough to make a good practice place and there's fresh water just over there too. It's like we're in another city, our own private city of trees.' Jago looked over at Caleb. 'You seem to be getting on with this lost boy, this Caleb?'

'I do, yes,' Eve said. 'It's odd because it feels like I've known him for a long time.'

The air was sweeter out in the forest. They were surrounded by the benign presence of the huge trees themselves. Great beings that stretched their arms upwards to the natural sky.

—————◆—————

They sat by the wagon, with a good fire going. They ate saffron rice and fish and fruit and even some wine taken from Mr Leighton's cellar that Jago had chilled in the stream, and afterwards they watched the dusk as it gradually got darker, a real dusk. Owls called in the twilight and other birds sang too.

When darkness finally came Jago took a lantern and went and washed in the stream. Caleb and Eve sat together and smelled the leaves and the chilled night air and looked up at the sky. 'Real stars,' Eve said, 'not something projected on to a dome but real worlds hundreds of light years away from us.'

⊰ CHAPTER 43 ⊱

FROM EVE'S JOURNAL

Recently I've had moments of feeling strange, as if my mind would suddenly flip and slip a gear and it frightened me. I had once told Jago that odd images came to me unbidden. I had told no one else of this before. I am sure that whatever happened to me before I was in that attic room with Jack, the something, the mystery that had caused my memory loss, is coming back now to haunt me.

The first night out in the forest I went to sleep in the wagon, while Jago and Caleb slept outside under a lean-to tent. I lay for a long time listening to the noises of the night and thinking about Bible J and Caleb. I had felt shy with Caleb but also comfortable. Now we were apart, surrounded by the night noises of the forest and by the stars and the wide sky.

There was a heady perfume in the air, the smell of leaf mould and woodsmoke from the dwindling fire. The wagon moved, as if someone had stepped on the little iron foot rest by the canvas opening. I sat up in bed. A breeze stirred the cloth and lifted my hair. It was Caleb. He stood in front of me all wrapped up in one of the velvet cloths. He was shivering. I could see gooseflesh across his pale shoulders and his upper arms. I reached out to him.

'Are you all right, Caleb?'

'I'm sorry,' he said. 'I just had to come and see you.'

His face was near mine and I could see him trembling.

'I understand, Caleb. Don't be sorry.'

'I can hear your heartbeat.'

'I can hear yours,' I said.

I reached out and took his hands in mine and raised them up and then I pressed them to my throat so that his hands were wrapped tightly around my neck. He kept still, his hands warmed my skin. I closed my eyes and tilted my head back and I waited. So did he.

'Tighter,' I said quietly.

He relaxed his grip then, and took his hands away.

'I don't understand,' he said. 'Doesn't that hurt you?'

'I don't understand either,' I said. 'I need you to hold me there tight. It's almost as if . . .'

'As if you want to be hurt? I don't want to hurt you, Eve,' Caleb said.

He looked into my eyes.

'You have oddly bright eyes, Eve,' he said. 'People often comment on my eyes being so bright.'

'It's true your eyes are like mine,' I said, 'and they crinkle at the edges when you smile, which isn't often.'

'I don't have much to smile about,' he said.

I reached my hand up and stroked the soft skin at the

side of his eyes and then for some reason I moved his hands over to cover my mouth and suddenly I called out, 'No,' and pushed him away from me. Something very odd was happening, and I felt impelled to make it happen, whatever it was.

He moved back from me, shocked. I had shocked myself. He had a frown across his face; his blue eyes were no longer smiling.

He pulled a velvet cushion into the centre of the space. He sat down on the cushion.

'Sit with me here, Eve. I won't hurt you. Did you think I wanted to hurt you? Do you want to hurt me?'

'No,' I said. 'I don't think you want to hurt me. I don't know why I did that, Caleb. I don't know why.'

I flung myself down on to the cushion beside him, down near to the ground. I could smell the intense scent of the earth with the grass and the leaves. I lay on my back and looked up at Caleb and his narrow chest and his skin, blue-white in the near darkness.

'There's a painted moon behind your head. You look like the man in the moon from one of Jack's nursery books,' I said. He lay down beside me and I cradled his head in both hands, and I looked into his eyes and said, 'In a strange way I feel for you, you know, but it is so different from the way I feel about Bible J. I don't want to kiss you or anything.'

'Yes, I do know,' he said, 'because I feel the same way about you.'

Caleb looked down at me right into my eyes and then I put his hands around my throat again. I felt his thumbs *pressing down. 'Like that,' I whispered.*

I closed my eyes and his hands rested there. He gradually relaxed his grip on my throat and then he lay his head on my breast and listened to my heartbeat. He pulled the warm velvet cloth about the two of us and I nestled against his shoulder and we lay still together in our strange new friendship in the warm darkness under the trees. Nothing else happened between us. As I drifted comfortably in his arms I thought of Bible J and his easy laugh and his smiling eyes. I remembered something else suddenly and very clearly. Another forest, and a bonfire, the smell of leaf mould, and rockets and fireworks bursting above the tree canopy, and then a line of people watching me jump over the sparks and remnants of a dwindling bonfire and I saw Jack there standing and clapping his hands and laughing, in celebration, but of what?

We spent two more days and nights in the forest. Caleb did not visit me again but stayed in the tent with Jago at night. We were completely relaxed with one another. I spent most of our last morning lazing, dreaming. I sat, or rather lolled, oh so dreamily, high up in a great oak tree. No one bothered me even when a storm came. There were dark thunderheads over the forest.

'A rare thing,' Jago said, 'in an age where the rainfall is carefully managed.'

I stayed up in the tree hidden among the dense leaves. I wanted to feel the storm, feel real, wild nature.

I was both thrilled and terrified as the thunder crashed around the forest. 'Oh marvellous tree, keep me safe,' I said in my mind, and my hand went at once to my throat where I had put Caleb's hands. I watched the real storm. Huge bolts of lightning sizzled in the wet, somewhere far over the trees. Below, seemingly undisturbed, Jago carried on working with his ropes. The rain fell in solid torrents, spilled across the leaves and scattered them. I put my face out from my deep shelter and let the rain fall on my skin and listened to it as it rattled on the leaves all around me.

I waited, high among the leaves, while the rain diminished. It was the tail end of the storm, and the remnants of the once boiling sky around me flew through the leaf spaces as wind on my face. The sound of the wind tearing through the yellow and orange leaves gave me intense pleasure. Occasionally, one or two big drops of rain fell through the leaves and splashed on to my neck, made me shiver.

If I concentrated hard enough, I found I could slow the drops of rain down just as they hit the leaves. I could watch them fall in a slower motion, I could study the light refracting through each one. There were little rainbows on the curve of the water. This was a new marvel. I decided at once to lock it away, deep inside myself; away even from Bible J, Caleb and Jago. I have surrounded the idea of it with a dense black box in my mind. I know instinctively that I should somehow shield it, that it shows once again that I am not the same as others.

I remembered something about that first visit to a forest. When the trails of smoke drifted up from the bonfire on the ground, and I breathed in the smell of the wood smoke and the wet forest floor, I saw cadets in red all lined up to watch me jump the flames of the bonfire. Perhaps that was why I enjoyed the smell of Jago's woodsmoke. Had that smell caused this memory to come bubbling up, and when would all this have been? It seemed somehow very distant but it couldn't have been.

I decided it was time to find Caleb and Jago.

I slid round the wet trunk and walked along the rope. The ropes linked all the smaller, younger trees, so that this, the old oak, was at the centre of a tree city that seemed as dense and populated in its way as that other city.

I climbed down the ladders, and when I hit the wet grass I ran with my arms wide, my long skirt billowed, and my feet kicked up little sprays of clean rain water.

I ran straight into the arms of Jago, lovely kind Jago. He swung me up and round and laughed at my wet hair and face. Now it seemed was the time to return. Jago needed to get back. There was to be a celebration of Pastworld's tenth birthday. Fireworks, a demolition, and Jago saw the chance to earn a lot of money in a few hours. It was too good to miss.

'I had a memory return to me,' I said. 'I was here in a forest just like this once before, perhaps in my lost childhood, the leaves were yellow and orange. Vivid like these, and there was a bonfire and I jumped the flames and there was a celebration, a firework display.' Suddenly I spun round and spread my arms wide. 'You shouldn't have hidden away from the storm. It was a blessing from the sky. We should have lifted our faces up to the sky and let the rain fall joyfully upon us. We should have savoured it, drank it in while we could. And just listen to that music, the last of the storm now rolling away.'

Jago went to fetch Pelaw and Caleb said, 'Eve, about the other night, I'm sorry. I shouldn't have let those odd things happen. I don't understand, I don't want to hurt you, Eve, but you know that.'

'I know. There's nothing to say sorry for,' I said.

'You forgive me then,' he said with the first big smile I had ever seen on his face.

'There's nothing to forgive you for, Caleb Brown.'

'Look at your wet clothes. You're mad,' said Caleb, laughing.

'Yes,' I said, 'I am mad, madly in love with all of this life all around us.'

We returned to the city by the same route and parked up with the rest of the circus family. Caleb went back to Mr Leighton's house. Dear Bible J came to see me. He stayed with me and now sleeps innocently beside me, with Jago in the back among the backcloths. I've been lying awake for a while, writing slowly across the paper. I was enjoying making the letters flow into words. My mind turns to the outside space under the trees and being there with Caleb and Jago. I think I would go there again with Bible J, although I can't see him sitting among all the trees somehow. It was so pure and strange out there and so beautiful, so unlike the city.

⊸⊱ CHAPTER 44 ⊰⊷

Catchpole spent a fruitless few days waiting for news, impatient for Hudson's reply, then finally in the early morning post, a brown foolscap envelope arrived from the Comms Centre. A hastily written note was attached to the file with a clip.

Hey Charlie,

Here it is, the very file you wanted. Appendix A. Sorry for the delay, but I had to steal it. There was no way that the records office at Buckland was going to let it out of their sight. However, with a little distraction and a swift substitution I copied it for you. You seemed that hell bent on it. What you do with it is up to you.

I didn't even glance at it. I would rather not know what's in it. They were mighty protective of it and all I will say is if they come looking, believe me, I will be in maximum denial mode.

Your old friend,

Hudson

PS Maybe you should burn it after you read it and go into denial mode too.

Catchpole sat at the desk in his rooms and poured himself a little whisky in a heavy glass, an old single malt – he had a feeling he was going to need it – and then he opened the file.

Appendix A File 2

STRICTLY CONFIDENTIAL /CLASSIFIED

NOT TO BE REMOVED

ATTN. ONLY: A. Buckland / C.I. Lestrade / L. Brown / J. Mulhearn /

PROMETHEUS PROJECT

Minutes of a meeting of Prometheus Project management held on XX/XX/XXXX

Present all named above

Mr A. Buckland in the chair

Logged from Tape 1 by secretariat / D.I. Prinsep.

Buckland: I am sorry we had to have such a private, distant and low key celebration but the reasons should be obvious looking at what we have made. I trust we are all recovered from the champagne. The subjects certainly lived up to expectations in themselves. I was astonished. Such beauty and skills from Number 2, from our Eve, such perfectly judged jumps and leaps and such dexterity and fearlessness. Did you expect that too? That level of achievement, was that built in?

Murmured replies, inaudible mutters.

Remarkable, not a spark on the dress at all. As for our Gentleman, well he looked the part all right and I think he would have done everything we have expected of him there and then if he were allowed to. If left to his own devices, quite a worry that one if he got loose eh?

Mulhearn: That's the problem Abel, both Brown and myself are very uneasy indeed about the Gentleman, Adam, Number 1. We have nurtured both of these, what — 'beings' shall we call them? People? And now feel we cannot allow the proposed scheme to go ahead as planned and budgeted for in the original proposal and Corporation briefing. Not at all.

Brown: I agree with Dr Mulhearn. It cannot be right now under any circumstances. Not now that we have known these creatures, these beings, and particularly Eve, our charming girl. We cannot continue with this under any circumstances. We cannot now see her hurt.

Buckland: Suddenly you have developed moral scruples? It is a shame you did not express the same feelings while you were spending my money like water on this thing. Think for a moment. You have achieved so much in the past five years, and I have spent so much to enable it. You have both made an extraordinairy breakthrough in biological science and now you are prepared to let it all founder through your own frankly misguided sentimentality.

Mulhearn: We hear nothing from our tame policeman so far, unlike him to be shy of commenting on such matters?

Lestrade: Numbers 1 and 2 are, strictly speaking, partly or is it wholly, artificial? If so, they are not covered by the normal criminal laws. The Gentleman is powerful and she is programmed to respond especially to him and to allow the events which he has been designed for to take place. Your plan, if I am right, is to revive the victim each time, to repeat the event?

Buckland: Yes precisely. Wipe clean and restart each and every time.

Lestrade: The laws that apply here, don't forget, are the old laws. There is no contingency or precedent for beings such as these . . . hybrids, clones, are they?

Mulhearn: Leave the description to us.

Lestrade: I am shy of calling them anything. After all I have only seen them the once at your secret celebration. If I were to witness as a paying customer what you have planned I would indeed be shocked. However, my belief is that once the word gets out that such a thing is available as part of a Pastworld visit, then you will make your research and development fortune back, and in my opinion all legally.

Buckland: You see, gentlemen, this is the secret desire, the dream that many people harbour. Especially about this

time and this place and those crimes.
The scenario has already been prepared,
you have produced your miracle, albeit a
secret one, leave them to us now. Let us
take care of them.

CONFUSED VOICES / SHOUTING.

Disc 1 RECORDING TRANSCRIPTION ENDS.
16:35 XX/XX/XXXX

Catchpole looked up from the pages of the transcript. He was troubled, shocked. It took him a little while to absorb what he thought he had just read. Hybrid people made as characters to enact a grisly tableau. Amusing automata were everywhere in Pastworld. Cheerful porters, stately butlers and flocks of picturesque pigeons were one thing; this was something else, clearly something of another order, and a revelation of the terrible greed and cynicism of a man like Buckland, a man Catchpole had always admired for his vision, and his genius in re-establishing the great city of the past. He had finally read between the lines, understood all the hints that Lestrade had dropped and it was suddenly clear. Lestrade had said only that the Fantom was 'supernatural'. No wonder! The 'Gentleman' was a sick construct: a hybrid designed at his inception to kill and eviscerate. Dr Mulhearn, the blind man, had been a bio-engineer working with Lucius Brown on an attraction for Pastworld codenamed Prometheus. At the same point they'd realised they could no longer support it. They had drawn a line in the sand, a line they would not cross. They had grown attached to one of their creations – the girl, Eve, known as Number 2. Number 1 was obviously the Gentleman now known as the Fantom. Who had given him that name, he wondered. Had he chosen it himself? He was designed to play the Ripper, the notorious East District murderer, and Eve was created to be his perpetual victim. It seemed so far-fetched, such sick ridiculous nonsense, and yet? A fire had destroyed the Prometheus project building, presumably along with all the research. Jack was believed killed and the creations had vanished, supposedly burned in the fire and dead like him. Except they weren't, any of them. Jack injured, in his own fire perhaps, took off into Pastworld with Eve to nurture and protect her. The Gentleman, built as he was, would have been too violent, too difficult for Jack to manage. He must have cut loose and become the Fantom. The Fantom who still searched for his intended, his perfect victim. And it seemed he had looked for his makers too, Brown and Mulhearn. He had dealt with poor Dr Mulhearn, and he had got his hands on his other maker now. Above all he was after this poor girl Eve, wherever she might be. She was in serious danger.

Catchpole did not burn the file as Hudson suggested. He tucked the sheets of typed paper back into the envelope and sealed it with the toggles. He went up to his room, took down his case from the top of the wardrobe and took out his police issue revolver. He checked the chambers and added the ammunition belt which strapped crossways under his cape. He replaced the case and went back down to the sitting room. The clock on the mantel read 8.15 p.m., nearly time for the big public demolition party. He could already hear the crowds. He turned down the oil lamp and the gaslight, so that the room was in half-light. It was time to pay a visit to Fournier Street.

Just as he was about to leave his lodgings there was a loud knocking at the front door.

→ CHAPTER 45 ←

Eve had been dozing, half asleep, half dreaming, but now she was awake suddenly, fearful and alert; she heard rough, low voices outside the wagon.

'Are they in there?'

'Far as I know.'

She looked out from under the edge of the canvas. Three ragged men stood outside the wagon. She burrowed herself under a pile of backcloths. It seemed that those who would do her harm had finally found her. Jago had been insistent that if such a thing ever happened she should save herself first. She wormed her way to the escape hole in the wagon board, lifted the trap quietly and dropped out under the wagon just as Jago had made her promise and practice over and over. She rolled silently, quickly, into the dense bushes. Then she watched from a distance.

One of the ragged men hefted a short length of lead

pipe in his hand. He read the words out loud from the painted canvas. 'Jago's Pandemonium Show. I'll give 'im pandemonium.'

The other ragged men, one skinny and one with broad shoulders, laughed at that.

'Kill the light,' the man with the lead pipe said.

The skinny man behind turned down the wick of his lamp so that its green glow faded out, leaving just dense, fog-smeared, Pastworld night.

Eve lay paralysed with fear, silent under the press of twigs and leaves. A baby started to cry in one of the other wagons.

The ragged man tapped out a little tattoo on the flimsy wagon step. After a moment Eve heard Jago stir and open the front flap just a crack. When he saw who was there, he tried to close it again. The ragged men were too quick for him. They grabbed his arms and pulled him out, then held him from behind with his mouth covered. Eve put her hand over her own mouth to stop herself crying out and remembered the feeling of Caleb's hands around her throat. She could see the fear on Jago's face as clear as day.

'Where is she?' the ragged man demanded.

Jago shook his head.

'Call her out, now.' He nodded to one of the other men to let go of Jago's mouth. The beggar trailed his dirty fingers across Jago's lips as he freed his mouth, and all poor Jago managed to splutter was, 'She's not here,' in a hoarse whisper.

The wagon flap swung open silently all on its own,

and Bible J stood bleary-eyed, framed by the entrance.

Eve's hand fell from her mouth in fear. 'Don't hurt him,' she whispered to the leaves.

The ragged man turned to Bible J. 'Where is she?' he asked quietly, breathing heavily now, a slick of sweat visible across his forehead. 'Where?' he smacked the heavy pipe against the wagon frame.

'Where's who?' said Bible J, quietly but firmly. Eve suppressed the urge to leap up out of the hedgerow and give herself up.

'You know full well who I mean. Your darkie friend here thinks he's being very brave and clever, trying to protect her, but he's not, he's being very stupid.'

Bible J stared back at him directly, his eyes unblinking. Eve's mind was working fast. She tried to take in how many had come, what chance they might stand if they fought against them. Two were holding Jago, and the other stood close to Bible J, his dark bulk looming like a shadow, like a stain.

She could see Jago's eyes wide, reflecting the low light, the whites silvery in the gloom.

The man turned from Bible J back to Jago. Then he did something strange; he kissed Jago very gently on the forehead and smiled at him. He looked into Jago's eyes as if savouring the moment, and then he struck Jago suddenly very hard on the side of the head with the heavy lead pipe. Jago slumped back suddenly, as boneless as a rag doll, his head twisted over to one side. That was enough. Eve pushed her way out of the layers of leaves and dirt where she had burrowed herself, and she stood up and stepped out right in front of them.

The ragged man, momentarily shocked, looked at her and then laughed quickly. It was a feral barking sound, and then covered his mouth with his hand and watched her walk forward.

She stood before them all in her long nightdress. Her hair had tumbled down around her shoulders. The beggar took a step forward and jumped up on to the wagon board, level with Bible J. He leaned forward and suddenly struck Bible J hard across the head with the lead pipe, and she watched Bible J fall down next to Jago. She managed to scream out a strangulated, 'No!'

The ragged man looked pleased at the outcome, at the release of fear and pain that he had caused. He looked at her and shook his head and then said, 'Used to run with Japhet in the old days. He's gone soft.'

One of the other ragged men tore the canvas flap all the way open and the man with the lead pipe helped push the slumped bodies of Jago and Bible J in through the open gap. He let them fall like two old sacks back into the wagon. He threw the pipe down hard and it hit the solid turf with a dull thud. He wiped his hands as if he had just disposed of something particularly filthy. Then he turned to Eve. 'Someone wants to meet you very badly, miss,' he said. 'He's been waiting a very long time and now he requests the pleasure of your company.' He laughed his horrible barking laugh again.

He pulled her away roughly by the arm but then the broad one stayed his hand and said, 'Remember what he told us, we are to go very gently with her, now.' The ragged man let go of her arm and bowed in front of her and said, 'If you would be so kind,' and ushered her forward. They walked past the wagon where the baby still cried. He stopped them for a moment as if to enjoy the baby's distress and then they took her right to the edge of the park. They went out through the tall iron gates which stood open. Eve was hunched and shivering in her night-dress. No one among the passing Gawkers took any notice of them. She was put into a dark, closed carriage. She could think only of the slumped figures of Bible J and of poor Jago lying together in pain back in the darkness of the wagon.

———•◆•———

When Bible J came to later, his head ached when he sat up and he felt groggy, as if he had been drinking bathtub gin and spike all night. Bright, stabbing beams of light pierced his eyes when he moved his head. He got up and staggered forward and then sat down again on Jago's bed. Jago lay on the floor. At first Bible J thought that they had killed him. There was blood on the sheet which had draped across his head where he had been thrown. Bible J put his head down close to Jago's chest. He could feel him breathing. He took stock of the caravan. Some of Jago's trinkets and holy figures had fallen from the little altar next to the bed when they had both been thrown back into the wagon, otherwise nothing seemed to have been taken . . .

Eve!

He went to Eve's little bed and steadied himself, looking down at the tangle of sheets. He saw the book she had been writing in lay open by the pillow. He picked it up and saw his own name written there in her neat hand. He took the book and went out and sat down on the steps of the wagon. He breathed in the cool air. Gradually his head cleared. He saw the length of lead pipe lying on the grass. If they were to get Eve back, they would need better weapons than that. He stumbled down the steps with Eve's book in his hand. He had to find help for Jago. He walked unsteadily across the wet cobbled path to the other caravans. Someone from the family would surely be around; if not then he would find help on his own. Then he would go to Fournier Street and rally Caleb and Mr Leighton, the time had surely come.

Most of the wagons were dark but a light burned in the window of the bearded lady's caravan. Bible J knocked on the door and then stumbled in across the doorway as she opened it.

Rose, the bearded lady had been talking to a friend over a late night pot of tea. The friend was a woman in a grey coat with a live spotted cat wrapped around her shoulders like a tippet. The cat stirred on the woman's shoulder, settled its head on its paws and looked at him.

'I know you, don't I, you're Mr Leighton's boy, his apprentice, you're Eve's young man. My, you gave us a fright. You all right? 'Cause you don't look too good.' She looked him up and down and took in the blood stains on his collar. 'You look that pale.'

'Jago's been hurt,' he said. 'They've taken Eve away

and Jago needs help, a doctor.'

'Where is poor Jago?' she asked.

'In his wagon. They knocked us both unconscious and they took Eve.'

'That poor girl,' the cat woman said. 'What is it with her? First her poor old Jack goes and gets himself murdered and now they've taken her away too?'

'Murdered?' said Bible J. 'Jack, who was Jack?'

'Eve's pa of course, least I think he was. Didn't she tell you about him? He was looking for her. I saw his body too, identified him in the morgue. The copper reckoned the Fantom got him.'

Rose fetched a clean towel and a jug full of hot water from the little range at the back of the caravan.

'Come on, you two, let's go and help poor Jago,' she said quietly.

Once outside, the cat strained on its leash, pulling them across the cobbled path, excited by the night smells. 'All right Kitty that's where we're going anyway,' the cat lady said.

The fog rolled in around them. Even with the gas lamps on the path it would soon be so dense that visibility would be almost nil. Bible J began to step backwards away from Bearded Rose and the lady with the cat.

'Where are you going?' Rose said kindly. 'Come on with us, you need looking after too.'

'I must go,' Bible J said. 'I must find her, where they took Eve.'

'But how? Where will you go? You don't know where they took her.'

'I don't know, but I'll look for her and with Caleb and Mr Leighton's help. I'll find her.' He ran further up the path towards the gates.

'Wait,' the cat lady called, 'take this.' She rummaged in her coat pocket while the cat tugged on the lead. She pulled out the calling card that Catchpole had given her.

'He knows something, this man. He's a detective, and he seemed all right. He was worried for Eve too.' She pressed the card into Bible J's hand. He trotted backwards away from her.

'Thanks for this, look after Jago,' he called out and then turned and ran and was soon lost in the fog.

→ CHAPTER 46 ←

The carriage drew up in Moorgate near the old Underground station entrance. The ragged men bundled Eve out of the carriage and after a deft movement they were through the hoarding and into the doorway and the stairwell that led into the old ticket hall. Eve looked around her. The place was dingy, its tiled walls covered with old advertising posters. Eve struggled in the arms of her captors.

'Gently now,' the ragged man said. 'Almost there, he's been waiting such a long time to meet you, just a moment or two more.'

'No, indeed. No more waiting for I am here *now*,' said a voice from the darkness above them. 'I am here, my Eve.' A figure approached them down the staircase. He seemed surprised by what he saw, for he stopped in his tracks and inclined his head. 'I had not realised that you would be so very beautiful. I had not remembered you well enough and my memories, such as they are, have not done you justice. Do you remember me, Eve?' He stood still before her for a moment while a group of ragged men surged forward behind him to try to get a glimpse of this fabled girl.

Eve looked at the young man. He was dressed in black evening clothes and had a charming smile. He also had bright eyes very like her own. In her state of shock she had no clear memory of this young man, but there was something, some attraction welling up from that pocket of hidden memory, a strange sense of liking, desire even.

'But where are my manners? You've heard me speak of young Eve.' The Fantom turned her by the shoulders to face all the ragged men ranged around the tiled walls. He kissed Eve tenderly on both cheeks and then tilted her head up by the chin.

'Ah, my Eve, it really is you.' The Fantom was trembling, a tiny betrayal of weakness. None of the ragged men had ever seen him tremble before. 'I would have known you anywhere, my angel, even though you've grown more beautiful than even I could have imagined.' He smiled.

The young man had a handsome, chiselled, pale face with those smiling sharp sea-blue eyes, like Caleb's. 'Oh my but you have grown,' the Fantom said.

Then he knelt down in front of her and looked up at her. Eve could not help but smile her mysterious smile. She felt entranced, enchanted. The man reached up and touched the tiny silver earring on the lobe of Eve's right ear, and then he smoothed her eyebrows with the tip of his finger. 'I looked at you when you were new. They showed you to me once. I am called Adam.'

'Of course, Adam,' she said again and the number one flashed across her thoughts. 'I do remember something,' said Eve. 'You wore white – no not white, it was more of a calico colour – and I called you something.'

'You did, that's quite right. You called me number one,' said the Fantom.

'Later we were in the trees together, it was night-time,' said Eve, 'and there was a bonfire party with fireworks and Jack was there.'

'Dr Jack Mulhearn, yes, poor old Jack, he was there and drinking champagne and so was Lucius Brown and they were all patting each other on the back because of us, my Eve.'

There was a sudden faint rumble, a distant noise from the tunnel below.

The Fantom ignored the noise. He was still mesmerised, looking into her eyes when Eve suddenly took his hand and lifted it up to her throat. There was silence among the ragged men who had heard the distant noises but weren't sure what to do as the strange reunion tableau unfolded before them.

The Fantom stayed still, his hand around Eve's throat. He looked into her bright eyes, so like his own.

He spoke quietly to his ragged men. 'It appears from those noises off, that someone, Lestrade possibly, has found us. The day has come. It seems almost meant to be. You can hear it as well as I can. You know what to do now, for we have long trained for and discussed this

possibility. I want you all to go now, all of you and deal
with them. Leave us – we will stay here for we have things
to do, and important people to meet.'

———————◆——————

The ragged men went in a crowd to the arms store which
was in a long corridor behind the ticket hall. They came
out minutes later bristling with weapons, rifles, pistols,
grenades and cartridge belts. The Fantom stood just
where they had left him, with the strange girl shivering in
her white nightdress as she stood patiently with the
Fantom's hands round her throat. The two were looking
into each other's eyes in a kind of daze.

The ragtag army of men clattered off down the steps
of the deep escalator. They headed down the platform
and then on to the tracks and up the tunnel itself towards
the source of the noise.

———————◆——————

'I am so sorry to have kept you waiting like this,' the
Fantom said quietly. 'You're shivering you must be cold. I
have some warmer clothes, clothes that were made
expressly for you. Come with me.' He lowered his hands
gently from around her throat and then he took her by the
hand, and together they went up a short staircase to a
long corridor. The entrance was closed off with
retractable iron grilles which the Fantom unlocked and
then opened wide. The tunnel had a high domed ceiling,

and instead of being lit by rows of oil lamps like the rest of the space it had a sequence of cut crystal chandeliers lit by bright electric candles which the Fantom switched on. The chandeliers stretched down the corridor in a long line and the prisms showered the curved walls with little reflections and slivers and rainbows of light.

'Like raindrops,' Eve said suddenly.

'Inauthentic,' the Fantom said, 'but so pretty.'

A dress rail and a floor-length cheval glass stood in the middle of the bright tunnel.

'As this is a special occasion, our anniversary and the birthday of this whole place, I think evening wear, don't you?' They walked together the length of the rail and the Fantom stopped by a black velvet dress with long sleeves and a scoop neck.

'This will do very nicely.' He took it from the rail and held it out to her.

He reached up and unbuttoned her mud-stained nightdress at the collar. She pulled his hand up to her throat again. He gently removed it.

'No,' he said, 'we're not ready, not just yet.'

The nightdress fell to the tiled floor. The Fantom stood back and appraised her as if she was a mannequin as she stood in her pale spectral nakedness. She stared back at him, strangely unafraid despite her obvious vulnerability. He handed her some underclothes from the rail, all white with broderie anglaise details and little velvet ribbons.

'They made all of this for you, Eve, just for you.'

She put the underwear on unselfconsciously and then

pulled the dress roughly over her head. The Fantom hooked the long line of fasteners together at the back of the bodice.

'There,' he said, 'perfect. Now come with me. I want you to meet someone very special.'

❧ CHAPTER 47 ❧

Bible J ran through the foggy streets, the dark hidden alleys, the fine squares and the parks of the city. It was crowded now, and a festive Buckland Corp. airship moved overhead through the dark sky. He was in a barely controlled fury at the loss of Eve, his bruised head, his bruised pride. He clenched and unclenched his fists as he ran. He ran on and on, his energy fuelled by his anger.

He found the address on the calling card easily enough. The door opened the moment he banged the knocker. To Bible J on the doorstep, it was as if his knock had simply flung the door open on the instant. He stood dishevelled and out of breath. While he caught his breath, he handed the card over to the man who had opened the door. Catchpole looked down at his own card and ushered the boy through into the dim parlour.

'Forgive the dark, I was just on my way out. Where did you get this?' Catchpole asked.

'The woman with the cat gave it to me,' Bible J said. 'She told me that you were looking for Eve.'

'Eve?' said Catchpole.

'Yes, Eve, they took her. Ragged men came and took her.'

'Who are you?' said Catchpole.

'I am Japhet McCreddie, known as Bible J. Eve is my . . . my friend. I work for Mr Leighton over in Spitalfields.'

'I know him, I was at his house. I am Sergeant Catchpole of the Yard.' He held out his hand and Bible J shook it. 'You were out with the houseboy.'

'Caleb, that would be.'

'I know,' said Catchpole, 'I was in fact there looking for Caleb. His father and your Eve are strangely linked. No time to explain now. Will you come with me? We have an important job to do. It could be very dangerous, I should warn you.'

'That's why I'm here,' said Bible J. 'Anything for Eve.'

They set off together, out into the crowded streets under the cloak of the fog.

⤜❊ CHAPTER 48 ❊⤛

Mr Leighton was at the big table in the seance room while Caleb polished the holsters and gun belts which were piled on the table beside him. Outside there was music from a barrel organ and the sound of crowds of milling people. Leighton sat loading bullets into a selection of pistols and guns from his collection.

Mrs Boulter came in with a tray of food.

'Put it over there please, Mrs Boulter. Thank you,' Leighton said, without looking up.

Mrs Boulter started in surprise at the gleaming pile of death metalwork scattered across the polished table. 'Whatever are you two doing?' she said. 'I was certain you would be going to the demolition party tonight, sir.'

'Defending myself, my home, and more, Mrs Boulter,' Leighton said cooly, sighting down the barrel of a Remington pistol. 'I have no time for any wretched demolition party. After that last event, that robbery, I am going on the attack. The Buckland officials do nothing, and honest, properly licensed persons like myself are targeted by illicit scum like the Fantom and his so-called "ragged men". Well no more, I will take vengeance myself.' He held her gaze as she backed out of the room, tutting and shaking her head.

Leighton waited until she had gone down the stairs.

'Food, young Caleb. I have things to say to you.'

They sat together and ate mutton pie and boiled potatoes with peas and gravy.

'I have enquired about your father.' He looked across the table at Caleb. 'He was a very important man, *is* a very important man in the history of this whole place. I believe it was no random robbery. Those ragged men took your father for a reason. I feel certain they have not killed him. They will be holding him for ransom, and they would have taken you too only you ran off. They obviously think that Buckland will pay up very big to get someone like your father back.'

'The blind man seemed to know my father,' said Caleb. 'And he mentioned a girl called Eve as well.'

'Eve,' said Mr Leighton, 'he mentioned Eve, the same name as that odd circus girl of Mr McCreddie's and you wait until now to tell me? Eve is in hiding from the ragged men too and your father was taken by the ragged men, and you didn't connect any of those dots?'

'No,' said Caleb, 'I didn't, I was so shocked by everything, I wasn't thinking straight.'

'Tell me,' Mr Leighton said, 'what do you make of the friendship between our Mr Japhet McCreddie and his circus girl?'

'They seem happy together,' Caleb said guiltily, and her face filled his mind again, her perfect face, her bright eyes and the feel of her throat under his hands.

'He took me to see her once,' Leighton said. 'A strange girl, very clever on the wire, very beautiful. She just struck me as odd, but then I am out of touch with the younger generation in here. I think she has dazzled him, almost like hypnosis. I could use her here in one of my scientific meetings. Shame she's a success up on the tightrope.'

'She is the best ever, Bible J thinks.'

'Why ever are you doing all this now, sir?' Mrs Boulter asked as she cleared away the tray, a puzzled look on her face.

'Mrs Boulter,' said Mr Leighton, 'take down the curtains and roll them and pile them in the hall with all the rest.'

The hallway was nearly full of chairs, rolls of fabric, paper, books and so forth.

'I have my reasons for all of this, Mrs Boulter,' he continued. 'I need to protect my investments here. This house has become too vulnerable. In fact soon I may close it down altogether.'

When they had finished and Mrs Boulter was back in the basement, Leighton said, 'The Fantom hates me and I hate him; tonight I propose to finish him off and free your father. I will claim my nice big reward from a grateful

Corporation, and you and Mr McCreddie will, I hope, help me. I have a dangerous job for you, young Caleb.'

'What do you want me to do?'

Mr Leighton went over to the corner cupboard and pulled out a wooden box with a brass lock. He unlocked the box and pulled out two mobile phones.

'Well, well,' Leighton said, 'look at them. Very, very strictly forbidden, and very, very inauthentic *indeed*. Old models I am afraid, though pretty reliable. I shall have one, and you shall have the other.'

'And?'

'I know that that there has been a traitor in my elegantly run little fortress here all along.'

'Who?' asked Caleb.

'Why,' he said, lowering his voice, 'Mrs Boulter I am afraid. Did you not notice her expression when she saw all the guns and her face change when I said I was bent on vengeance and would soon be closing down the house?'

'Not really,' said Caleb.

'Well trust me, I did,' Leighton said. 'I want you to follow her. As sure as eggs are eggs, she will soon be out of here and looking to be taken to the Fantom, to warn him what I am up to. You follow her among the crowds and then when you see where she ends up you call me. I have a general idea where his lair is, but I need to know the exact location. Do you think you can do it?'

Caleb's heart leaped at the thought of doing something positive to rescue his father. *I will be the one to do it*, he thought.

'Of course,' he said.

'The phones have only one number keyed in, each other's,' said Leighton. 'When used they will of course set off an alert at Pastworld Security but we will be beyond worrying about that by then. Besides it will be busy out there this evening, what with the demolition and all. As soon as you find where it is press one and call me and I will get there with the arsenal. One more thing. Here, take this.' He handed over a Remington service revolver and holster. 'You may need it. It's fully loaded so take care. Are you sure you want to do this?'

'Sure,' said Caleb.

'We might make a footpad and a liar of you yet, young Master Brown,' said Leighton. 'Take this house key as well in case I am gone if and when you return, and Caleb.'

'Yes.'

'Go carefully now.'

'I will,' said Caleb. 'I will.'

Mrs Boulter slipped away from the house a few minutes later and Caleb followed behind her. He had his hair stuffed under a cap, which he wore pulled down tightly on his head, so that it cast a deep shadow across his face. He looked like any regular 'Ollie Twist' street boy. He was at once swept along by the busy throng on the pavement. He had to struggle to keep his eye on Mrs Boulter. She walked surprisingly quickly. Mrs Boulter stopped a ragged man, and they turned away from the crowd into a doorway. Caleb watched their heated conversation, Mrs Boulter gesturing back towards where she had come from. Then Mrs Boulter and the ragged man moved off together. Caleb followed behind them as close as he dared through the crowds. Every movement of every beggar in the shadows promised a possible betrayal, and perhaps even a painful death. He moved on through the streets, the mobile phone heavy in his pocket, the revolver ready at his hip.

⇸ CHAPTER 49 ⇷

Catchpole and Bible J arrived in Fournier Street, just two among the excited crowds of Gawkers. Bible J opened the front door to find Mr Leighton sitting fully armed in crossed holsters and cartridge belts in a muddle of furniture and piled-up boxes.

'At last, Mr McCreddie, there you are,' he said, 'and I see you bring Sergeant Catchpole with you.'

'Expecting trouble, it seems? These are all licensed guns I presume, sir?'

'You Corporation people do nothing about the Fantom,' he said, 'so I am forced to do something myself.'

'That is why we are here, man,' said Catchpole. 'We have come to enlist you to just that purpose. We intend to find the Fantom at once.'

'He has taken Eve,' Bible J said desperately.

'Has he?' said Mr Leighton. 'We shall mount a two-pronged attack then. The game is afoot. I have already sent young Caleb out as a scout to locate the Fantom's lair.'

'But I know where he is hiding out already,' said Catchpole. 'At least I think I do. I believe he is in an abandoned Underground railway station at Moorgate. It's not far from here. There is no time to lose.'

'Wait,' said Bible J, and he ran up the stairs, unlocked the gun room and put Eve's journal carefully down on the table. If only he had time to read it. Then he took a pair of pistols from one of the cabinets. He locked the gun room, took the stairs two at a time, and was soon back in the hallway.

'Right,' said Catchpole, 'let's go.'

Leighton handed a rifle and a grenade to Catchpole, who tucked the gun across the broad shoulders of his ulster coat.

'Take these, you'll need them. I am staying here,' Leighton said. 'I am not a coward, I just fear they might come here. I must defend this beautiful house and its contents, they mean more to me than life. By the way,' he said with a grin, 'I am expecting a nice chunk of the reward monies for helping to save Lucius Brown's son at least.'

'You shall have your share,' Catchpole said, 'although I doubt there will be any reward.'

'Why do you say that?' Leighton said.

'Another time, not now,' Catchpole replied. 'Come on then, young man,' and with that Bible J and Catchpole went out into the dark street.

Bible J had his two revolvers and a desperate feeling of loss overlaid with anger and excitement. Catchpole had his own burden of fearful knowledge, a secret which filled him with dread and with pity for poor Eve.

They moved unhindered through the crowds. There appeared to be no one in pursuit of them and none of the jovial red-faced bobbies challenged them. Catchpole felt Gawkers' eyes watching as they passed. He acknowledged some through force of habit, just once, with a quick nod, and then they turned off into Commercial Street. An iron eagle-head finial on the crest of a railing turned very slightly, and very slowly, and seemed to follow them.

The gas lamps were lit now, and there were more crowds of busy people. Cabs, carts and horses, passed and clattered to and fro. Bible J noticed a single ragged man. They followed him, playing cat and mouse, dodging in and out of the crowds along the length of the street. As far as they could tell he was unaware of being followed.

The fog was lifting. The deep mechanisms had shifted again, and another gear had been engaged. The great street was full of people on their way to the fireworks and the demolition. The Gawkers were now close and all around them, as they went beyond a rumbling cart towards the bright windows of the Lyons Corner House. It was then that Catchpole realised they had lost sight of their ragged man.

'I think we should change tack,' Catchpole said. 'Enter

the Fantom's lair via another station in the old Underground system and make our way towards it through the tunnels. We can pull off a surprise attack.' He pulled a book from his pocket, opened the back cover and pulled out a folded Underground railway map.

'We could get in at St Paul's and make our way from there.'

'Won't it be dark down there?' said Bible J.

'Yes, pitch black. A little comandeering is in order.'

A bobby with a drooping moustache and a cheery smile on his face was patrolling the kerb not far from them. Catchpole approached him and flashed his warrant card. He was soon back holding a police lamp.

'This should do the trick.'

✦ CHAPTER 50 ✦

Abel Buckland sat in part of the Buckland Corp. head-quarters that was very strictly off limits to all but himself and his personal security staff. It was a high-ceilinged room on one of the upper floors. One wall was lit up with a bank of a hundred or so live monitor screens and feeds. Buckland had earlier launched an Espion camera to follow Sgt Catchpole, and Catchpole was no longer alone. With him was William Leighton's accomplice Japhet McCreddie. Buckland kept the camera moving just behind them. They had found their way to one of the old, boarded-up entrances to St Paul's Underground station and they appeared to be making a forced entry into the disused station itself. They vanished suddenly into the darkness one after the other. The Espion camera lingered on the blank, open entrance way, hovered there as capering Gawkers and children with balloons streamed past heading for the fireworks display and the demolition.

Buckland shut off the live feed and turned to Inspector Prinsep.

'We will take my private airship, Prinsep. Lestrade is off on his own agenda, he has a job to do, he will brook no arguments. You and I have someone to rescue. We must go now. Time is of the essence.'

'But Mr Buckland, sir,' said Prinsep, 'the celebrations start in just one hour.'

'The fools will have to wait if necessary,' Buckland replied, getting to his feet. 'This is a matter of life and death. It is something we have to do.'

✹ CHAPTER 51 ✹

The Fantom guided Eve in her velvet gown up a further stationary escalator. They walked into a large room at the top of the rusted steps. A man was tied to a chair, watched over by a ragged man with a rifle. He leaped to his feet at the sight of the Fantom. The figure in the chair was suddenly bolt upright too, as if he had just been woken up.

'Ah look,' said the Fantom, 'they were dozing up here, not enough excitement. Perhaps I can change all of that right now. Come with me, my dear, and meet a very special person in both of our lives. Come on now, don't be shy.'

Eve and the Fantom stood before Lucius Brown, who looked up at them and then immediately closed his eyes and lowered his head.

'I've met this man before,' Eve said in surprise. 'I know him, I made tea for him at home once. He is "the smart visitor", an old friend of Jack's.'

'Yes,' said the Fantom, 'that's right, an old, old friend of Jack's.'

Lucius looked up at the Fantom. 'Let me speak to you alone, just for a minute, please.'

The Fantom let go of Eve's arm and he pulled at the sleeve of Lucius's coat, tugging it up to reveal the neat little bar code on his inner wrist.

'Look there,' he said, 'the mark of Cain. Dr Jack had one just like it, for security you see. Now he wants to talk to me in secret. Forgive me but I will hear him out. Wait for me, dear Eve.'

He gestured to the ragged man.

'Take her over there and keep her with you for a moment.'

'Well?' he said to Lucius when Eve was out of earshot.

'Is there any way that I can appeal to any part of your better nature to simply let her walk away and vanish again?'

'My better nature?' The Fantom laughed. 'How funny that you of all people, my designer, my maker, my only true father, should enquire as to my *better nature*. You would know my nature better than anyone else. *You* tell *me*. Do I have a better nature?'

'You might have developed one quite naturally since your freedom. It's been a long time.'

'Really, has it? It seems like only yesterday that you and Jack tried to burn me alive, my own dear surrogate parents. Boring was I, not enough for you?'

'Please, there really is no need to harm the poor girl. Surely you have had your fill of killing by now?'

'She wants me to kill her. It is what she was made for. It will be my apotheosis to kill her over and over again. The odd thing is that each time I kill it is so very different from the time before. The sensation is different, and not only that, it is also very hard to recall. Oh I can remember the general feeling but not that precise exquisite moment of the soul's release. I am told it's a little like the crisis in the human act of love, but then I wouldn't know about that, would I?'

'Love, now that is the word, *love*,' said Lucius. 'Hold on to that word, that idea. Eve is in essence your own sister. You should protect her, you should love her, not destroy her.'

From the other side of the ticket hall Eve watched the exchange between the two men, focusing on their mouths as their lips moved. Whispers echoed in little intangible susurrations and flutterings from the tiled surfaces of the old station. Watching their lips every word was as clear to her as if it had been printed on a page. She went cold inside; she felt that she was in a waking dream. Nothing that they said made sense to her and yet all of it did. Then as suddenly she was snapped out of the dream. She thought of Bible J. She saw his smiling face, his crinkly eyes. 'Love', the man had just said. That was it. She loved Bible J. It was clear to her now. She must get away and find him.

'Oh but I do love her,' said the Fantom. 'I have been looking for her these past years, looking and waiting, for that brave, lovely girl that you so cleverly designed for me, *Father*.'

'I didn't design her. I merely enabled her, just as I enabled you. I am not her maker, nor your maker, Adam. God made you and her, just as he made me. You have a soul somewhere inside you, a ghost in your machine, I know it. There is good in you despite what you have done, what you might be planning to do.'

'Oh, Father, it is so touching that you imagine there might be some good in me after all.' He laid his hand on Lucius's head. 'Your other son now, my brother, I wonder where he is tonight as the city celebrates its birthday. Is he at the big party? Will he enjoy the fireworks do you think? It would be quite something to meet him but so far he has eluded me. What greater present could I have been given though, on this anniversary, than to find her at last, my victim, my true bride in death, my Eve?'

'She does not need to be your victim. You have a choice, you have free will.'

'Do I really? Strange then that I feel predestined to please her and she wants me to be her killer. You made sure of that, you and Dr Jack, didn't you?'

Eve had been watching their mouths. She turned to the ragged man next to her. Her mind was clear now, like a freshly washed pane of glass. She raised her arm in its black velvet sleeve and smashed the ragged man very fast and very hard in the face with her elbow. The ragged man reeled and fell silently to the ground and everything slowed down in front of her, just as the raindrops had suddenly slowed in the forest. There was a shout, but the voice of the Fantom was distorted, was low and slow. She ran away back down the escalator, her feet barely touching the grills of rusted metal. To the Fantom in the ticket hall she had appeared as a dark streak, a whisper, a blur of sudden movement.

'What did you do to her?' said the Fantom, caught off guard by the sudden shift in Eve from complacent victim . . . to what, he couldn't tell.

He put his hands around Lucius's throat, his face a mask of rage, his eyes burning bright, cold greenish blue. 'What the hell did you do to her? Why has she run off like that?'

Then he let go.

'I'm sorry, Father,' he said in a small voice. 'I don't want to hurt you, but how could that happen?'

'It may be that Jack put something extra in her programming, during all that time they had together,' Lucius coughed out.

'She has been dancing high on ropes, for God's sake,' said the Fantom, 'the circus. Thirty feet in the air and never fallen once. *Someone* did something special for her.'

'I have no idea what Jack might have done,' said Lucius, 'and it's too late now to ask him, you've seen to that.'

⇢ CHAPTER 52 ⇠

Caleb stood in a still space outside the old Underground station. The ragged man he had been following had vanished here a few moments ago. Crowds of Gawkers pushed past on their way to the fireworks. This was surely the place. He pulled the phone out of his pocket, turned it on and pressed one. A Gawker stopped and looked at him.

'Look at that, how much have we paid for all this authentic immersion and in the street right in front of us there's some bastard kid using a damn mobile phone?'

'You're kidding me?'

'I kid you not, look at him, large as life and twice as ugly.'

Caleb listened desperately to the ringing, over and over in his ear, but there was no reply from Mr Leighton.

He looked up in time to see two large Gawkers coming towards him, about to carry out a citizen's arrest on authenticity grounds. Time to go. He ducked under the hoarding and fell into a dark space. He rolled down some hard steps, dropping the phone. Then he hit a stone floor and lay there waiting for a moment.

No one followed him down.

He sat up and looked around, his eyes gradually growing accustomed to the dark. He was on level ground, at least. He heard a faint voice crackling from the phone somewhere near him in the dark. He scrabbled around and found it.

'Hello.'

'Caleb?'

'Here.'

'Where are you?'

'Underground, an old station I think.'

'Can you see anyone?'

'No, but I can see a staircase going down.'

It was an escalator, only it wasn't moving. He could see light coming faintly from somewhere below. He stood up and walked to the top and looked down. The steel stairs fell away sharply to another floor way below, and down there was where the light was coming from, a very dim light.

'I'll walk down,' he said.

'The signal will go,' Leighton said.

'I know but I can't help that. I must go down,' Caleb replied.

Caleb started to walk down carefully, his free hand resting on the grip of a pistol just in case. On the next level the phone went dead. He was on his own now.

Down here the light was better and he could see through a curved archway to another conventional staircase. He walked down the next set of stairs and found himself on the platform. He had arived at the aftermath of a fierce battle. Smoke was still drifting in a haze over the lights that were strung along the walls of the platform and then further on into the tunnel itself. The station tiles had recently been shattered with rounds of bullets and grenades. Dead ragged men were lying in heaps across the rails at the mouth of the tunnel. The platform was streaked with smears of blood. He could hardly look at the bloodied, twisted men on the tracks. He sat down on the edge of the platform and took a gun out of its holster ready and then waited. He could hear quiet scuttling noises from among the old rails and track systems below his dangling feet: rats arriving among the bodies, and they were not mech ones either.

He sat for a moment trying to make sense of what might have just happened, listening for any sound, anything other than the rats. The rails stretched in both directions beyond the platform into darkness. After a moment or two he heard voices from the tunnel to his right. He stood up and raised the revolver, remembering what Bible J had said, and he held the gun out straight with both hands, his finger lightly on the trigger. He stood at the edge of the platform and waited for what might come out of the tunnel.

Eve dashed on through dark tunnels and passageways. She came to a set of stairs and she took them three steps at a time, racing down as sure-footed as a deer and as lightly as a feather. She found that she could see as clearly as if all the lamps had been full on. She ran fast with no hesitation all the way down another escalator and arrived at an area which opened down on to the train platform.

A boy stood with his back to her, his arms extended holding a gun towards the tunnel entrance.

'Caleb,' she said.

Caleb turned and saw Eve in a black dress standing framed in the platform entrance.

Her eyes shone as if they were lit from within.

'Eve,' he said, 'but how did you get here?'

Before she could answer him a shot rang out from somewhere down the tunnel. Shots came at them from the darkness. Caleb couldn't see who was shooting and didn't wait to find out. He ran towards Eve still holding the gun in both hands. Another salvo of bullets came from the tunnel. Eve reached out, grabbed Caleb and pulled him away into a side tunnel. He stuck the revolver back in the holster and they went back down a short corridor away from the ricocheting bullets.

'Oh, Caleb, I am so glad to see you. Is Bible J all right? They hit him and left him for dead with Jago.'

'I don't know. I haven't seen him today.'

'I have so much to tell you,' Eve said, 'but there is no time. The Fantom is very close to us and he means me harm, and you too, and yet I . . .' She hesitated. 'Oh nothing,' she said. 'Come on.' She ran with him, tried to pull him along at her new speed, but he slowed her almost back to normal. When they reached the top of the escalator, Caleb was propelled by the force of her speed across the floor of the ticket hall. She pulled him up to his feet.

'Sorry,' she said, 'I just thought we should move fast.'

'How do you do that?' Caleb asked, brushing himself down.

'I don't know,' said Eve. 'I just can.'

A voice rang out from above them.

'Don't move either of you. It would be a mistake. You see I am holding a very sharp blade to the throat of a very important person, isn't that right, Eve? Unless I miss my guess, that boy you are with is Caleb Brown, our brother. Perhaps you should tell him who it is I am holding.'

The Fantom walked down the escalator towards them into what little light there was. Caleb saw his father in front of him, with a knife held at his throat.

'Dad,' he said involuntarily.

His father could say nothing, but his eyes widened with panic.

'Yes,' said the Fantom, 'it's Papa, our dada, our father, our pater, clever, clever old Lucius Brown.' The Fantom reached the final step.

'I see that you are armed, young Caleb, and authentically armed too, with a fine looking Remington revolver. I wonder where you got that? Not that it matters, because it is time to throw it down now, go on. You, Eve, will not move as much as an eyelash or I will slit this throat here, with some sadness admittedly, but also with some pleasure. Imagine that hot geyser of the familial blood that will wash over us all, will wash us in the blood of the lamb. The gun, Mr Brown, the gun.'

Caleb threw the revolver and it skittered across the tiled floor.

The blade of the knife at Lucius's throat caught in the light with a dull glint.

'Are you all right, Dad?' Caleb said.

Lucius lowered his eyes.

'Step forward, young Caleb. Let me get a good look at you,' said the Fantom.

'I can see resemblances between us all, isn't this nice? We are a little family and all together at last. I am sure you are puzzled by what I mean. You see, Caleb, your clever father here,' the Fantom pulled up Lucius's head so that his throat showed white, '*our* clever father made me, and he made the lovely Eve here too; he made us one for the other. Isn't that right? Nod, Daddy. Tell him the real truth.'

Lucius nodded his head.

Caleb could make no sense of this; his head swam. His father had a second family, had children; Eve was apparently his own sister; this other figure, the Fantom, was his brother? What did it mean? His father had never said anything about such a thing, even after Caleb's mother had died. All Caleb could say was, 'You're the Fantom?'

The Fantom flipped his free hand back up to his face and it was suddenly covered once again in the black full face mask.

'I am now,' he replied.

Eve said, 'You talk of family, Adam. Well I have a family already. My family is Jago the harlequin who rescued me, and Rose the bearded lady and Bible J. I don't know that man you're threatening at all. I've only met him once when I made him a cup of Assam tea. You seem to have some strange power over me, but you are not my family. Let that poor man go.'

'You are meant for me Eve and for me alone. You raised my hands to your own throat. You know you want me to take your life, to complete the circle. It is built into us, preordained.'

Eve took her chance. She lunged forward suddenly, a black velvet blur and pulled the knife away from Lucius's throat. She threw it hard so that it clattered across the floor. Caleb dropped down and rolled along the ground. He got hold of the revolver. He sat up, eyes closed in terror and pointed the gun to where he imagined the Fantom would be . . . But when he opened his eyes, the Fantom had gone and so had Lucius.

'He went up to the street,' said Eve. 'Come on, Caleb. We will save your father. Our father,' she smiled her open smile at him and reached for his hand.

There it was again, 'our father', he thought. He looked at Eve's face, her eyes were like his – she really could be his sister – but the Fantom his brother? His father had nodded, had agreed, but then he had had a knife at his throat. Caleb took Eve's hand and they dashed together up the stairs, Eve's hand tight in his.

❧ CHAPTER 53 ❧

Once up out on the street Eve and Caleb caught sight of the Fantom pulling Lucius through the crowd. They followed, one pair just behind the other, dodging and tucking into doorways, sometimes holding back, sometimes moving forward. The Fantom hurried up a rising street and veered off suddenly and Eve caught sight of the two locked figures stumbling down towards the side of a towering building. It was surrounded by hoardings which were plastered over with 'Grand Demolition' notices. There was a wide cordon sanitaire around the base of the building, where the Fantom had stopped. Eve held Caleb back in the shadows and they watched as the Fantom looked around, waited a moment and then pried open a door in the surrounding fence. Caleb looked down at his hand clasped in Eve's. It felt right to be holding it, as if he were protecting her, like a sister, and she were protecting him. She turned to him and they looked up together to the top of the tower. The huge building loomed over them. Its iron bones showed dark black against the misted sky. There were two airships docked near the top.

After waiting for a moment they followed the Fantom in through the fencing and a gaping entrance way, then set off together up the wide staircase, which was in almost complete darkness. The darkness did not slow Eve down; indeed she seemed to welcome it as if it were her natural habitat. She seemed able to see everything as clearly as if it were daylight and she held Caleb tight as she ran upwards.

The sound of swift bootsteps echoed down from higher up, as the Fantom climbed somewhere above them.

The Fantom crossed a landing dragging Lucius with him. They reached the dark upper hallway. The floor was densely covered with dust and sharp fragments of old cement and plaster. The hall was lit with a series of low emergency lamps left by the workmen. Their light revealed boxes and huge explosive charges piled one on another, tools and trestles, huge metal barrels, sledge hammers and damaged internal walls with more charges laid in the supporting pillars. Then the Fantom felt something by his feet, a flicker of movement. He looked down at the large brown sentinel rat, its eyes red, its tail swishing. 'Restricted area,' it said in its flat mechanical voice. 'Restricted area.' The Fantom lifted his foot and then hesitated. He thought of the man he was holding around the neck: had Lucius made him in the same way that someone had designed and made this mech rat? He looked at the rat up close. The mouth was open and working, its little jaws moved up and down, the voice repeated its mantra over and over. He looked closely into its red eyes and then he heard the sudden sound of someone clapping and the Fantom lifted his head. Abel Buckland stepped out of the shadows in front of them.

'Nicely done, my dear special Gentleman,' said Buckland. 'You showed restraint. You could easily have crushed that poor sentinel of ours into oblivion as you usually do and have done before, but you are, I see, growing, becoming sympathetic. Don't go too soft on us, will you? Of course you won't, you are as impetuous and as reckless as ever,' he went on. 'We missed you recently. I wondered where you were, and then you dealt with that unfortunate ragged colleague of yours and left his head on top of the tower up here. This place is like a magnet for you. Come on now, Adam, and Lucius, my old friend, just come with me.'

The Fantom stared at him with his bright piercing eyes. 'You're here to finish me and my black-hearted father here,' he said holding Lucius closer to him, an arm thrown protectively around Lucius's throat. 'You are trying to keep me from Eve, have been all these years.'

'No I'm not,' Buckland said with an attempt at a reassuring smile. 'Far, far from it, I've found you. Aren't you the least bit curious as to how I managed to be here waiting for you, my boy? You're a very clever young man.

I wonder how on earth you think I did it?'

'I have no idea,' said the Fantom, one hand now clamped firmly across Lucius' mouth.

'I have been following you since very early this morning using some of these,' Buckland turned on a powerful torch and the bright beam picked out several needle-thin Espion cameras floating in among the dust motes and debris of the corridor.

'You see, my boy, I try to keep watch over you just as a good godfather should. I am not as authentically of the past as I make out. Privately I use the new technologies when I have to, and I don't mean steam power. I am your true father, Adam – you were always my idea. Lucius here contributed and poor Jack helped. They were your enablers, but I conceived the idea of you,' said Buckland. 'Come on, three more floors to the roof and safety for you both. I fear that the forces of reaction are biting at our heels. Lestrade is even now acting to destroy your ragged men. It is too late for them, but not for you two. Come on, both of you, now.'

Outside in the night sky two airships hovered near the roof, one a Buckland Corp. passenger vessel, the other a smaller security model. Both were tethered by taut anchor wires to the girders of the exposed roof. Buckland walked towards the edge of the building and raised his arms up. He turned to the Fantom and Lucius. 'Soon one more of my dreams will be realised. There will be a double celebration. You have come back to us and this hideous building is to be finally destroyed, blown from beneath us in a huge fireball.'

➨ CHAPTER 54 ❧

Sgt Charles Catchpole and Bible J made their way through the dank tunnels towards Moorgate station. The police lamp lit their way effectively enough. It also lit up the wildlife, the scavenging rats, the skittering mice, even one or two feral cats who seemed to thrive in the musty disused spaces. Catchpole spoke to Bible J quietly as they walked, weapons drawn. 'I have learned something about this Fantom, something very disturbing,' he said.

'What, that he cuts people up and takes their hearts out? I could have told you that.'

'No about the real nature of him. The person himself.'

A shot rang out from the tunnel ahead of them. Catchpole turned out the lamp and dived down amid the filth between the tracks. A wavering light was coming from ahead spilling over the curved vault of the tunnel. Distorted shadows soon followed, looming over the curved brickwork – armed men, several of them too by the look of it.

'Ragged men,' said Catchpole. 'Keep still, lie low.'

Three ragged men appeared at the turn of the curved tunnel. They slowed as they entered the straight stretch. They shone their lantern around and in a moment the beam picked out Bible J, who was still defiantly standing up, his two pistols raised straight out. The lantern moved away and then almost immediately swung back on to him but from his position flat among the steel rails Catchpole took careful aim with his rifle at the lantern. He knocked it out in one clean shot and the tunnel was plunged into darkness again. Bible J fired wildly with his revolvers at where he thought the ragged men had stood. Answering fire followed; bullets ricocheted from the walls, one buzzing past Catchpole's head like a wasp. The three ragged men retreated back down the tunnel. Catchpole laid down a barrage of fire with his rifle. The sound echoed and rolled deafeningly around the tunnel walls. They sounded like an army, especially when he stood and bowled a grenade further down the tunnel at where he supposed the ragged men were running. The explosion knocked him back among the tracks with compressed force, fragments of tiles and bricks clattered around them.

'That's it,' said Catchpole, 'he'll know we're coming now. Let's move on. Are you all right, young man?'

'I'm fine, 'cept I can't hear any more.'

They moved further down the tunnel, picking their way through shrapnel and twisted rails.

They met no more opposition on the tracks, no stray

ragged men anywhere further down the tunnel. Instead of gun fire there was now a sort of deafening and uncanny silence which seemed to fill the dark tunnels all around them. Then there was a warm wind and a roaring sound and the clattering of wheels. It sounded exactly like an underground train heading for them, but here the tracks were plainly unused and indeed had not been used for years. The clogged dust at their feet remained undisturbed. Catchpole hurried on ahead in case he had to head off some approaching danger. He arrived at the junction of two tunnels in time to see a line of brightly lit Underground train carriages rattling towards him sparking on clean electrified tracks. He pressed himself against the walls of the tunnel and the train swung past him on the bend and rattled down the side tunnel which joined theirs. The carriages passed close by him and he was able to see the passengers inside. Policemen and Buckland Security. Dozens of them stuffed into the carriage like the rush hour. Some were bloodied and obviously wounded. There were bullet holes spattered and raked along the side of the carriages, and he could see grenade damage and some of the men were holding their weapons as they passed him by; they looked like weary soldiers returning from the front.

He scuttled back down the tunnel to where Bible J waited in the dark.

'What was that?' said Bible J. 'I thought I heard a train.'

'You did,' said Catchpole, 'a fully electric one too. Someone has got to them before us, someone official.

Come on.'

They walked on down the disused tunnel past the section of clean and maintained track which led off to the side and vanished into the darkness. Their way was soon blocked by twisted rails and lumps of masonry, and then at the mouth of the tunnel there were the bodies and bits of the bodies of dead ragged men everywhere.

'God,' said Catchpole, 'it's a slaughterhouse.'

Bible J walked through the dark, bloodied mass hardly able to believe what he was seeing.

'Who did this?' he said, looking around the walls and the blood-washed station platform as they emerged into the half light.

'Buckland Corp.,' said Catchpole with disgust. 'I saw an underground train full of police and cadets, it must have been them. This was an organised surgical strike. Someone in authority wanted the ragged men gone.'

'Look over here,' said Bible J. 'It's Ma Boulter, shot through the head. What's she doing here?'

'Reporting to her boss, the Fantom, of course,' said a voice from the shadows and Inspector Lestrade stepped out in front of them. 'I hope those weapons are licensed. I am sorry you had to see "beneath our skirts" so to speak, Sergeant Catchpole, but we have been forced to act, to cleanse the hive. This mess will all be gone by morning and few will be the wiser.'

'Mess?' said Catchpole. 'They were people – men and women. Shouldn't they have been brought to trial? It's savagery, pure and simple.'

'I thought you were a company man, Catchpole?'

'I am a policeman, and I thought you were too, Lestrade, not a cold-blooded killer?'

'They engaged us in battle. We had little choice, and there is still the head of the snake to attend to,' Lestrade said, pointing above.

⇢ CHAPTER 55 ⇠

Eve and Caleb waited on the staircase. They could hear the voices on the floor above. Someone was there with the Fantom and Lucius. Eve pressed her finger to her lips. Then the voices stopped.

They crept up the last of the stairs, into the corridor where a red-eyed mech rat tried to stop them. 'Restricted area, restricted,' it said. They ignored the rat and continued up a final set of temporary wooden steps which led out on to the roof of the tower.

Caleb went first. He put his head up into the wind and darkness. The noise of a crowd drifted up from far below. He could see three figures standing on a level surface among the exposed and dangerous girders of the tower top: his father, the Fantom, and an older man he did not recognise. Two airships were tethered some way away, rotors idling, ready for business.

Caleb turned and gestured for Eve to come up. She

joined Caleb on the roof girders. Her hair blew about her perfectly shaped face as she stood to her full height.

Eve strode forward across a narrow girder towards the temporary platform where the three men stood together.

Caleb tried to follow her across the broad steel beam, holding his revolver out as a balance weight but he stopped immediately in terror. He had taken one misguided look at the crowd six hundred feet below them and that was enough to make him freeze, to lock him solid.

'Oh good, look who has joined us,' said the Fantom.

'Eve,' said Buckland, 'at last. Welcome, I am Abel Buckland, CEO of the Buckland Corporation. It is a long time since I have seen you, my dear, and I doubt that you would remember me at all. My, but you are certainly more beautiful now than I could have ever hoped or remembered. We met only the once and that was when Lucius and Jack and the rest of us were out celebrating your,' he paused, 'your *completion*, might be the word to use. We had a celebration, with fireworks, just like there will be tonight.' He raised his arms as if to take in the whole of the artificial night sky. 'Another celebration tonight, a demolition, the last building to leave us, and not before time. It seems so right and so appropriate that you should have been found now and reunited with your Adam. Now we can enter a whole new phase of special entertainment in Pastworld, and you and Adam will feature brightly at the centre of it.'

Lucius wrenched his mouth free from the Fantom's hand.

'It is wrong now, Buckland, and it was always wrong,' he said. The Fantom clamped his hand back over Lucius's mouth.

He turned to look at Caleb balanced some yards away, stuck on the high girder unable to move forward or back.

'Our father is becoming a bore, young master Brown. Shall I pitch him down to the ground? One shove from me and he will fall like a stone.'

'Hush, Adam, calm yourself. Just keep hold of Lucius for now,' Buckland said. He signalled with the device he was holding and the passenger airship moved further away from the tower and the anchor wire tightened. He made another adjustment, and the second smaller airship moved closer.

'We will soon be ready for the fireworks,' he said. He pressed the device in his hand once again and part of the gondola floor of the larger airship dropped open. Thousands of sheets of paper fell out and scattered in the air like giant wedding confetti; they spiralled slowly down to the grasping hands of the eager crowd gathered far below. The countdown had begun.

⇥ CHAPTER 56 ⇤

Catchpole and Bible J finally pushed themselves out through the hoarding at Moorgate station. They had searched the remains of the Fantom's lair. There was nothing but a chair in the middle of the ticket hall with ropes attached. There were the remains of some food stores and enough weapons and ammunition for a siege, but nothing else, not a living thing except some newly emboldened rats.

They had no direction to follow now and the crowds were dense. Even getting through them was likely to be difficult let alone catching sight of The Fantom. There was a moment of silence and anticipation. The crowd around them pointed and looked upwards, raised their hands, excited. High above them a tethered passenger airship was dropping thousands of leaflets that fluttered and swung around in the cold air. Catchpole picked one out of the air and read it aloud to Bible J.

A GRAND
DEMOLITION!

WELCOME TO THIS TENTH ANNIVERSARY PARTY IN CELEBRATION OF **PASTWORLD**. THE MOST SUCCESSFUL THEME PARK IN HISTORY. THE PLACE WHERE PEOPLE COME TO LIVE THE LIFE OF THE PAST, WITH ALL ITS CERTAINTIES, PLEASURES, AND DELIGHTS; BUT YOU DON'T NEED TO BE TOLD THAT, BECAUSE YOU ARE HERE ALREADY!

THE **SPECTACULAR** DESTRUCTION OF THIS, THE LAST OF THE **20**TH-CENTURY BUILDINGS, TOWER **42**, WILL SHORTLY TAKE PLACE. YOU ARE ADVISED TO STAY WELL BEHIND THE SAFETY BARRIERS. PLEASE ENJOY THE FIREWORKS AND THEN JOIN ME, ABEL BUCKLAND, FOUNDER AND **CEO** OF THE BUCKLAND CORPORATION, IN BIDDING FAREWELL TO THE LAST ARCHITECTURAL ANOMALY STILL STANDING IN **PASTWORLD**.

ABEL BUCKLAND

Catchpole threw down the leaflet. 'Tower 42. The Fantom was there just recently. He was caught by our security cameras. That will be the place.'

They moved off through the crowd towards Tower 42. Danger signs were everywhere, but luckily the bobbies on the perimeter were all distracted, looking up at the two passenger airships in the sky and the still scattering leaflets.

Catchpole and Bible J squeezed in through the fence and the hoarding and on across the wasteland into the stairwell of the building.

Catchpole led the way up the first staircase using the beam from the borrowed police lamp. They continued to climb floor after floor until eventually they found themselves in a long corridor full of debris, abandoned tools and carefully placed explosive charges. Catchpole kicked aside the mech rat that scuttled over and it hit the wall. 'If you're monitoring any of this, then that's for you, Hudson old friend,' he said.

———◆———

Outside, on the temporary platform Abel Buckland stood enjoying the muted sounds of the crowd rising up from the city far below them. Using his hand-held device, Buckland set off the first rocket of his great firework display. It shot upwards and exploded high in the air in a great white burst of light. The light revealed the Fantom who stood fully masked, his cape billowing in the wind.

It was then that Eve stepped forward. She walked

almost to the very edge of the building and held her black-sleeved arms out wide from her body. 'No, Eve,' Lucius called out, fearing that she was about to leap or fall from the building.

'Eve,' said the Fantom, and he let go of Lucius carelessly and in a rush so that Lucius lost his footing and slipped down on to the uneven surface of the roof itself. He huddled there, holding tight to a twisted steel beam.

'Dad,' Caleb called out in fear.

'I'm all right, ' Lucius called back. 'Hold on and don't move. I'll save you.'

'Rather save yourself,' said the Fantom and aimed a cruel kick at Lucius. His boot flicked across the top of Lucius's head, narrowly missing him.

Caleb shouted from his frozen position. 'Leave my father alone or I will use this.' He waved the long-barrelled gun uncertainly in the Fantom's direction.

The Fantom laughed. 'Sadly the recoil will send you straight down to the ground, my poor little brother, so go ahead and fire.'

The Fantom reached over and held on to Eve. He lowered her arms carefully, slowly, tenderly, so that finally they stood close together, on the very edge of the building, like lovers in an embrace, high on the very edge of the world.

Buckland called out excitedly, 'The charges have been set, and in a short time, after the sirens, the building will simply be no more.' He switched something on the device. More fireworks, bright rockets and fountains of colour lit the sky. Buckland raised his device and signalled with three quick flashes of white light across the gap towards the smaller of the airships. The ship moved out from its position and slowly approached the building.

Lucius Brown crawled gingerly back from the edge, keeping low to the platform on his knees, his elbows tucked in and his head down.

Catchpole and Bible J stepped out on to the roof. Catchpole shouldered his rifle, and aimed it in the direction of the Fantom and Eve. Bible J called out, 'Eve,' and she turned her head a little and smiled across at him.

'Let her go,' said Bible J.

The Fantom swung round and saw a man with a rifle and another boy with a gun, a rough-haired boy with a familiar face. 'Of course, the black book, the Bible – the boy is called Bible something,' said the Fantom.

'Let her go, come to me, Eve. I . . .' said Bible J.

'Eve is mine,' said the Fantom, 'made for me. You have no understanding of this creature. She and I are linked for ever, linked in love and death in a way impossible for you to understand.' He turned Eve so that she faced Bible J back across the jagged roof braces.

'This young man has called for you to go to him. Perhaps you should show him who you love. She has been made, programmed especially to respond to me. She can never resist me no matter what happens.'

Then Eve took the Fantom's hands and placed them around her own throat. She tilted her head back with her eyes closed in an image of surrender, of submission. Eve and the Fantom teetered together on tiptoe on the brink. The Fantom, inscrutable behind his mask, and Eve seemingly the swooning, willing victim.

Lucius Brown, unnoticed, had crawled over to Caleb who still stood on the girder. Lucius stood and helped his son down on to the more solid roof platform. Caleb hugged his father fiercely.

Sgt Catchpole picked his way across the roof and stopped some feet short of Abel Buckland. He spoke. 'I now know the truth about this whole sorry mess, Mr Buckland. I have read Inspector Lestrade's files and personal notes and I know about the Prometheus project.'

'I do not have to answer you, Sergeant Catchpole. You are an employee of the Corporation. I order you to arrest these youths, who are threatening my life and the lives of my characters.'

'Do they really have lives?' Catchpole said.

The small airship had reached the edge of the building. Inspector Prinsep's pale face loomed out of the cabin port. He raised the vessel up so that the gondola door was easily accessible, directly above the roof platform.

'We are leaving,' said Buckland. 'You must arrest Lucius Brown and his son for their own safety. Take them somewhere secure. The other youth is a known criminal, a felon, and may be shot at will. I should hurry if I were you. This building will not be here for much longer.'

'Caleb,' Catchpole shouted, 'take your father now and get off this roof. Go now, straight down and don't stop, save yourselves at least.'

'So,' said the Fantom, 'you will run away, Father, and leave us. Well you may run, but you cannot hide for ever from me. I will find you.'

'They'll be under tons and tons of modern rubble if they don't get out before this place goes down,' Buckland shouted.

Sgt Catchpole fired his rifle once so that the bullet struck Buckland's hand and his remote control device shattered. Fragments of it sprayed out into the darkness beyond the roof. Blood streamed from Buckland's hand and he fell on to his knees moaning.

'You will regret that,' said the Fantom calmly.

'It was inauthentic,' said Catchpole, 'it didn't belong in here at all.'

'I will cut you and then take out your heart while you are still alive.'

Catchpole swung the rifle across to point at the Fantom.

'You won't risk a shot, surely not with the lovely Eve so close to me.' The Fantom pulled her closer still.

'Go, Caleb, and go now,' said Bible J.

Caleb took his father's hand and pulled him towards the narrow staircase to begin their descent. Lucius called out, 'All my fault, all my fault, the ghost in the machine.'

The cabin door stood open on the hovering airship. Inspector Prinsep stood in the doorway. 'This way, sir,' he said.

Buckland crawled his way across the roof, whimpering and holding his damaged hand in pain, and Inspector Prinsep managed to pull him into the cabin.

Buckland, out of breath, called back to the Fantom, 'Come with us now, and bring your Eve with you. This thing holds four very comfortably.'

Caleb took a last look back at Eve. She was outlined in a sudden green burst of light from an exploding firework. Her bright eyes were fixed on Bible J. *Eve is his girl*, Caleb thought, *I must let him save her.* He gave a little wave at Eve as if he were leaving her standing at a bus stop, not teetering on the edge of life itself, six hundred feet in the air.

⇢ CHAPTER 57 ⇠

Bible J kept his pistol trained on the Fantom. It glinted in the reflected light of the continuing fireworks.

He took a step forward and the Fantom took one step closer to the edge, pulling Eve with him one step closer to the abyss.

The Fantom gestured out across the city rooftops. 'Ah,' he said, 'look at the marvels of Pastworld.'

The gun trembled in Bible J's hand. The Fantom hummed a tune to himself, under his breath.

'Have you ever jumped from this high, ever fallen free?'

'No,' Bible J said through clenched teeth. He was furious, powerless, armed but with no chance of taking a clear shot.

'I have many times. Why just the other day I jumped from this building. You should try it. It's quite a feeling.'

'No thank you.'

'Put it this way. It's either jump now or stay and be swooped up by my ragged men. Come on now, lad,' he said. 'Join us.'

There were repeated shots from the stairwell.

'Here come my reinforcements,' the Fantom said grinning.

'All of your ragged men were slaughtered tonight,' Catchpole called out, 'every last one of them. Lestrade's work.'

For a split second the Fantom hesitated in his reaction. He looked down at the city far below them, and tightened his grip on Eve.

A brighter white light flared up for an instant, and there was a roar from all the Gawkers milling about below.

Buckland called out from the airship, 'That was a warning signal. There will be a siren or two and then the building will be blown. Come inside, Adam, and bring Eve with you.'

The Fantom moved to step up into the gondola of the airship, but at that moment Bible J jumped forward and held on to him with one hand as tightly as he could, bunching the windblown flapping cape around the Fantom's waist.

'Let her go,' Bible J screamed. 'I love her.'

The Fantom turned, one arm still firmly wrapped around Eve. He raised his free arm. An ivory-handled razor flicked open and the blade caught the light. The razor flew downwards towards Eve's exposed throat just as Bible J thrust his own head in the way.

'Adam,' Buckland shouted from the airship. 'Now. Quickly.'

Bible J fell down on to the roof. He slipped forward, blood pumping from his neck. The Fantom raised both his arms. He still held the razor. It was high in the air, and it dripped an arc of blood. Eve stared up at the Fantom as if she were magnetically attached to him. She was aware Bible J had fallen injured, possibly dead, beside her. It was then that something was released in Eve, and the spell was broken. She screamed fiercely in the Fantom's face. She resisted him. She broke free and crouched down next to Bible J, cradling his bloodied head. With the sudden chance of a clear shot at the Fantom, Catchpole fired his rifle several times.

Inspector Prinsep threw a stun grenade from the airship. A muffled explosion shocked the air around them. Catchpole was knocked off his feet. The crowd below roared.

The Fantom, with almost calm deliberation, just stepped off the edge of the building out into the open air. He made no attempt to climb into the open door of the airship gondola, which in any case had been pushed clear of the building by the shock wave from the grenade.

He went into free fall.

Buckland screamed out something which was lost to the wind as his creation fell. The swirling air rushed past the Fantom, and his black cloak billowed out behind him. The Fantom pulled at something, a little hooked handle on a lanyard across his chest. He was jerked upright as his bright scarlet parachute rippled and blossomed above him in the surrounding grey air. He slowed in midair. He became for a moment, a puppet dangling on a string. He drifted towards the crowds and the cobbles with a strange slowness, floating towards the Gawkers and the wet roadway below. Inspector Lestrade watched the red blossom as it fell and signalled to his army of cadets to move in.

———◆—

Amid the noise of the cheering crowd came the rattle of cab wheels, and a black closed cab driven by the last of the ragged men swept through the crush. The harsh scrape and rattle of iron rims rang unnoticed against the cobbled road. The warning siren sounded again. From somewhere close, echoing from the high hard walls came the sound of police whistles. Then another siren sounded, and was answered by another. The Fantom ran forward across the wet cobbles, a ragged sleeve reached down from the closed hansom cab and pulled him up, and then the cab careened off down an incline and away from the crowd and into the fog with a great panel of scarlet fabric trapped and flapping behind it.

→ CHAPTER 58 ←

Eve picked herself up and stood tall. She breathed in deeply and opened her eyes. Buckland's little airship had moved off now and was hovering away from the building. Her mate, her would-be killer, her Adam had gone too, vanished in an instant in his black cape somewhere over the edge. Her love, her Bible J, lay at her feet in a spreading pool of blood. The other man was getting up.

'We can't stay here,' he said. 'I am here to help you. We must get down to safety.'

Eve crouched down next to Bible J. She kissed his forehead, it was warm. She felt his pulse. There was a faint fluttering movement.

'Save yourself, Sergeant,' she said. 'I will save Bible J.'

'The building will be blown at any moment,' said Catchpole.

Another siren sounded.

'There's the warning,' he said.

Eve put her arms under Bible J's warm back. She picked him straight up from the roof in her delicate black velvet arms as if he weighed no more than a feather. She walked forward to the very edge of the building. The big Buckland Corp. passenger airship still hovered, some yards from the tower. The anchor wire was stretched tight. It swayed in the wind but no more and no worse than the high rope she was used to.

'Where are you going?' Catchpole called out.

'Wait and I will come back for you.'

She looked across at the airship, at the word *Buckland* written along the side. She held her Bible J between her arms. He was her life, her balance. She stepped out over the abyss towards the wire and put one foot forward.

Her feet were firm on the swaying anchor wire. Some of the crowd gathered below could see what was happening, and they called out. She did not falter. She walked forward as if she were carrying poor Bible J along a wide road just as Jago had taught her. She moved fast, but time seemed to slow down for her. All of her movements were careful and deliberate, but to anyone looking on she resembled a black streak, a blur of speed.

The cadet piloting the airship opened the door of the passenger gondola in disbelief at what he was seeing. Eve laid Bible J out on a sofa in the gondola. She went back across the wire in a blur of speed for Sgt Catchpole. He protested and made to run for the staircase but then the final siren blew. She held her arms out to him. There was no time to argue. He allowed himself to fall back into her arms. She stepped out on to the wire with a six-foot-tall police sergeant balanced across her arms and carried him too across the chasm.

The cadet cast off and the airship moved back and away just as the first explosions split the night and Tower 42 shuddered on its foundations. The crowd cheered.

The building slowly toppled and sank to the ground in a great cloud of dust and shattered debris. Caleb watched it all from the safety of the street. The collapsing building reminded him of the way poor Jack had fallen when the knife had entered his heart.

When the dust had settled and the crowds had dwindled his father managed to hail a hansom cab. They set off for Fournier Street. Caleb watched and thought about Eve as the horse's grey hooves flew over the wet cobbles.

'I must just tell you one thing, Caleb. You are not as them. You are my natural son, the son of your dear mother. They are, well, they are genetically linked to you, and no more. Their DNA was based on ours – but modified of course.'

'Later, Dad, not now. Just tell me one thing. Did you tell me to run when you were down on the ground that night?'

'Of course I did, Caleb. I wanted you to save yourself. Any father would.'

Caleb closed his eyes, he rested his head for a moment on the seat of the cab in relief. They ordered the cab to stop near the great church. Before it had even come to a complete stop, Caleb threw the door open and jumped down. He skidded across the damp cobbles and slid to a stop, gesturing back for his father to follow and for the cab to wait. Then he ran across Fournier Street. With his father behind him, he opened the door of Number 31 with the key.

Mr Leighton stood in the dark hallway bristling with guns. He had a rifle raised ready on his shoulder.

'Oh it's you, Caleb,' he said, lowering his rifle. 'Thank God, I thought that the Fantom had finally come for me.'

'I doubt that will happen now,' said Caleb. 'This is my father, we found him.'

'Both of you together,' he smiled. 'Now I can claim my enormous reward from a grateful Corporation.'

⤜ EPILOGUE ⤛

FROM EVE'S JOURNAL

The leaves are full and green. It is summer again and I am writing this under one of my favourite trees. It has a soft moss waistcoat creeping up from the roots. There are more flowers now, white with a yellow centre, all scattered among the grass, the soft grass which tickles my bare feet when the breeze stirs it. Jago says it will be a long hot summer for me. Brother Caleb came out to see me a few days ago. Jago brought him. And here I am writing once more in that very book he so kindly kept for me.

A red admiral butterfly has just landed on my hand and I have waited, paused in my writing. I let it just sit and dry its wings. I have plenty of time now. No one has seen the Fantom, my mad, sad brother, Adam, since his jump. He has disappeared, the cadets tried to follow his cab but effectively he has vanished. That doesn't mean he has gone away for ever but I feel safe here. I think that I could resist him now. Knowing exactly who I am has helped me to under-

{ 352 }

stand everything. Mr Brown told me that my memory was cleared and locked by Jack after the fire. He told me that my speed and abilities had surely been put there by Jack to protect me. He says that when time appeared to slow down for me it was just that I was going so fast. In a way I am lucky. I am, I suppose, the first of a new step in evolution. I have been engineered, assisted. I try not to overuse my skills and I am certainly lying low here in the forest far away from everyone and everything. Caleb says that Mr Buckland has been charged under the Misuse of Genetic Science Act and that Lucius Brown will give evidence at the trial about the nature of the Prometheus project. Inspector Lestrade has been retired and Sgt Catchpole has been promoted into his position at Old Scotland Yard.

Sgt, sorry, Chief Inspector Catchpole, will write an official account to set things straight. I will be living quietly among the beautiful trees here in the forest for a long while yet, well at least until the baby is born. What kind of a child will he or she be I wonder. What new gifts will they bring?

I want to find the perfect name for this blessing, our child, this new and doubly welcome entry into Jago's broad family. I have two favourites if it is either a boy or a girl, and so can't decide. I will have to let my darling choose, my dear funny Bible J, who lies comfortably resting and restored in the hammock above me, his dear face patterned and shaded by dappled leaf shadow. He will have the last word on that matter.

All in all, Pastworld London lives up to all the stereotypical images that the traveller may have of that very old and literary place. A city of twisted streets and quaint old buildings. A city of mystery, a city of shadow and fog. A city like no other.

Perhaps it will first work its recreated magic on you when you turn a corner into a side road near the murky river and see the cranes and wharves, and hear Big Ben strike the hour over the bustle of river traffic. Perhaps it will come over you the moment you step aboard a horse-drawn hansom cab and feel the floor dip as your weight springs the supports. Perhaps it will happen when you slam shut the heavy door of a railway carriage and catch the intoxicating smell of the steam smuts and the hot oiled metal of the engine. Or might it be the moment when a respectable-looking gentleman in an opera cloak tips the brim of his evening hat to you as you pass him, his face shadowed under a gaslight, and a shiver of apprehension goes through you, and your senses quicken to the thrill of possible adventure . . .

⤜ ACKNOWLEDGEMENTS ⤛

I should like to thank my agent, Hilary Delamere, for believing in, and encouraging me to write, this story. Valerie Brathwaite and Sarah Odedina of Bloomsbury Children's Books listened to my original idea with enthusiasm, and then waited for the book to be finished with an equal, and almost monumental, patience. I should also like to thank various friends and family who listened to my ideas or read and commented on the various drafts of this book, including David Fickling, Juliet Trewellard and Lily Beck.

No book is ever the work of the author alone and I must especially thank my marvellous editor, Margaret Miller of Bloomsbury USA, who suggested so many ways to shape and improve my muddled drafts and ideas, and for whom no praise is high enough, and also Isabel Ford who fine-tuned the result with such care and attention to detail.

Pastworld is a work of fiction, although I have borrowed, for the purposes of the story, my good friend Rodney Archer's house and secretly lent it to the roguish Mr William Leighton. Any errors of fact and geography among the murky underground railway lines and the ruined platforms are the fault of the Buckland Corporation and any complaints should be addressed to them.

Ian Beck
2009